PRAISE FOR *DARE TO KNOW*

ALSO BY
JAMES KENNEDY

The Order of Odd-Fish

DARE
TO
KNOW

A
NOVEL

QUIRK BOOKS
PHILADELPHIA

JAMES KENNEDY

First paperback edition, Quirk Books 2022
Originally published by Quirk Books in 2021

Library of Congress Cataloging in Publication Data
Names: Kennedy, James, 1973- author.
Title: Dare to know / James Kennedy.
Description: Philadelphia : Quirk Books, [2021] | Summary: "After a nearly fatal accident, the most talented employee at a prestigious death-prediction company forecasts his own death day and finds he is already dead"—Provided by publisher.
Identifiers: LCCN 2021004469 (print) | LCCN 2021004470 (ebook) | ISBN 9781683692607 (hardcover) | ISBN 9781683692614 (epub)
Subjects: GSAFD: Suspense fiction. | Dystopias.
Classification: LCC PS3611.E5633 D37 2021 (print) | LCC PS3611.E5633 (ebook) | DDC 813/.6—dc23
LC record available at https://lccn.loc.gov/2021004469
LC ebook record available at https://lccn.loc.gov/2021004470

ISBN: 978-1-68369-316-1

Printed in the United States of America

Typeset in Sabon, Parqa, and Trade Gothic

Cover and interior designed by Ryan Hayes
Production management by John J. McGurk

Quirk Books
215 Church Street
Philadelphia, PA 19106
quirkbooks.com

10 9 8 7 6 5 4 3 2 1

TO HEATHER

YOU KNOW

have death in my pocket. Folded up, ready to go. Ordinarily I wouldn't take on a client like this, but I have to make this sale.

Driving up 290 through gray December slush to Starbucks. My own office is long gone. Now I've got to do business at a cruddy table for two—not ideal, but three bucks for coffee beats thousands of dollars a month on rent, upkeep, a secretary . . . did I really use to have a secretary? What'd she even do? In any case, the margins aren't there anymore. Took a while for me to understand that. Reality is, this is no longer a classy business.

I'd done the initial calculation in advance. Checked it again. Stuck it in my wallet. I need this to go smoothly.

Once upon a time, this business was strictly referral. We'd pick and choose. Ads? Please. We wouldn't even give you a follow-up meeting if we pegged you as obnoxious or, worse, "delicate"—because we weren't just salespeople; we had to be on-the-spot therapists too. Had to handle the client's reaction. Got special training for that, way back when. Unpredictable, the way the client would take it. You might tell some successful pillar of society "thirty-one years" and he'd freak out and spiral into a nervous breakdown right in front of you. Whereas to some loser you might say "two years" and he'd actually shape up, get his life in order. Finding out was the smartest move he'd ever made.

I developed an eye for it. Could sense how someone would react. Got consulted on hard cases. No sale's worth a meltdown. It's bad for business, that's why management gave us discretion back then. I mean the old management, Blattner and Hansen, before they cashed out. Anyway, I'd make my judgment. Jack up the price if my client wasn't taking it seriously. Raise it until they *did*. But cut them a discount, too, if I sensed the need. Not purely out of altruism. If customers are running around bitching they wish we'd never told them, that's bad PR. But those times when it worked out—we loved those inspiring stories. Or marketing did.

We could afford to turn away business back then, back when the calculations could take several days to complete and we charged upwards of twenty million a pop. Now any joker who can scrape up twenty *grand* can get their answer in an hour. And believe me, if I don't jump on that sale, Martin McNiff will. So even when I'm at some dingy food court, looking in a client's eyes, and I know that when I say "three years," it'll destroy her, I think of alimony, college for the boys, the condo, this joke of a car—I just need that shitty fifteen percent.

Parking at Starbucks, I shut off the engine. Sit there a minute. Drizzle flecks the windshield. Not even four o'clock and it's already dark. Never thought I'd end up here, right where I started. Always thought I'd make it out to California or something. Julia did.

Put my game face on. We used to give it a sense of occasion. Called it the Moment. I still prefer to give it a sense of occasion. Not pretentious, just basic self-respect, respect for the client, respect for what I'm selling. It's part of the service. Outdated philosophy, I know. Still, it doesn't feel right to me, to tell my client in this mini-mall coffee shop, barely a step up from a McDonald's. Here's what surprises me, though: *clients don't care*. Some actually complain: "why can't you just tell me over the phone"—well, Martin McNiff will tell you over the phone, sure. He'll even text it to you. But I don't. Look, I get it. I'm old-fashioned.

When you have your Moment, there should be a sense of occasion.

So many treat it like it's no big deal now. I've had clients actually call up their friends as soon as they find out. Blabbing it in a lighthearted, isn't-it-funny way. That's the worst. When they joke about it. Baffles me. Back when I was starting out you'd actually get to see the client's face change in front of your eyes. Disbelief. Terror. Relief. Hopelessness. *Something*. Now: nothing. Like I'm giving them a quote for drywall.

When we started out, when we were still Sapere Aude, it was hard for us to get taken seriously. But one hundred percent accuracy makes the skeptics shut up.

It was most satisfying when the skeptics shut up permanently. On precisely the time and date we predicted.

Nowadays I keep the prediction books in my car. They look like a bunch of phone directories, cheap paper packed with columns of tiny type. I keep them in the trunk along with a couple of pressed shirts and an extra suit. With no office, I have to lug the books around everywhere, but the thing is, I can't help but feel that having these books *with me* all the time, instead of on a proper bookshelf, makes the whole enterprise feel low rent.

We used to keep the books in a special room at the office: People mock that now, I know. But still, I kind of miss it. Back then the books were leather bound with sheepskin paper. Beautiful fonts. Medieval-style illuminations, even. We'd bring them out with a kind of reverence. Not grandiose, just an unfussy recognition of the seriousness of what was about to occur. Like a sacrament. A priest doesn't freak out every time he makes bread turn into God. It's just his job. He's a professional.

To do the math makes the math come true.

So we'd unlock the glass case and bring out the books. People always wanted to peek at what was on the pages. We showed them because why not? To anyone except a trained professional it's incomprehensible anyway, just endless, closely spaced columns of tiny numbers and symbols, like a phone book translated into cuneiform got infected with calculus and then mated with the Egyptian *Book of the Dead*. That's what we nicknamed them: the Books of the Dead.

After the client gawked at the books, we'd get down to business. Leaf through the pages, cross-reference the client's info, ask the questions, do a calculation, flip back and forth through the different volumes, more questions, more calculations, closing in on a number— until I would actually *feel* the number, like I could physically sense the number drawing closer to me, until it was almost trembling in my hand. This was the Moment; this was the Moment that made a professional.

Because you don't just blurt it out.

It takes tact, sensitivity.

Different people want a different kind of person to tell them. Blattner and Hansen figured that out early on. Some folks want a trustworthy older banker type. In that case they'd send you to Hutchinson. If you preferred to keep the information at an ironic arm's length, if you wanted to find out just for a lark (early on that was most of our clientele), they'd send you to Ziegler. If you wanted a pretty woman to tell you, they'd send you to Julia. Part of Blattner and Hansen's old-school cluelessness was that they'd only hired one woman at first. The sexy sell, right? Of course Julia knew her shit, as we all did, but there's no denying that a certain type of rich asshole would rather be told by a redhead who would maybe, oh just maybe, let him cry on her shoulder. That was Blattner and Hansen's angle, anyway. Once they saw Julia's numbers, though, they woke up. More women got hired.

But none of them were quite like Julia.

Me, I got the skeptics. The engineers, the professors, the cynics, people who wanted it all clearly explained. I was their man. Starting out, I was the only one in sales who even had a proper scientific background, though for all my reputation, no, I wasn't really a working scientist. Abandoned my physics doctorate to take this job, don't get me started. Still, I could explain the way it worked, or as far as the clients' understanding would go.

We were the first ones. The pioneers. But so what? You can't keep the fundamental science secret. What we were doing with thanatons, it's not magic, though when it's first explained to you, sure, it certainly *sounds* like magic. So does quantum theory, right? I was amused at the objections to the process at first. "It doesn't make sense that you have to calculate everything with a pencil and paper. Can't you have a computer do it?"

As if *that* were the weirdest thing about thanatons.

In any case, the computer inevitably fucks up somewhere. On a theoretical level I can demonstrate to you, step by step, why the computer *must* fuck up—how the calculation can't help but go off the rails if it's performed purely mechanically—but would that really help you? I had to study thanaton theory for years for a reason. No shortcuts. Suffice it to say that something irreplaceable is generated in the give-and-take between the client and me, the interview and the calculations, as we work through each step of the algorithm together. Something that swings the result, makes it correct. Crazy, yeah. But no crazier than Schrödinger's cat, both alive and dead at once.

The upshot: shut up and calculate.

And as for the thanaton of thanatons—the eschaton—

Shut up and calculate.

Still, I should've seen it coming. Me of all people. Because soon enough, other companies also solved the engineering puzzle of how to tease information out of thanatons (or, as the media dubbed them, "death particles"). We could file all the patent infringement suits we liked but competitors flooded the market. Made it cheap, easy to access. What started out as a sublime privilege for millionaires became an upper-middle-class luxury. Then slipped into being a middle-class necessity. Now it's a stupid curiosity for any schlub who doesn't mind credit card debt. Downmarket. No sense of occasion. We ditched Sapere Aude—people didn't get the reference, and it turned clients off. Rebranded the whole thing. Now we're just Dare to Know.

Like I said: not classy anymore.

But I've got to make this sale.

The lady who'll meet me at this Starbucks today, she's my only promising lead. Truth is, I'm on the ropes. Martin McNiff is eating my lunch—isn't that how an over-the-hill salesman like me would phrase it? Sure, whatever, I'm forty-nine, I admit it, I can't hustle the way a twenty-eight-year-old can. And in some law-of-the-jungle corner of my mind, I accept this, I agree that Martin McNiff *should* be eating my lunch, I acknowledge the old must step aside and make way for the young, that I've had my chance, etc., etc. A sage perspective, maybe, but that doesn't change the fact that *I need the money.*

Things seemed unlimited when I was young. To the point that I felt that I stayed objectively young for longer than other people, that I kept my freshness, my promise longer than them. Like I stayed parked at twenty-eight years old for fifteen years. I'd see friends from high school, college—they aged early, they seemed forty-five when they were only thirty, they lost their hair, got fat, dressed like shit, and it was hard for me not to suspect that it was *their fault*, that they'd made some obscure mistake that triggered the aging process. A mistake I'd somehow avoided. Wishful thinking. Still, the idea seeped into me. Turned into an unexamined principle upon which I based my life.

Until recently, the facts were on my side. Way into my thirties I seemed like I was still in my twenties, with a flat belly, plenty of hair, and a quick mind. But then of course I lost it, one day I woke up and I realized it was all gone, that it had been gone for years. I wasn't a young go-getter. I was a corny uncle.

And now the Martin McNiffs are coming.

Martin McNiff works for one of the new start-ups. Companies that tell you not only *when* you'll die but also *how* you'll die.

It's like high school physics, Heisenberg's uncertainty principle— the idea that the more accurately you determine a particle's position the less you can know that particle's momentum, and vice versa, right?

That's how McNiff's system works. Except instead of measuring the position and momentum of a particle, he's measuring the when and the how of your death. And the more accurately he can tell you one, the less accurately he can tell you the other.

Well, I can tell you this: Martin McNiff uses hack algorithms. My algorithms? The precision of a geometrical proof. Bulletproof like Euclid, one hundred percent. Martin McNiff—he's got heuristics, he's got rules of thumb, he's got glorified actuarial tables, but he's no scientist, he's no artist. Though sonofabitch is fast, and yeah, he's cheap.

But even McNiff will admit that if he sells you solely when you'll die, or solely how you'll die, his algorithm degrades. McNiff can only hit eighty-eight percent accuracy max. That's my in. That's what I remind clients about. McNiff hustles statistics. I provide *certainty*. We all know that we'll die someday. When I tell you exactly when that someday is, I'm relieving anxiety. Right?

Wrong. Turns out that's not what clients want. Not really. People like their range narrowed down thrillingly, but they also like to keep that wiggle room at the end. And the addition of the "how you die"—McNiff's twist—it's clever.

But come on: if McNiff tells you that you have a 67.2 percent chance of dying by drowning on June tenth next year, and a 10.8 percent chance of dying of cancer on September fifth five years from now, etc., etc., I'd argue that you're still always wondering which of those half dozen ways or days you're going to bite the dust. And so even though Martin McNiff is eating my lunch (which he is, brutally), I'd argue the extra "information" McNiff gives you only leads to *more* anxiety—but, well, try explaining that to a client. It's too many dots to connect and you can see where that pitch is going, i.e., straight into the toilet.

Long story short: Martin McNiff is eating my lunch.

I met him at a party once. McNiff. He joked that if there came along a company that told you not just *when* you died, and *how* you died, but also *why* you died, it'd drive us both out of business. "The philosophical why, I mean," McNiff said, smiling, and by this point I didn't know if it was a good-natured joke or if he was slipping the knife. I didn't know how much McNiff knew about me personally. That's the thing about being on the ropes: you second-guess yourself; you suspect everyone else; you don't want to be a prick that can't take a joke, but then again you don't want to be the chump that anyone can mock; you lose your instincts; you laugh vaguely and change the subject; subtext becomes opaque; you can't banter; in short, you're a bore.

I get out of the car and hustle across the rainy, slushy parking lot. No umbrella, of course. Why didn't I think ahead this morning? Rookie mistake. I'm going to look all bedraggled and damp. Nobody wants to hear the information from a wet, disheveled, middle-aged man. That's what Ron Wolper would say, Ron Wolper who's ten years younger than me, Ron Wolper who's been breathing down my neck for the past year since I haven't been able to make quota. Ron Wolper, one of the new hard-asses who came in when Sapere Aude was restructured into Dare to Know. Blattner and Hansen wouldn't treat me this way. Blattner and Hansen wouldn't say make quota this month or it's my job. They'd let a couple of months slide.

Not Ron Wolper.

I'm early. I have fifteen minutes to go to the men's room, fix myself up, find a table, get everything composed.

When I'd opened the book at lunch to do the preliminary calculation, crammed in the back seat, eating a drive-thru cheeseburger, I felt that familiar tug we all feel, that everyone in sales must resist: *What if I looked myself up?*

But of course that's the taboo. That's what you must never do. It would be impossible ever to do your job again, we were warned, if you knew the time of your own death. The number would inevitably loom too large in your mind, would disrupt your client's calculation . . . Anyway, it's technically theft, unless you intend to pay for the service of knowing when you'll die, which, guess what, I can't afford. Twenty thousand on credit? Guess again. The humiliating truth is my clients can afford this service and I can't. Don't think they can't sniff that out, either. And the minute they know you need the sale, you're sunk.

So dress like you don't need the sale. Negotiate like you don't need the sale. Hard to pull off when they see my car. When we're meeting at a coffee shop. When I'm still wet from the fricking rain.

No umbrella. Jesus.

I broke up with Julia at a Starbucks just like this, like a shithead. She was moving to Bloomington and wanted me to come with her. I was in line to move up at Sapere Aude. If I stuck it out in Chicago one more year, Blattner and Hansen hinted, there was a good chance that I'd be promoted to the head office in San Francisco. I wasn't about to sabotage my career by running off with her to Bloomington. I actually said to her, like a dick, "Who moves to Bloomington? Bloomington is a place you move *from*." So I dumped her in a coffee shop just like this one, and bang, these coffee shops began popping up on every street corner, until in no time at all the country was blanketed with identical memorials to how I was a shitty twenty-five-year-old who couldn't take his head out of his ass long enough to move to Bloomington and be happy with someone who loved him.

Julia lives in San Francisco now.

I'm still in Chicago.

Forget it. Make this sale.

I come into the Starbucks lugging my case full of Books of the Dead. I scan the tables. People tapping on their laptops, checking their phones.

The nausea. The cloud of sickness clinging around each glowing screen. Not as bad as sometimes. I can deal with it. Even still, I take a roundabout route through the tables. Buzzing static in my guts. No need to make it worse.

Multicolored string lights in the windows. Christmas carols playing. Candy cane decorations. Lisa Beagleman's not here yet. Good. I brought my fresh suit out of my car, too, because I'd been taking meetings all over suburban Chicago nonstop in these wrinkled clothes since seven this morning. I looked rough. What I needed: fresh-pressed suit, ironed shirt, quick shoeshine, get my hair in order. In a negotiation, these things matter. It's when I'm changing (in the men's room, in the big handicapped stall, with my suit on the hook on the back of the door, hopping around on the pissy floor in my black socks, getting into new trousers) that my phone buzzes. It's Erin.

Buzzing head static.

Just to be clear, I don't hate Erin. The guys who, when I go out drinking, refer to their ex-wives as *that bitch*, implicitly inviting me to speak that way about Erin—I don't respond in kind. It wasn't a "good" divorce, but why hate her? Hating Erin would erase the good years when we were starting out, when the boys were young. I can't help but feel those good times still exist, that those previous versions of Erin and me continue to inhabit a real location in space-time. I don't want to deny or dishonor what was, probably, maybe, one of the better times of my life, or better than I'll ever manage again. In short, Erin is not *that bitch*.

I touch my phone. Brace myself for the sick. Everyone who works with thanatons eventually gets this feeling, this queasy sensation around computers. And of course your phone's just another computer. In the old office we had workarounds. We actually installed analog rotary-dial phones, Bakelite antiques with copper wiring. Good luck finding those nowadays. But how ridiculous is it to be a salesman who can barely use a phone or email? That's why we used to have secretaries, of course. Computers feel like nails on a chalkboard when we walk in a room, the way they *calculate* creates a repellent aura—no matter how sleek the interface, how stylish the design, their math stinks up the room. Jabbing, stabbing, primitive, brutal.

I answer the phone, all business. That's the deadening thing. Erin has to rearrange her work schedule and wants to know, can I take the boys this weekend instead of next? I can. Our voices, which used to be ecstatic together, or laughing together, or furious at each other, are now just working out scheduling details. In a way, ordinary conversations like this debase the old memories more thoroughly than if I had complained about *that bitch*.

The boys, sure, I care about them, but by some genetic fluke, both of them look and act just like Erin's lunkheaded brother Bryce. Go ahead, admit it. Bryce's DNA dominated mine. As the years go by, and especially since the divorce, I have less and less in common with the boys. Stopped recommending books to them. They don't read anyway. They gave up trying to talk to me about sports. I never cared about sports, there's no point in faking it now. So yeah, I'm disengaged from my sons' lives. Yeah, I should make more of an effort. I try to reengage, but I don't know how. I see myself fading in their eyes.

A few weeks ago, I was speaking at their high school for Career Day (and here I thought I was doing them a favor), trying to explain the rudiments of thanaton theory to their pizza-faced classmates, to convey to these teenagers some clue about the history of Sapere Aude, of Dare to Know, of what our company actually meant and stood for in the early days. But as I looked over the assembly gathered in the school gym, children with their eyes glazed over, children who were bored by scientific miracles, children for whom the startling implications of thanaton theory were yesterday's news, irrelevant, quaint—I realized I couldn't see either of my sons. I continued droning on with my PowerPoint, my mouth moving on autopilot as my eyes roved the crowd, as I began to understand that both of them must've simply skipped my presentation. And yet when I dropped by Erin's that night and asked them about it, they were impatient that I even brought it up. No, they said, it wasn't because of some dramatic reason, no, it wasn't because they were ashamed of me—they both had just had something else they'd rather be doing. Okay, then, what were you doing? God, Dad, it doesn't matter, let it go!

They were ashamed of me.

I hang up. The phone's algorithms calm down. Put it in my pocket.

The queasiness clinging to the thing ebbs. My stomach relaxes.

I come out of the bathroom, buy a coffee to justify my existence, and sit down at one of the larger tables near the window. I start unpacking my Books of the Dead, opening to the bookmarked pages, arranging my papers of preliminary calculations, prepping for the assessment.

It's only once I'm fully settled in that I see that Lisa Beagleman is already there.

In fact, I realize, Lisa Beagleman has been there all along. I must've walked straight past her on my way to the bathroom. There, in the corner—a large sour-looking woman with a gray sweatshirt, off-brand jeans, and squinting, distrustful eyes. Well, I'm no prize either. I should've recognized her but her nothing-colored hair was in a ponytail last time. Never could remember a face.

I am here to tell Lisa Beagleman when she will die.

She's looking at me from her table, quietly amused. I understand right away that this sale isn't going to go the way I want. She smiles at me and it's a predatory, stupid smile.

"Freshening up?" she says as I sit down at her table.

"Thanks for being patient." Off on the wrong foot; she has the upper hand already. She knows it. How to play it? Lighthearted. "And here I thought I was early."

"You still are." Lisa Beagleman makes it sound like an accusation. I check my watch: yes, I'm still six minutes early. Her smile says it all. *You really need this.*

"Before we start, just to confirm—" I make a show of going through some papers but who am I fooling? I produce the invoice. "If you can sign off on this and a few more pieces of paperwork . . ."

She doesn't even look at the invoice. "Well, the thing is, I just got off the phone with Martin McNiff—you know, Martin McNiff?"

Don't take the bait. "Uh-huh."

"And after talking to him, well, I just don't know about twenty thousand *dollars*." Seriously, even the littlest things about Lisa Beagleman are irritating, like why'd she put that meaningless emphasis on the word "dollars"? She'd prefer to pay in what, Krugerrands?

Shut up. Let her talk.

"You know?" Lisa gives a put-upon sigh. That nasal, wheedling voice. Quacking her midwestern vowels. "It's just that for twelve thousand *dollars* Martin McNiff said he could tell me both *when* and *how*, and I thought, here I am with you, spending twenty thousand on just *when*."

Is Lisa Beagleman for real? Does she really want me to explain it all over again? How I provide certainty while McNiff can only give her statistics? I'd explained it to her on the phone. I'd mailed her the brochures. Well, I'm not going round and round on this. Nickel-and-dimed by a Lisa Beagleman. Christ.

I let the silence sit there.

"You know?" she says.

Hardball. "I'm sorry to hear that. I suppose you must've gotten off the phone with Mr. McNiff just now, or else you would've canceled our appointment and notified me sooner." I gather my papers and rise. "I'll let you go then—"

A lie. But it works. I see it in her eyes. She's overplayed her hand.

"No, calm down, sit down," she says. Trying to regain the initiative by implying I'm overreacting. Telling me to sit down is giving me an order. Putting me in my place. Obviously a dim bulb, but she might be a savant at small-time wheedling. Everyone's good at something.

I don't sit down. "Twenty thousand."

"Okay, okay, okay," she says, which isn't an agreement but I sit down anyway.

– – – – – –

She got me down to sixteen thousand.

Is it a smell that I give off? Some chump pheromone? It can't have always been the case. I used to close multimillion-dollar deals. Must be like the invisible desperation you emanate when you haven't been laid yet. Only when someone finally fucks you does the stink vanish. But still, even after that, fail too many times, accept too many nights alone, that stink sneaks back. Deep down I don't really believe I'm a loser, although for the last few years the world's been informing me otherwise. My problem is I don't listen. I keep expecting everything will turn my way.

Fifteen percent of sixteen thousand is twenty-four hundred, I'm thinking, as I start in on the standard introductory spiel for the millionth time. She's almost certainly already seen actors recite this spiel on TV; by now it's as ingrained in pop culture as the reading of Miranda rights.

"I'm going to say some sentences that will seem like nonsense," I begin. "I'd like you to respond to each sentence with the first words that come into your head, no matter how seemingly odd or random. Please don't try to be clever or funny. Please don't try to beat the system. The algorithm has taken those possible responses into account and it will only result in a longer session. None of the statements touch upon conscious personal information, and the responses we aim to elicit from you will also have no conscious personal content."

"Yeah, yeah," says Lisa Beagleman.

Spiel over. I initiate the stage one calculation I'd calibrated for her in the car. "Blue lady lays, a wending way around away, eels conceal the puck."

"Oh come on," she says impatiently. "It really *does* work like this?"

I make a note in my book. "Marry fluorescent chatter, romping willowy hunger flash."

"So stupid. Beep bop boop. I don't know."

Another note. "Ornery ourobouros, kill sky love shield, raw throat lizard eyes."

Lisa Beagleman just shakes her head.

I put my pen aside. Just use the scripted response here. I don't have the energy to meet this woman on her own terms.

"I'm going to pause the assessment," I recite, "and remind you that you voluntarily asked for this information, were fully briefed on the process, and already paid your deposit. When we complete the assessment, I will be able to predict the date and time of your death to an accuracy of one hundred percent. If you continue to resist the questions, that will only make the assessment longer."

Challenging eyes. "And what if I don't want to know now?"

"That's perfectly okay if you don't want to know anymore," I lie. "But you've already paid your ten percent deposit, and that's nonrefundable."

I don't mention to Lisa Beagleman that if she quits now, I only get a reduced five percent of that ten percent. My full fifteen percent only kicks in if she goes all the way, finds out when she'll die, and coughs up the full twenty thousand—strike that, sixteen thousand. Bottom line: if she walks away now, I'd only be netting . . . Jesus, eighty bucks.

I have to, *have to* close this thing.

"Quintile merryman main bus undervolt," I say.

Lisa Beagleman wavers, then: "Hawaii."

- - - - - -

O nce I get them in rhythm, I'm good at keeping them locked in.

"Salt hum winter cream," I say.

"Treat aunt cottage door," she says.

Time flies. I'm in the zone. After every exchange of seeming gibberish I consult the books, make the necessary calculation, derive the next words to say, then it all starts over again, faster, until we're just jabbering letters and numbers at each other—"D 4 T G 8 9," I say, and Lisa Beagleman rattles off "X 4 2 9 X 3 E"— and the thing is, I'm good at this, I enjoy it. Even though nowadays the assessment is standardized to the point where you don't even have to be a real mathematician anymore—any technician can just execute the script—I get results faster using the original methods, plus a few custom shortcuts of my own. So I do it my way, which requires a bit of creativity, finesse, skipping and combining steps, closing off loops, and anticipating the algorithm's zigzags, which keeps life interesting. But although it all seems to be going well, I sense it starting to go wrong.

An inkling. But I've been trained to notice it. The twitch of Lisa Beagleman's eye. The way she's answering quickly but not eagerly. As if she's rushing through it before she can change her mind. That's it. She's on the verge of changing her mind. But I have to make this sale. She *is* changing her mind. The difference between eighty dollars and twenty-four hundred. She's changed it.

Shit.

I'm still zeroing in on a number, ping-ponging between six or seven different possibilities. A baby is crying somewhere in the coffee shop. Keep it together. Down to four possibilities. Lisa Beagleman herself might not know it yet, but I know it: she doesn't want this anymore. The crying baby belongs to this man I can see over her shoulder. It's just him and the baby. Maybe he's a single dad, trying to take a break at this coffee shop and his baby is freaking out. Down to three possibilities. The baby is a girl. A handful. Last calculation, simple, just multiplying two numbers. Always thought I'd rather have a daughter.

I have the answer.

Lisa Beagleman is trembling. I clear my throat. She doesn't want to know. Well, make her want it. I see her eyes darting, trying to get out of it. I'm about to tell her exactly how much time she has to live. She's backing out. Don't let her. Afraid. The naked fear. What I used to see.

Lisa Beagleman opens her mouth but before she can say anything that would nullify the contract I say, "Lisa, you're going to die in six years, eleven months, four days, and nine hours."

– – – – – –

Oh Jesus, I fucked up. Shouldn't have forced it.

She breaks down crying. "I *told* you I didn't want it," she weeps, nearly screams, and it doesn't matter that it's not true, that she never explicitly told me she didn't want it, but no, I messed up, it *is* my fault, because after all I *could* read it in her manner. Now she's making a scene—this is why we used to do it in an office, not in public—and she's wailing! Breaking down! I've never misjudged so badly, but I'm ashamed to admit that when her smug mask broke my first thought was, at least here's someone who *feels it*. And when most people cry, it screws up their face, makes them look abject, but for some people, like Lisa Beagleman now, there's a hidden dignity that's unlocked when they cry, her eyes no longer so verminous, so calculating, even though I can't understand what she's saying through her tears except, "And I'm never even going to see Mandy go to high school, to puh-puh-puh-puh-*prom*," standard shit. When they're spiraling they always latch onto some random life milestone that they just then realize they'll never experience. The man with the baby comes over from the other table, "Is everything all right?" and oh Lordy, now super-dad is sizing me up, like we might have to "take this outside," and I'm too stunned to do anything other than offer a handkerchief to Lisa Beagleman, but she swats it away and howls, "*Six years.*"

"Practically seven," I say, stupidly.

"I *told* you I didn't want it," she weeps. From the way she's interacting with super-dad as he comforts her and I sit there like a stone, it becomes apparent they know each other, that super-dad is "David," that their kids go to preschool together, that "David" is stepping in as a protector. He turns to me and says, "It's probably time you left."

Oh hell no. "I need Mrs. Beagleman to sign this confirming that she's received the information."

"You can get her to sign it later, buddy." Buddy! Now I'm "buddy." David is hugging Lisa Beagleman now, comforting her. I'd judge her hysterics as over-the-top if I hadn't witnessed the exact thing before, so many times—never on my watch, but when less adroit salesmen fail to stick the landing, amateurs who don't have the balls or the backup to walk away when you're supposed to walk away—well, this is why Martin McNiff does it over the phone, right? McNiff doesn't care. Mandy and her puh-puh-puh-puh-prom . . . did you know McNiff has moved into the market for under-21? Used to be an unwritten rule you don't do that, but it turns out the testing goes even quicker with babies and toddlers because there's zero self-consciousness fogging up their assessment responses. Well, if you can look into the eyes of brand-new parents and inform them their child will die of cancer when they're four years old (72.3%) or in a car crash when they're twelve (23.8%), etc., and then have the transcendent balls to bill them for the pleasure, you're welcome to it.

In any case, McNiff has no problem picking up the check.

Neither do I, apparently.

I have the paper out, the pen out. Lisa Beagleman's got to sign if I'm going to get my miserable twenty-four hundred dollars and I am not walking out of this shitshow without my twenty-four hundred dollars. Everyone is glaring at me, even the baristas. I'm the bad guy, I'm the scum of the earth. Well, you know what? I've got a signed contract. She asked for this. She went through the assessment. She paid her money. I kept up my end. Am I always going to be the good guy in life? No. Learned that ages ago.

"You're still here?" says super-dad David.

I don't move. "Sign."

– – – – – –

Wet white flakes flying at my windshield. Slush world changed to snow world while I was inside. December in the suburbs of Chicago, where am I even? Schaumburg or Palatine or purgatory, swinging out of the parking lot, blasting down the avenue, onto the highway, like a criminal getaway minus the charm. Lugging the Books of the Dead out of the Starbucks, nobody asking "Can I give you a hand with that?"—everyone knew what had happened, they'd seen similar scenes before. But it had never happened to me. Lisa Beagleman screaming me out the door. Shouldn't have told her. Too eager. Like a chump franchisee. Like some asshole who'd just earned his license, who rents his Books of the Dead by the week.

And to think I'd been one of the first ones.

It's death-dark and I'm driving around in a shaken-up snow globe. Two lights come blazing out of the blackness, zoom past, another idiot stupid enough to be driving in a slushy shrieking blizzard. But I had to get out of there. Not just out of the Starbucks. Out of the parking lot. Out of town. Out of that whole world. Lisa Beagleman and super-dad David, turning the crowd against me. Won't be doing business in there again.

She'll call headquarters. She'll make a complaint.

Ron Wolper.

Oh, Christ.

But that's what you wanted, wasn't it, Wolper? For me to be more aggressive? To push that sale? Oh no, don't blame Wolper, it's you, you knew it was a dick move even while you were doing it, you didn't listen to your own judgment. Because be honest: you *would've* held back, you *wouldn't* have told her if you'd liked her. But from the minute you saw Lisa Beagleman you didn't like her. She didn't like you either. Natural enemies. Who would win. Well, I won. She's the one crying. I got my percentage.

Dick, dick, dick.

This blizzard is something else. Dumb being out here. The flying white streaking by in the blackness swallowing up the car, like I'm blasting through hyperspace. Brutal wind. Car hard to handle, the wobbly way it takes the curves. Well, you said you wanted a white Christmas . . . You say that every year. Weaving, almost fishtailing. Careful what you ask for. Home still miles away, why in such a hurry to get there? Nobody's waiting for you. Complain if there's no snow in December it doesn't feel like the holidays; complain if there *is* snow in December it's too much to handle—digging your car out in the morning, hours of traffic—

I hit the skid.

Fly off the road.

— — — — — —

A car crash doesn't feel the way you think it'll feel. Or it didn't for me. Not enough time for panic, for freaking out, not enough time for your body to catch up to what's happening, for your brain to zap the right chemicals out to the right muscles—when I hit the skid and fly off the road, I am calm, I do everything correctly, I keep control as much as possible, try to minimize the damage, even as I think in a resigned way, *This is it. Now I'm dead.*

Crumpled in a snowy ditch. Car totaled.

Then the rush comes, the useless adrenaline.

All the emotion I should've felt, too late.

MY NAME

The kid who was my roommate at eighth grade physics summer camp was Renard Jankowski, and—well, it's physics summer camp, right? It's going to attract a certain type of kid. We were all nerds. I use that word in its damning original sense. None of us identified as such. It was 1987.

The "camp" wasn't real camp, no bonfires or canoeing, no forest hikes, but basically just more school, a way for the college to turn a profit in summer using its deserted dormitories and cheap labor pool of grad student instructors. Renard and I shared one of those cinder block, linoleum-tiled dorm rooms. When I arrived with my stuff on the steamy first day, Renard was lying on the top bunk as if he'd always been living there, reading something from the shoeboxes of 1970s science fiction paperbacks he'd brought from home. Renard spent the summer plowing through those boxes, book after book, though I never saw him get enthusiastic about anything he read. Whenever I read a book that I loved, I always had to urge everyone else to "read this! You *have* to." And if I hated a book, I'd rant to everyone about how crappy it was—but Renard Jankowski read without comment, steadily, passionlessly, paperback after paperback, like a cow indifferently masticating its cud.

Renard's daily outfit was one of his many black souvenir T-shirts from various national parks, with something like an eagle or a grizzly on it, tucked into dark blue jeans with a belt with a big elaborate country-music-singer buckle. He had an oxlike build and straight dark hair and a little bit of a mustache and the kind of tinted sunglasses that are supposed to work as normal glasses indoors and turn into sunglasses outdoors, but in practice were always semidark. When I came into our dorm room that first day Renard didn't say a word. He ignored my hellos. I unpacked my stuff in silence, puzzled and almost angry. Maybe there was something wrong with him. But then, after an hour of quiet, Renard began talking to me as if we'd always known each other. His literal first words to me were, "So, anyway . . ."

– – – – – –

There was a particular science fiction author I loved. An Englishman who had only written a handful of funny sci-fi books. A writer you wouldn't find in Renard's box, because Renard had zero sense of humor, but I loved this author—not just for his goofy best sellers but for his big personality. He made for a garrulous interview, lived a fascinating life, was a world traveler, was generous with his money, was an early adopter of new technologies, and was curious about everything, the kind of author whose tossed-off ideas were better than epics other writers had sweated over for years, whose throwaway jokes turned out to make better predictions about the future than the prophecies of earnest futurists. Anyway, one of this author's unfinished stories (he had so many, he seemed to workshop them aloud in interviews) was about a character who had forgotten something crucial that had happened in his life. So this character jumps off a cliff on the theory that on the way down, while his life is passing before his eyes, he'd remember that important thing he'd forgotten, the thing that would show him the real meaning of his life.

As for what'd happen to him when he inevitably hit the ground? Well, he'd solve that problem when he came to it.

The author died before he could write that story.

But as my car is flying off the highway, as I'm crashing into the snowy ditch—here's my story.

— — — — — —

Renard and I became friends. Maybe that's the real reason all of our parents sent us to gifted-kids camp—so we could meet people who were our own speed. Not just intellectually but, for lack of a better term, philosophically. One night, as we were sweating in our bunk beds that humid July, Renard asked me what I thought happened after you died.

"I guess you just switch off," I said. "Like a computer."

"Do you really think that?"

"I don't know. What do you think happens?"

Renard didn't speak for a long time. I thought maybe he had fallen asleep. But then, after a while, Renard said, clearly and deliberately, "After you die you will be staring down that tunnel of red circles at the end of a *Looney Tunes* cartoon. And you will hear a voice that's like Porky Pig trying to say *that's all, folks!* but he's stuttering so much he can't even get past the first word. And that *Looney Tunes* ending music keeps repeating, too. But then you realize it's not Porky Pig's voice, it's somebody else's. And then you notice that the words superimposed on the tunnel don't spell out *that's all, folks!* like they're supposed to. They spell out something else, but the letters are backward, and you're trying to figure out what the backward letters are saying, but you don't want to, because you know it will be a nightmare word, but that nightmare word is also the secret of the universe, and it's right in front of you now, it's in your face, you can finally read the secret of the universe, but that voice is babbling at you, and the music is playing again and again, and that's what you must sit through, for all eternity."

Try talking like that all the time. See where it gets you. How weird do you have to be to be bullied at *physics camp*? Renard was that weird and I was his roommate. One night after dinner we returned to our dorm room to discover that both our beds had been pissed on by the other boys, and shaving cream was smeared all over our stuff. Renard sighed and began cleaning up the mess without complaint. I was furious for revenge. Renard took it with a quiet shrug.

"Why don't you get mad?" I said.

"No point."

Scrub scrub scrub.

I said, "Renard. Your books all got pissed on."

"Throw them out."

"Really?"

"I don't want piss-smelling books."

"But maybe some of them are still good."

"Just throw them all out."

This felt wrong to me. I thought Renard loved those books. He was letting them go with zero emotion.

I held one up. "What's this one about?"

"It is about an artificially intelligent prison planet that doesn't have any prisoners. So the planet manufactures its own prisoners. Then it tortures them until they die."

"Oh."

"The prison planet devours those prisoners and recycles them to make a new generation of prisoners. One prisoner escapes, hero's journey, et cetera."

"Did you like it?"

"Uh."

"What do you mean?"

"It's a metaphor for the universe, I guess."

"Was it good?"

Renard shrugged.

"What?"

"I don't know. Define 'good.'"

In retrospect, that physics camp let us all run wild. Nowadays you couldn't get away with running a kids' program that lax. In the mornings a rotating cast of instructors taught us seminars and did labs with us, but in the afternoons and evenings we were more or less free to work on our own weird projects. The social contract seemed to be that parents were looking for a place to dump their clever-but-not-outdoorsy offspring for July and August, the university was happy to take their money, and as children of the eighties we were used to filling up hours of unprogrammed time on our own.

One night Renard asked me in the dark, "What are you afraid of?"

– – – – – –

When I was a kid I was afraid of the Beatles.

To me their voices sounded mechanical and insinuating, their music shaggy and wrong. My older sisters had an LP of *Sgt. Pepper's Lonely Hearts Club Band* and its cover was unnerving to me. It was too busy, its collage of dozens of famous people seemingly pasted in from various universes, and the four hairy men in brightly colored circus-military uniforms looked smug and gleeful and threatening. My sisters played *Sgt. Pepper* all the time, on the little gray portable record player they got for Christmas. It sounded devilish to me. I remember one day, hanging out with my sisters in the basement—I was probably four or five years old and was rolling myself around the carpeted floor on a wheeled ottoman—I saw that record lying on the carpet and sensed that this was my opportunity, the moment that I could take action, and so in a blind rush I rolled my ottoman right over *Sgt. Pepper's Lonely Hearts Club Band*, cracking it into pieces, and then it was like I was floating, I felt this incredible surge of well-being, and even though my sisters were screaming at me now, I was relieved I'd never have to listen to that music again, I was certain that I had done a righteous act.

For me the eighties meant a time of clean lines. Top 40 music sounded cleanly synthetic. Eight-bit computer games were constructed of sharp, neon pixels. Movies and TV shows got taken out of the hands of weird hippies and put in the hands of pros who knew how to please. Things that were meandering, bearded, shaggy, bloated, natural, organic: out. Things that were straightforward, lean, engineered: in. This was good. I hated the druggy, ugly seventies, or my child's-eye impression of it. Charles Manson looked like a Beatle to me. As a child, I felt like the devil walked the land in the seventies, because when I'd overhear adults talking seventies stuff, or see it in newspapers, it'd be about serial killers, or hundreds of people committing suicide using Kool-Aid or whatever, or drugged-up soldiers massacring villages, or Andy Warhol ghouls lurking in discos. Why were they acting like that? I felt lucky to come of age after America had flushed all that gnarly viciousness out of its system and bequeathed to me a world that was clean and safe and reasonable. I'm older now and realize that *Sgt. Pepper* is a fine album, and of course all kinds of worthwhile things happened in the seventies—and yes, I'm aware that I sound like I had been some weird reactionary child who read the *National Review* instead of *Garfield*, but I wasn't, not really, because just remember, a child has no political context, only an impressionable imagination, and to be fair, when Bob Dylan is demanding at you over the radio that "Everybody must get stoned," it frankly sounds scary to a child, especially with Dylan's apparent nasal delight in the idea, with the creepily wheezing old-time harmonica, and you vaguely know that being "stoned" has to do with drugs, and you know drugs are bad, but Bob Dylan is so maniacally insistent about it, why is he so *invested* in everybody getting stoned? Especially when he goes on to say, "They'll stone you when you" do this and that—what does that even mean? If you don't get yourself stoned on Bob Dylan's fucking schedule, he'll send somebody to *do it to you*? These are your big heroes of the seventies—shaggy weirdos like Cheech and Chong, Bob Dylan, and the Beatles? You know who'd be a better hero? Pac-Man! Here's a hard-working guy who clocks in every day without complaint, who plays by the rules, and if a ghost kills him, he doesn't protest the system, man, he just gets himself born again.

I didn't say that to Renard in so many words. But when Renard asked me, "What are you afraid of?" it would've been stupid to say "I'm afraid of heights" or "I get nervous about public speaking." I wanted to say something particularly true about me so I said something similar to the above about not liking the Beatles and how I had broken my sisters' record on purpose.

To my surprise, Renard felt the same way. He said that music on the radio sometimes freaked him out, too, but for him it was the sleek, artificial eighties anthems that were haunted; to Renard those songs sounded reptilian, sinister, metallic; he remembered one time, late at night in bed listening to the radio, when Don Henley's "The Boys of Summer" came on, he had felt a chill at the lyric about seeing a deadhead sticker on a Cadillac. Renard had no idea what a "deadhead sticker" was but it had sounded to him like a satanic emblem—and since the sticker was displayed on a Cadillac, that implied that even the wealthy were in on the satanism, that society's spiritual corruption went all the way to the top. Renard had also imagined the "little voice inside my head" referred to an actual voice that broke into the singer's consciousness, hissing behind his ear, *Don't look back, you can never look back.* So the question is, should you obey this demon voice or defy it? Should you actually look back? But wait, what if it's a deliberate taunt, what if the voice's intention is to goad you into looking back? In that case, you really *mustn't* look back, right? Like how Indiana Jones tells Marion not to look when they open the lost ark? Because maybe the deadhead sticker wants to do something worse than melt your face off, it wants to infect the world with its evil, and if you *did* turn around to look at the deadhead sticker on the Cadillac it would find its way into you, it would place its evil in you.

So don't look back.

Renard and I understood each other.

— — — — — —

Not long after physics camp was over, I found out that lyric wasn't what Renard and I thought at all. "The Boys of Summer" wasn't about wealthy satanists with cryptic death glyphs on their expensive cars. It was about lame middle-aged nostalgia, and the "deadhead sticker" merely referred to a decal for the band the Grateful Dead. But that discovery didn't make it any less creepy because the name "Grateful Dead" was still disingenuously ghoulish, and their music was still noodley seventies garbage, and everyone in that band still looked like scary bearded drug men—basically just another bunch of fucking Mansons.

Renard and I made a theory together, a theory we half pretended with each other was true, and that I still sometimes think of when I hear shitty classic rock on the radio: that something vast and invisible and evil permeated America, an unseen presence that sprawled across every state and dwelled in every person, and that this entity was always trying to speak, that it was always attempting to announce itself, and thus it sought out and used the biggest megaphone it could find, manifesting its voice in Top 40 music—though it could only manage to speak in spurts and starts, in disconnected phrases across songs, across decades. Nevertheless, its demon phrases were repeated infinitely and everywhere through that inescapable classic rock radio, the voice of a vast invisible thing who was going to do awful things to all of us, a voice who in fact relished telling us exactly the tortures it planned to inflict on us, a voice who demanded to be heard, and that was the terrifying thing, it was all out in the open, you could turn on the radio at any time, and sometimes the sinister thing would speak to you directly.

– – – – – –

My radio is still on somehow.

I switch it off.

I sit there in the snowy ditch for a while, being alive.

The car is wrecked but I'm okay. Seat belt on. Airbag didn't even deploy. Not a bruise on me. But the engine won't start. I open the door, experimentally. Cold and snow whoosh in. I shut it.

Keep the heat in the car for as long as I can.

Blood pounding through my body. Brain buzzing. I feel like I'm far away from here. In a kind of daze I dig out my old AAA card and call for a tow truck. The world blinking, blinking around me, then settling down.

The tow truck place says it'll take an hour.

Snow whips wildly around the car. I'm off the road, pointing down into the ditch at maybe a twenty-degree angle. Headlights flash by. You wouldn't see me if you weren't looking for me. Or you'd think the car had been abandoned.

I glance over at the books.

Alone in this wrecked car. All the time I need.

Don't.

The rule. Even more: the taboo.

But nobody would know.

But no salesman is ever supposed to look themselves up.

Still, I had almost died. Just now. And right at the moment I thought I was dead, I had pretty much thought: *okay, fine*.

I take one of the Books of the Dead out of the back seat.

Open it.

But—

Only one thing stops me.

— — — — — —

I remember the first time a salesman broke the taboo. The first time any of us in the company did an unauthorized assessment.

It was at the first Sapere Aude conference in Minneapolis, where we started out—though to call it a "conference" makes it sound much more buttoned-up than what actually went down at that hotel that weekend, with me and Julia and Ziegler and Hutchinson and everyone else. When they made the documentary (much of it using Hutchinson's fuzzy old VHS home recordings) they had referred to us (and I know it sounds self-mythologizing for me to repeat it) as the *freaks and dreamers and geniuses* who started Sapere Aude. The Minneapolis conference had taken place my first year working for the company, when we were just thirty employees—really, selling the time of your death is the only real job I've ever had. But back then it wasn't a real job. Or didn't feel like it. The public still didn't fully believe or even understand what we were up to. We were still cutting edge, revolutionary, punk rock, whatever you want to call it. Young.

We were all extraordinary. Everyone who was smart and ambitious, who knew which way the wind was blowing, wanted in.

The fact that they wanted me was a fluke, in retrospect. Everyone in the physics community was talking about thanatons, of course, but outside academia a lot of it was irresponsible talk: techno-utopians claiming that controlling thanatons would grant us immortality, hippies with their self-serving woo-woo, religious nuts spinning their wheels trying to fit thanatons into their dogmas. More than once I had to be the killjoy at an undergraduate dinner party, the guy who cleared his throat and said, well, actually, I *study* thanatons, and the facts don't quite support *that* interpretation.

SOMEONE: So wait. If there were no thanatons, there would be no death?

ME: Thanatons don't cause death. They just react to it. Think of it this way: if you got rid of the mercury in thermometers, would the temperature stop changing?

SOMEONE: But what *are* thanatons?

ME: Thanatons are subatomic particles that seem to be what we call "quantum-entangled" in human death. We don't know why yet, but they change state in a complicated way in response to future mortality and—

SOMEONE: Then how come we've never detected thanatons before?

ME: What do you mean?

SOMEONE: I heard there's no evidence of the existence of thanatons before, like, a few years ago.

ME: That's kind of like saying there were no quarks in ancient Greece because Socrates never saw a quark. The only reason we haven't seen thanatons before is we weren't sophisticated enough. We didn't have the math or machinery.

SOMEONE: But I heard there's evidence that all the thanatons just appeared recently. Like they were called into existence, somehow.

ME: I guess we're going to have to agree to disagree on that one.

You have to decide when to insist on accuracy and when to let it slide for the sake of the dinner party. Nobody likes the "well, actually" guy, especially when he takes it upon himself to shut down the fascinating cultural theorist holding court with their oh-so-mind-blowing speculations . . . But here's the thing: when I did correct them, I always did it gently, with humor. I gave the blowhard an out, and so I got a reputation as that rare bird: a science person who could relate to laypeople. But in reality I was closer in temperament to, or so I wanted to believe, Henrik Stettinger, the discoverer of thanatons, the "reluctant revolutionary" who looked uncomfortable in every photo you saw of him. Stettinger didn't even want to believe in what he had discovered, didn't publish a word about thanatons until he had checked and rechecked and exhausted every single possible alternate interpretation. Stettinger logged countless late nights tracing other possible trajectories in the bubble chamber and tried his hardest to disprove his own discovery. That was noble. I admired that.

I'd first heard of him when everyone else had. I was a senior in high school when the discovery of thanatons was announced.

As it turned out, Stettinger had been a professor at the same university where I had attended physics camp.

I was surprised at that. Not that it wasn't a good school. I mean, it was okay. But you wouldn't expect a fundamental shift in physics coming from a just-okay school in the Midwest. Still, that's how science advances sometimes, right? From outsiders. That old saw about Einstein being a patent clerk when he hit upon special relativity.

In any case, I never met Stettinger that summer. He probably wasn't even present on campus. The "reluctant revolutionary" didn't teach classes, and certainly wouldn't have been wasting his time with eighth graders.

Though, looking back, Stettinger would've been making his breakthroughs on that campus around the same time Renard and I were there.

— — — — — —

The university hosting the physics summer camp was a new kind of environment for me. I had grown up in a bucolic suburb of strip malls and golf courses, populated by engineers and small business owners. Everything in my hometown was new and clean and air-conditioned and worked on the first try. The university's fake Gothic architecture and ivied brick was like nothing I'd experienced; it was the first time I'd hung out at a place that was dirty and not up-to-date, though those typically negative qualities seemed part of the premise of the place, the lack of air-conditioning and the occasional cockroach and the slightly broken-down agedness of everything somehow feeling like eccentric privileges and not cruddy inconveniences.

In the back of the university's library was a converted storage space where they kept TVs, VCRs, movie projectors, and a bunch of computers—Apple IIes with primitive modems that I guess some millionaire alumnus decided the library should own but the librarians clearly had no idea what to do with.

A trio of girls from the physics camp seized control of the AV Room, running it as their own fiefdom. No other camper got access to the computers without their say-so. These girls bonded early over some kind of early BBS stuff with the computers and modems. Most of us other campers were boys and we didn't care much about the computers—this was before the internet was a thing. We were more interested in building robots or blowing stuff up. The boy campers dubbed the girls the FARGs, for the "Fat AV Room Girls." Typical awful teenaged boy shit, and for what it's worth, I don't even remember any of those girls being fat (one of the girls had significant breasts and dressed to hide them, so maybe that read as "fat" to the boys). In any case, these computer girls fundamentally did not give a fuck. They shrugged and called themselves FARGs, too, so they could return to their darkened, glowing AV Room to ignore the rest of the goings-on at camp and do God knows what— if it were us boys, we'd be downloading ASCII porn at 2,400 baud or something similarly gross. Long story short, the FARGs ruled the computers.

But those girls liked Renard. Or at least they'd achieved a certain détente. I don't know why. Renard didn't act any differently around them. It was more like two species of fish in an aquarium who don't have a predator-prey relationship so they just ignore each other. In any case, the FARGs allowed Renard access to the AV Room, and under his aegis, I was admitted as well.

There was a video game on the Apple IIe that Renard played that he introduced me to. You controlled an Indiana Jones–looking man who walked around what seemed like an endless house, which resembled some kind of Aztec or Mayan ruin filled with spiders and scorpions and crocodiles and giant octopus things. You dug through garbage piles in the house and opened boxes looking for something, but what were you looking for? The wanderings didn't seem to have any point; you just kept on walking and walking until you were overrun by the monsters and you died. You controlled your guy not with a joystick but with the keyboard, with a bewildering combination of keystrokes that had to be done lightning-fast, and you spent a lot of time getting killed unfairly.

The game was boringly addictive in that 1980s way, back when the unspoken subtext of every game was: oh, like you have anything better to do? The "puzzles" you were expected to solve all presumed you had hours to grind away, punching each individual identical brick on a wall of what seemed like thousands of bricks to find the one random brick that would open a secret door into the next level. Back then you often played games without documentation, because you'd rarely buy games—the games came to you via someone cracking its copy protection and pirating it onto a blank disk, the game getting copied from friend to friend. So you often played games without knowing what, exactly, you were actually supposed to be doing. Renard said the object of the game was to find someone called the Flickering Man, but neither Renard nor I saw the Flickering Man; the Flickering Man's appearances were rare and random, Renard informed me, occurring only on the highest, most inaccessible levels.

I didn't spend as much time in the AV Room as Renard. Nevertheless, both he and I were dubbed "FARG fags" by the more popular boys, which was a nice bit of projection since everyone knew the dominant boys organized brutal group jack-off contests in their rooms.

As for the official camp activities of building rockets and blowing stuff up, I did participate in all that, but it was always a relief to escape from the summer heat into the air-conditioned AV Room, where the girls were muttering darkly over the birth of the internet and Renard was ascending level upon level in the strange house of his game, searching for the Flickering Man.

– – – – – –

That was back when I could still tolerate computers.

Like most bright kids in the 1980s and 1990s, I spent a lot of time programming and playing video games. But as an adult I discovered, to my discomfort (along with the others at Sapere Aude), that the more time I spent immersed in thanaton mathematics, the more computers rubbed me the wrong way.

We knew thanaton theory was weird. We knew that gaining proficiency in its subjective mathematics changed you, that it altered your modes of perception. We knew that the very act of calculation subtly distorted space-time around it.

We just hadn't expected certain distortions to be so nauseating. The way it *feels* as computers suck up and spit out data, chop it to bits, yank it back and forth, bully it around—

Look. We were all technical people. Tinkerers, part-time programmers, nerds. And yet many of us, after calculating our first few hundred death dates, began to feel an aversion to computers. The relentless jabbing and shivering in the way computers process their calculations—we started to feel it like a physical cloud around the machines, a constant low-grade electric shock, exponentially spiking in proportion to the number of calculations swarming through its CPU.

Thanaton theory wasn't just a new branch of physics. It had opened up a whole branch of subjective mathematics as well—certain kinds of calculations that computers simply couldn't perform.

But once you've immersed yourself in enough of this subjective math, you begin to perceive the math of others.

And the way computers do math feels like chewing tinfoil.

We thought our acquired distaste for computers was just a minor thing. For some of us it remained minor. For others, though, the nausea became overwhelming, and they were obliged to quit. Especially as the years went on and using the internet became necessary for living a halfway normal life.

This is all to say that, for the past twenty or so years, the internet has felt like a continual house party that I can't attend. At best I'm hanging out in the front yard, peering in the windows. But the more glimpses I take into that window, the more the partygoers seem like monsters, the party more frantic and sick-making . . . and no, not in a prudish or judgmental way. I don't mean I'm sickened by what people do online—I don't care about selfies or porn habits or nasty tweets—as far as the actual calculations are concerned, it's all the same. I mean the nature of the calculations. I glimpse a screen from afar, and for a moment it's alluring, it looks smooth and crisp, it seems to offer so much. But then I get closer and I feel the loathsome speed and inanity of the computer *thinking*, the jagged jackhammer calculations happening every second, the *bang bang bang* of TCP/IP and HTTP and TLS/SSL, the numb way numbers are shunted around—and then the nausea comes, the dizzy sour feeling, the vomit inching up my throat.

This happened to almost all of us at Sapere Aude. Unease with computers, revulsion toward the internet, even a disinclination to use smartphones. Most of us can manage it if we have to. I can kind of muscle through it. But it always feels wrong.

Other guys of my age, of my disposition—that is, curious, smart nerds—built the internet, or populated it with their creativity. In any case, they became millionaires.

I helped build something else.

And so here I am.

– – – – – –

have to piss.

There's a blizzard outside the car but there's no getting around the fact: I drank two coffees during my Lisa Beagleman session and nature calls.

I bundle up. Hat, gloves, scarf, everything. Crack open the door. Immediately snow and wind blast into the car. I stagger out, make sure I have the keys (that would be classic, locking myself out of my car right now), and slam the door. The emergency flashers blink red and white against the fluttering dark.

Survey the damage. Just as I thought, I'd slammed into the concrete embankment at the bottom of the ditch and the car's front is totally crumpled and twisted. It's finished. Surprised its electrical system still works.

I fumble with my pants with gloved hands. Can't do it. Have to take off the gloves. Fingers immediately numb with cold. Stand with the wind at my back, open up my fly, fuck this is cold, then I'm pissing into the darkness, into the snow, steam boiling up and swept away in the flashing light. Already my dick is freezing. Finish, finish, finish this.

Are you going to look yourself up?

The books are in the car. You could do it.

And what then? If I do a thanaton assessment on myself and find out I'm going to die in like thirty years, what would I change? Or if I'm going to die next week, what would I do differently then?

Never a good idea.

Suckers like Lisa Beagleman, with her Mandy and her puh-puh-puh-puh-prom, learn that too late.

Resist it.

But Stettinger must've looked himself up. He had to have, right? It's hard to think he could've not done it. Stettinger never explicitly denied that he had. And if looking yourself up was good enough for Stettinger . . . Well, you always aspired to be another Stettinger, didn't you? The whole eschaton thing, right?

Right?

A car comes barreling by. Doesn't even slow down. Slush flying. I'm standing out in the snow, dick out like an idiot.

No Stettinger.

– – – – – –

S tettinger was why I chose to commit to physics. Thanaton theory hit me at the exact right time, late in high school, when I was at maximum ambitiousness. I even made a point of enrolling at the university where Stettinger was a professor, the university where I had gone to physics camp with Renard. The joke was on me, though: Stettinger soon became world-famous. For my entire college career, I never even saw him on campus.

But full disclosure: in my junior year, I actually *corrected an error* in one of Stettinger's derivations of thanaton theory.

In the grand scheme of things my correction had no practical consequences; it turned out that what Stettinger overlooked in that part of his derivation (an unbounded series that, potentially, could've blown up to infinity) coincidentally canceled out elsewhere (a new set of vectors that zeroed out the term). I hadn't proven that Stettinger's equations were false—that would've been a career-making discovery—I merely showed that they had to be derived in a slightly different way, which mathematicians more skilled than I promptly did.

But the episode gave me minor notoriety at a young age. Nothing big. A footnote in the history of thanaton theory.

Anyway, I didn't follow it up with other scholarship. The embarrassing truth is, the only reason I even discovered the mistake was because I found it so difficult to follow Stettinger's knotty, labyrinthine, idiosyncratic math, and so I had forced myself to laboriously check and recheck every step of his proofs—that's how I noticed the minor error that others had missed. I wasn't a straight-up physics major anyway—I was a physics and philosophy double major, not so much interested in finding practical applications for "death particles" as in writing papers about what thanatons *meant*. The other physics majors were concentrating on applications. I secretly believed they were philistines. I'm sure they judged me as a lightweight.

In the long run, they were right.

But back then I had buzz. When Sapere Aude started up, Blattner and Hansen called me "the youngest and most notable scholar of thanatons," which is what they wanted me to be. In retrospect, what they really wanted was an aggressively young face, someone who didn't look like a classic nerd or a middle-aged duffer, someone who could explain this mind-blowing stuff on TV and at conferences. Back then I had mojo and knew how to talk about thanatons with authority, I knew how to make thanatons accessible—and even more importantly, I knew how to bullshit about them, too.

I'd already been accepted in my first-choice physics doctoral program. I remember hanging out with Julia in my dorm, hemming and hawing on what to do. If I stayed in research, I said to her, maybe I could make new discoveries, push the field further. If I went to work for Sapere Aude, for all its flashiness, for all its financial upside, I'd fundamentally be a salesman.

A few days later Julia told me she got her own job at Sapere Aude.

"You're kidding," I said.

Julia said, "You know me."

That's what the documentary got wrong. Julia didn't follow me in.

I followed her.

I joined Sapere Aude, and school was out forever.

— — — — —

Julia was different. Everyone else at Sapere Aude in the early days—both in sales and in research—they were all kind of like me, upper-middle-class strivers with an abrupt, confrontational, this-is-the-future-get-used-to-it attitude. Because after all, we *were* the future. Arrogant in a suburban way. It was only natural and expected that the universe should rearrange itself around us. (In time, of course, the universe did rearrange itself around us, but we didn't have to be such dicks about it.)

Julia had an affectionate semicontempt for us. She went to our college but she was also a "townie" and from the beginning seemed to have more poise, because, after all, this college town was her territory. When she was still in high school, Julia had already done her drinking at off-campus parties, had already stayed up all night in the dorms, had already done her drugs, already had her sex. College thrills were yesterday's news.

Julia smoked. My first kiss was with a girl who smoked, Hannah Rhee. A cold November day, eighth grade, on the bleachers by the empty football field. Hannah chewed gum and the combined taste of grungy cigarettes and cloying bubble gum was so distinctive I can taste it even now.

I never smoked, but I liked the girls who did.

When I first asked Julia out during my sophomore year, I was surprised she said yes. Maybe she surprised herself, too. Motivated by curiosity, probably. She was a business major. I was physics and philosophy but hung out with the artier crowd. Julia and I had zero friends in common, and what passed for scruffy charm in my clique was embarrassingly shabby in her more conventional circles. When I showed up for our first date on my bicycle, she said, "Oh, you poor thing."

But she was game. "Okay, yeah, you know what? We'll do it on bikes." Julia got hers out of the basement (she lived off campus with three other girls; I lived in a dorm all four years), but I was pretty sure that this was no longer a real date.

The restaurant I had picked was a disaster. It was an oyster place and there was "live jazz" playing. We could barely talk.

I shouted, "I wouldn't have picked this place if I'd known they were playing jazz."

Julia said, "You don't like jazz?"

"I hate jazz."

"Good. If you did then this night really would be over."

"What?"

"Let's go."

"Our food isn't here yet."

"Fuck it."

That was when my date with Julia really began.

We rode around our college town on our bikes in the dark. Some of the same roads Renard and I had biked down, years ago. Biking the streets at night was something Julia used to do in high school, she said, but she hadn't done it in a long time. She gave me her local-kid's tour: the houses of her childhood friends, the parks where she had played, her high school. We rode through downtown, which always seemed kind of empty, past the ominous-looking water plant, through the gardens next to the river.

We stopped at a gas station. Julia bought cigarettes and a lottery ticket. She bought the ticket like it was a routine thing, reciting her numbers like she'd said them a million times. I had never seen anyone buy a lottery ticket before. It was the kind of thing poor people did. Julia turned to me and said, "Let's buy a ticket together." Probably at any other time I would've called buying a lottery ticket "a tax on stupidity" or something math-snotty like that. But this time I didn't.

I just said, "I've never bought a lottery ticket."

"Of course," said Julia. "Deep down you're already a millionaire."

At first I thought it was a compliment. It was anything but. In that gas station I thought maybe Julia meant I had the confidence of a millionaire. Or that I was already on the fast track to becoming a millionaire.

It was only later that I realized her real meaning: that I habitually acted with all the entitlement, with the oblivious assurance, with the bland assumption of resources of a millionaire.

It was pretty cutting, in retrospect.

And a prologue.

─ ─ ─ ─ ─ ─

Julia and I ended up at a party that night. Later I found out she'd meant to go to the party all along. Probably she'd intended to cut me loose early. But somehow I hung on, or she let me hang on.

It wasn't a college party. None of Julia's friends from campus were there. At school, I'd see Julia hanging out with the rich kids, the athletes, the model-level girls, but this party was different. These were Julia's townie friends. Some of them were much older, like pushing thirty. Men with mustaches. The music wasn't carefully curated as it was at the parties I went to, parties thrown by the indie rockers who hung around the campus radio station. This was unironic classic rock and bad metal. Some guys were burning a couch in the back yard, stripped to their boxer briefs. The stink of bad weed floated around. The music blasted, embarrassing and trashy. I was dressed wrong. Too college. Didn't belong there. Dudes looked like they wanted to kill me. Contempt. Probably my imagination. Probably nobody noticed me at all. Julia separated herself from me, was talking to some other friends, hadn't invited me into the conversation. Where was I supposed to go? Was this even a date anymore? I was ridiculous. A puppy tagging along, not taking the hint. In over my head. Shirtless guys shouting back and forth. They were my age; they already had jobs. I felt like a child. Wait, here was a real child: a literal kid who looked like she was twelve years old "manning" the keg. What? Now I was in the kitchen talking to a tattooed woman in a ratty pink tank top. She was drinking a beer and I had a Coke, and she was bored to death of me. She said something about her husband, about her baby. But she couldn't be more than twenty-one. A baby at twenty-one! A different world. I had nothing to say to her, to anyone. The elaborate system of ironic references I had honed with my friends was obnoxious here.

Out of strained politeness, the too-young mother had asked me what I did. I said where I went to school and she snorted, "of course," and when she asked what I studied, there was no reason to lie. She was obviously looking for a way out of the conversation, but then a grizzled metalhead who was at least twenty-eight, rooting through the refrigerator, said, "You study *what*?" and when I repeated, "thanatons," he said, "Let me get you a beer—I gotta ask you something," and when I said I didn't drink he responded, "Good idea, professor, gotta save those brain cells." If the young mother had called me "professor," it would've sounded contemptuous, but this guy—I suspected him to be the type, and I was right—was one of those intellectual metalheads, an autodidact who preferred metal in part because of its complex time signatures, its mathematical virtuosity. In another life, he'd be sitting next to me in a physics seminar and not working in some stockroom. Anyway, he had earnest questions about thanatons.

So I explained thanatons to the metal guy. The young mother hung around, looking irritated. But she didn't get up and leave, either, like I expected she would, like I kind of wanted her to. The metalhead—his name was Carl—and I sat at the kitchen table and I explained to Carl, with pen and paper, how Stettinger had discovered the existence of thanatons and deduced their properties. Carl was no fool, either. He asked good questions, even some questions scientists didn't have answers for at the time—thanatons were still a young field with no practical applications yet. At that point, all anyone knew was that Stettinger had discovered bizarre subatomic particles that were intimately connected with human death.

I didn't know where Julia had gone off to. Assumed she'd ditched me. Fine, I'd make my own way back home. I don't know how long I had been talking to Carl, maybe forty-five minutes, when I heard a noise behind me.

I turned.

Julia, smoking. Her eyes on me. As though she had been standing behind me for a long time. Looking at me almost as if puzzled, a different way than she had before.

— — — — — —

Somehow that date with Julia led to another date. Then another date. When I asked her later why she kept going out with me, even though we seemed so mismatched at first, Julia said it was because I actually *asked* her out on dates instead of just calling her up to "hang out." She said, in a way that was hard to read, "You wooed me."

But it was something else, too. The way Julia's expression changed when she watched me explaining thanatons to Carl. Like she saw something capable in me.

Those first few weeks felt like a miracle. Julia was out of my league, or at least I thought so. I convinced myself I had to savor everything I could before the clock ran out, before she wised up to the fact that I was beneath her. I developed rituals to keep it going. On my way to meet her, I'd always pick up cigarettes and a lottery ticket with her lucky numbers. I liked it particularly, the seventh or eighth time, when Julia just took the cigarettes and lottery ticket without even saying thanks. Accepted them as routine. We were a couple.

Julia was a small-time drug dealer. Weed and ecstasy, occasionally cocaine. That's why we went to that party on our first date; she was picking up her supply. The clueless kids in the dorms were too scared to buy drugs from a real townie, but they'd readily buy from the pretty girl in Econ.

When Julia was dealing, she was all business. She never used. Getting high was part of her high school experience, that was kid shit. Now she had a car. She was paying her own tuition. That's why Julia had said "Oh, you poor thing" when I showed up for our date on a bicycle. I was always short of money because I didn't work, I just studied. Julia was already running a business, essentially.

Always pointing herself upward. Always dressed fashionably while other girls were still stomping around campus in their comfort sweatpants. I started dressing differently too. Everyone else at our university was still acting like children. Julia and I were adults, or on our way. Or so we thought.

We weren't really.

— — — — — —

When I was an undergraduate I didn't really think about Renard. About the weird things we used to do on that very campus. I never visited the dorm that Renard and I had stayed in.

There was a reason for that.

— — — — — —

Renard and I would sneak out of our dorm at night. Nothing was secured back then. It was summer and the campus was skeleton staffed. We weren't yet in the era of electronic surveillance systems and ubiquitous cameras. In 1987, if you did something under the cover of night and got away with it, you'd really gotten away with it.

Renard and I got away with a lot.

We crept out of our room after midnight and explored the hidden parts of campus. We figured out how to get on the roof of the chemistry building, and from there we could open the windows into professors' offices that were seemingly abandoned for the summer. The art building, full of junked sculptures and installations and bulky kilns and pottery equipment, had an agreeably disorderly air during the day, but at night was full of menacing silhouettes. Steam tunnels made a labyrinth underneath the campus, and from there you could access the basement of the physics building and even get close to the disused particle accelerator.

I was terrified of being caught. But exploring was too exhilarating to resist. Even when Renard and I got in over our heads, like when some adjunct professor working late into the night was walking down the desolate linoleum hallway after buying a snack from the vending machine, passing us as we hid behind a door holding our breath, our hearts exploding, it almost felt like a real-life version of the video game Renard played so obsessively, with its ruined house full of endless stairs and secret doors and traps and spiders and snakes. Like maybe a real-life Flickering Man was wandering around late nights too, waiting for us to find him.

One night Renard and I found our way into the college's auditorium. We climbed onto the stage and looked out onto the rows of dark, empty seats. Backstage were heaps of old sets and props and a queer half-sized door that led down rough wooden steps into what looked like a costume storage room. I couldn't quite tell what was down there because it was so dark.

I flicked the light switch. Nothing.

A scratching noise came from that darkness.

"Go down there," Renard said.

The way he said it was unexpectedly abrupt. In the darkness the figure of Renard suddenly seemed ominous, almost threatening. He was the kind of nerd who worked out, who had muscles, though not the kind of all-around muscles you get from actually playing a sport but a kind of specific unnatural definition that I guessed came from working out exclusively with machines. The combination of Renard's weirdly muscled physique and his pimply nerd face always looked jarring to me. Maybe it was physical intimidation that compelled me to go down the stairs, or the brutal edge of authority in Renard's voice—anyway, I obeyed him.

Only once I was at the bottom of the stairs did I feel alarmed.

I looked up at the square of light, with Renard's shadow in it.

I couldn't see his face.

A scuttling noise around me. Now I was truly freaked out. For the first time I thought, why am I down here? Why did I obey Renard? But this was a thrill, too. Everything around me felt sharp, alive, hyperreal. The dim racks of fancy dresses and pirate costumes and soldier uniforms and a hundred other theatrical outfits packed in tight rows to my left and right looked like a fascinating maze. The stinging smell of mothballs went to my head as the scuttling got louder, and I braced for a rat to run over my foot, for tiny jaws to bite my ankle, but nothing did. When Renard said, "Keep going, go further," I actually wanted to keep going, deeper into the labyrinth of costumes. I pushed through the walls of silk shirts and fur coats and gangster suits until I was in the middle of it, until I couldn't see the light from the top of the stairs anymore, or Renard, although I knew he was still up there. I was surrounded and packed in tight on all sides by the costumes, and I stood very still, and the scuttling in the darkness came closer, and the thought came to me, with a kind of pleasure, that this is what death is like; death will be exactly like this.

– – – – – –

I t became a regular thing. Renard and I would be exploring the midnight campus and then suddenly he would order me, in a rough way, to do something.

I would always do it.

Sometimes Renard would command me to do something dangerous, like walk along the edge of the roof of the chemistry building, where one false step would've made me fall five stories and probably killed me. Sometimes he'd dare me to do something subtly destructive, like sneak into a professor's office to remove the forty-fifth page out of every book on his shelves. Or something jokey, like replace the hand soap in a public bathroom with mayonnaise.

I liked these night missions. I could almost sense the atmosphere charging up just before Renard gave the order. The thrill being that, according to some unspoken rule, there was no way of getting out of it. I *had* to do it.

That was the fun.

We didn't overanalyze why we did this. I didn't follow Renard's orders at any other time. But when I accepted Renard's special dares, there was almost a kind of solemnity, and for those few minutes it felt like we were in a separate reality, each one of our completed missions feeling like another step in a long, complicated ritual that was somehow touching our vast and invisible and evil thing. That through our actions, inch by inch, we were bringing something new into the world.

One night Renard said, "Have you ever been to Cahokia?"

— — — — — —

G et back in the car. Fast as you can. Out of the howling blizzard.

Slam the door.

Jesus, it's cold. So cold. Cold cold cold.

Still no tow truck. Rub hands together. Don't feel a thing. Blow on them. That piss in the freezing cold wasn't worth it. Why didn't you just piss in the car? It's not like you'll ever drive it again. It's wrecked.

Christ. Have some self-respect.

But going outside distracted me at least. Bought me time against myself.

Because I don't want to look myself up. Not really.

Really?

The books are right there.

I want to know.

Why not? I don't care anymore. Everything is fucked anyway. It doesn't matter. Go. Look.

I open the first book again, to start the calculation.

But Minneapolis.

But Julia.

— — — — — —

'd never gone out with a girl like Julia before. Partly because girls like Julia weren't interested in me. Partly because I was suspicious of girls like Julia who had their shit together a bit too much.

Julia didn't entirely understand me either. Wasting a hundred-thousand-dollar education on something as impractical as thanaton theory—a rich kid's indulgence, Julia obviously believed, though she didn't say as much to me out loud. Julia was the first in her family to attend college. She wasn't going to fuck around. I met her parents, who lived close to campus, and I liked them. Her dad was an electrical contractor who drank shitty beer and walked around the house with no shirt on and blew glass in the garage, really beautiful pieces. Her mom was a vet tech who got off on smutty romance novels and clipping coupons, something I realized I had never seen anyone actually do before. When I first visited

Julia's small childhood home, I remember thinking its cramped size was exotic. Living in such close quarters with your whole family, practically on top of each other, seemed like a kind of adventure!

I had the sense not to say that out loud, though.

On maybe our fourth or fifth date, Julia and I went to a house party that had an ironic prom theme, the idea being everyone would go to Goodwill and buy dorky suits and hideous prom dresses, and we'd dance all night to bad music from our high school lives that we secretly still liked. Julia and I had our first kiss to "Into the Groove." I was in a blue velvet tuxedo with ruffles and Julia wore a ludicrous satiny pink bridesmaid's dress. But Julia made the cheap dress look unironic. She shone in it.

Walking to the party, on an icy hill, one of her high heels broke.

She went skidding down hard into the muddy, half-melted snow.

I was horrified. I dashed down the hill to her, helped her up. I couldn't understand why she got so quiet after. Julia told me later that one of the reasons she ended up liking me was that I hadn't laughed at her when she fell that night. I couldn't understand—who laughs when a girl falls on her ass? A lot of people would laugh, said Julia, and after a while she admitted, "Maybe I would've laughed." I said I didn't think she would. Julia said, "That's why I love you"—and I thought, holy shit, had Julia just told me she loved me? Or did that not really count yet? Did I have to wait for the magic words to be their own sentence: *I love you*, just the bare declaration, no qualifiers? Julia eventually did say *I love you* to me properly, later, of course, and I said it to her. Still, maybe this was her way of sneaking it in early.

Do you fall in love with someone because you understand them? Not at nineteen. It's their otherness that draws you in. At nineteen you're collecting people. Trying on different ways of being. When I was young, I always scanned girlfriends' bookshelves, full of dead giveaways. Of course she would have that book . . . but they would surprise me, too. Challenge me, expand me.

(During my affairs in my thirties? Didn't care what they read.)

Sports, for instance. Julia played high school tennis and was a scratch golfer; she actually attended our college's dull football games. My relationship to sports was limited to a manifesto I'd written for my high school newspaper arguing for the abolition of school-sponsored athletics (which, you need not remind me, is extremely charismatic and not at all obnoxious).

And yet Julia made even sports enjoyable for me. One time we went golfing together, even though golf was the kind of stupid shit my dad did. Somehow Julia made it a blast. Granted, we were both wasted, we'd smuggled whiskey onto the course, Julia having long ago undermined my personal no-alcohol policy. But on the sixth hole I accidentally sliced the ball hard into a flock of geese. One of the birds plummeted out of the sky.

The goose hit the grass and lay there, motionless. A bunch of other geese gathered around it, honking. Staring at me like I was a villain.

Julia thought this was hilarious! I felt terrible. But here's the thing that might be hard for me to convey to you: Julia's laughing at an animal getting hurt and maybe killed was . . . attractive? From anyone else, the laughter would've repulsed me. But a goose getting whacked out of the sky by a golf ball *is* kind of funny, maybe. And even if it's not, I didn't want to be the kind of guy who's more sensitive than his girlfriend about it. "It's just a goose," said Julia, moving on to the next hole. Her heartlessness was refreshing—or was she just pretending to be heartless? Was she trying to be kind of badass? Or maybe she just didn't want me to feel bad for killing a bird? The explanations were all irreconcilable, but I liked Julia even if she was playing a role, and whatever, by the end of the ninth hole we had forgotten about the goose anyway and we were just laughing, who knows what for, I just remember the fuzzy hilarity of the afternoon.

I did sports stuff for Julia's sake. She did arty stuff for me, though she persisted in her terrible taste. For movies, she didn't like "anything foreign or black-and-white," and definitely not the plotless weirdfests my friends and I preferred. She'd watch crappy blockbusters, and I'd have to go with her. Movies for children. Dumb computer effects. And yet she would turn around and mock any good movie that was halfway challenging as "oh *so* deep." For Julia, taking art seriously was an embarrassing stage that real adults moved past as soon as possible.

That should've irritated me. But from Julia it was a liberation. By that point my indie rock friends and I had devolved into a passive-aggressive cultural bullying of each other; our once-exciting underground scene had become sexless, inert. With Julia, I might've been dancing and fucking to shitty music, but I was dancing and fucking.

Julia had the biggest room in the group house she lived in, a long room that stretched the width of the place. Her bed was in the middle of the room, a natural center stage, surrounded by books and clothes and candles and CDs strewn on the floor. Unsentimental with me in the beginning. The first time we had sex, she said, "But if we have sex, some chemical will be released in my brain that will trick me into feeling like I love you." Sounded heartless to me. We did it anyway, but what she'd said wounded my little vanity. I remember that first time, how she turned her head to the side, eyes closed, lip curled as if suspicious, as if still withholding judgment, and as her head bobbed against the pillow she giggled a little, as if our sex didn't involve me but was her own private joke that only she understood, that she wasn't sharing with me . . . until she then looked at me, eyes wide, baffled but happy, like we had figured out something incredible together.

That's the way I remember Julia.

Used to think of her all the time.

Now, not as much. But sometimes.

Gross old man.

‒ ‒ ‒ ‒ ‒ ‒

Back to Sapere Aude's first conference.

The conference was more than a conference. Looking back on that week in Minneapolis, the intense debates, the technical breakthroughs, the engineers mixing with the flakes—and by flakes I mean genuine weirdo occultists, kooks in hooded cloaks, crackpots with capes and tangled beards, witches with accents—who even invited them?—and then of course the sudden tragedy, it all felt larger than life. All the recklessness and brilliance and catastrophe that Sapere Aude ended up being famous for was already there.

Back then we were just getting off the ground. The world didn't know yet what was going to hit it. But we knew. And even though now, years later, we've all gone our separate ways—some to success, others . . . well, others like me—for that week in Minneaopolis we were all pure potential.

Now I know that potential is a disease. It betrays you. These days, whenever I feel that limitless exhilaration, that wild fresh hope welling up—I kill it.

Keep your eye on the ball. Do the work.

In Minneapolis, Julia and I were young and in love and everyone was on fire, including the rest of the old gang, Hutchinson and Ziegler and Hwang and Wiesnewski and Kulkarni, all of them, even Hansen and Blattner, who were still idealistic, and we'd been down in the hotel bar all night, raving it up, before moving the party to Hutchinson's room, all more than a little tipsy when the idea came up—I don't even know who said it first—hey—let's look ourselves up.

Even back then it wasn't allowed. The specific taboo hadn't developed yet; it was merely against company policy. But what Blattner and Hansen didn't know wouldn't hurt them, right? And even though ordinarily it'd take hours or even days to complete the calculation, we'd all drilled the algorithm so many times that week on each other, and we knew each other so well, which made anything feel possible, and we were punch-drunk enough to think that if we all did the calculation together, it would be an hour's work max, and come on, when you're half in the bag in a strange city in a strange hotel, you do things you ordinarily wouldn't, so why not, okay, let's do it! Julia was the only one who seemed iffy but once we had the idea, the rest of us wanted to do it quickly before anyone chickened out. Nobody volunteered to be the subject, so like a bunch of high school dorks, we put an empty beer bottle in the middle of the table and spun it—and it landed on Hopkins, the kid! The only one in sales who was even younger than Julia and me.

Everyone laughed! Even Hopkins laughed, though already he looked a little pale. I could tell he didn't want to do this but he was a good sport. We had all become close that week. In those early days Sapere Aude was more than a company. It was shaggier and weirder, more intimate, especially at this conference, which I had thought was going to be a kind of standard sales or training conference. Instead it was a combination brainstorming session, emotional debate, supernatural invocation, and collective freakout. I knew there were things going on behind closed doors in that hotel that were suspicious yet might've been indispensable in getting Sapere Aude off the ground, and indeed, once we shaved off the rough edges and got the math right, Blattner and Hansen flushed the self-proclaimed occultists out of the company, quietly paying the hotel thousands of dollars to look the other way regarding whatever unnatural activities had occurred in their rooms—I remember drunkenly opening the door to the wrong room, which was pitch-dark except for a metallic glow coming from the bathroom, there was the sound of an animal's cry or a squeaky laugh, and I caught a glimpse of a ragged figure in the bathroom mirror staring at me before a woman with no eyebrows and an empty stare shut the door in my face. I was told some of those rooms were permanently locked after that, never to be used again, but really, the most disturbing thing that happened that week happened in our room.

We were all so tipsy it was a miracle that any of us were able to perform the calculations on Hopkins, we were slurring the assessment I'm sure, scrawling out the equations on pads of paper emblazoned with the hotel's logo, pawing through our brand-new Books of the Dead, half out of our minds, but then again we all knew the algorithm cold at that point, knew it backward and forward. Running the assessment calculations was second nature. Not everyone there was from Sapere Aude; Hutchinson had picked up the pretty-boy bartender and lured him up to our room, though we knew Hutchinson had a wife and kids, but his wedding ring came off that week, and he picked up that twentysomething boy so smoothly and matter-of-factly that we all figured this was Hutchinson's normal MO, maybe even a tacit understanding of his marriage; it wasn't our business anyway, nobody cared about Hutchinson's wife. Hutchinson seemed so old to me back then, so sophisticated. He probably wasn't more than thirty-five. A kid to me now. Still married, I hear.

We lit candles around the darkened room—standard operating procedure in the early days, the black candles, the carefully toneless repetitions, etc., we cut all that stuff out when engineering zeroed in on a purely mathematical method, and even I forget how unsettling it could feel when we were first starting out; it gets omitted from the histories so people think our algorithm runs on pure logic, but no, something hungry and invisible around us demanded to be acknowledged and sated—we closed the curtains and the room felt small and special, becoming our whole world, all of us in giddy sync, rapidly chanting the nonsense sentences to Hopkins and Hopkins firing back nonsense just as quickly, his dimpled face laughing, having fun now, even Julia was into it, though I wonder what the pretty-boy bartender thought of us—he'd probably come up to Hutchinson's room expecting a quick blow job but now he was stuck with these weirdos engaged in some combination of math problem and pagan ritual, and yet he lingered, maybe feeling the thanatons buzzing in the air around us, all of the particles together slowly turning and pointing at Hopkins—back then I could still feel it; as you get older, you lose that feeling of thanatons, their queer prickling as they flit and flicker through the air, just like how, as you grow older, you lose the ability to hear very high-pitched tones, like how when I was a kid the green monochrome monitor for my Apple II clone in the basement continuously emitted a high whine—anyway, thanatons are like that, they tingle when they're charged up, and the atmosphere was flooded and buzzing with millions of tiny quivering invisible arrows, sharpening, blowing through us, millions every second . . .

We had our answer.

Pencils down. We all arrived at it more or less at the same time. The only one who didn't know was Hopkins. The bartender too, I guess. But nobody wanted to say it.

"What?" said Hopkins, his smile fading.

"Six minutes," said Ziegler.

- - - - - -

O f course Ziegler was the one to say it. Because it had to be a joke, right? But it was no joke. The number was correct. We'd all come up with the same result. No chance of all of us making the same mistake in the same way. Hopkins was going to die in six minutes, no, five now, and some jackass (maybe the bartender) had set the timer on the kitchenette's microwave oven, and it was already steadily counting down. Not funny, guys, come on, Hopkins said, and Ziegler and Hutchinson and the others said, No, this is the result. Someone open the drapes, blow out those stupid candles, said Kulkarni. Four minutes. All the lights flicked on, mercilessly bright. Hopkins said, You're reading it wrong, and Julia said, No, we're reading it right, and I remember the way Julia's face screwed up, I think she was the first one who fully understood what was about to happen, she wouldn't even look at me, at Hopkins either, and Hopkins said, It's wrong, you calculated wrong, you're reading it wrong. Three minutes. Kulkarni said, Do you have any medical problems? No! shouted Hopkins, and then, this is ridiculous, but his eyes were on the clock too, all of our eyes were on it, I reached out to Hopkins and said, Come on, relax, but he wrenched his arm away and said, No way, maybe you'll kill me, and I said, Come on, Hopkins, you know me, and he shouted, I don't know you, I don't know any of you, oh my God I've got to get out of here, I need to call my, I need to call Mom, holy shit I'm going to die. Two minutes and everyone was freaking out and someone knocked over the wine bottle and it glugged out in a red stream on the carpet, Mom, somebody, Julia tried to touch him but Hopkins twisted away, snarling, then suddenly he was doubled over, gasping, and the room went silent for a second and then we were all screaming, Someone call a doctor! Kulkarni was on the phone and Julia tried to hold Hopkins but he wouldn't let her, he was heaving, he couldn't breathe, something was wrong, something was very wrong, but we knew it would happen, thirty seconds now, twenty, Hopkins fell to the ground, calling for someone, anyone, to help him, and the microwave went off, beep beep beep.

— — — — — —

Ruptured cerebral aneurysm. Hopkins's brain exploded in his skull. The aneurysm had been lurking there for who knows how long, the coroner said, just waiting to blow. So it's not like we had killed him.

But it felt like we had. Blattner and Hansen should've fired all of us, if only because the optics were terrible. Stettinger quietly disassociated himself from Sapere Aude, of course—he'd never been directly involved in our day-to-day workings, though he did sit on the board to lend us legitimacy. Blattner and Hansen had paid through the nose for that, had wined and dined "the reluctant revolutionary" for months before they wore him down and got him to sign on in the most limited way.

Well, that was over now.

And yet—insensitive as it is to say—from a business point of view Hopkins's death was the best thing that could've happened to us. Kicked Sapere Aude into the public consciousness. All of us swore never to reveal how we'd looked up Hopkins's death six minutes before he died, how we'd predicted his death to the minute. But of course word got out. Maybe it was the bartender. Or maybe one of us—Hutchinson?—correctly guessed that such a story would make Sapere Aude notorious before we'd closed a single sale.

The Hopkins incident became a kind of instant urban legend. People knew what we claimed to be selling, they knew that we'd had a conference at that hotel. And the coroner's report was public record. Reporters couldn't resist connecting the dots. The story fit the larger narrative about us, especially in those early days when the public looked at us as a bunch of sinister oddballs and geeks. At any rate, the myth took off.

People began to take us seriously.

Blattner and Hansen probably were surprised we decided to stay on, considering how freaked out we all were. But then orders began rolling in, and then Blattner and Hansen couldn't fire us anyway because now there was too much business, even before we officially went live, and Sapere Aude had to make hay while the sun shined. Hopkins wasn't forgotten, obviously; we talked about him all the time. A kind of mascot, a sacrificial lamb. Nothing brings a group together like a shared death or shared guilt, and we had plenty of both. Felt crass, but the opportunities were huge and we rationalized to ourselves, Hopkins would've died anyway, whether or not we predicted it. I don't think anyone was so boorish as to say, "We must keep going for Hopkins's sake" or "Hopkins would've wanted us to continue," but the result was the same: we made a shit ton of cash.

We hadn't killed Hopkins. But we knew thanaton theory. We weren't purely innocent, either. Because the time of Hopkins's death didn't technically exist until we measured it. By running the algorithm, by forcing the waveform to collapse, we pinned Hopkins's death down to one particular time among many. In a way you could say we *had* killed him, by perhaps demanding the time of his death before the universe was ready to tell it. To do the math makes the math come true. This was where thanaton theory began to get murky, unnerving; it was where Julia stopped the conversation. She didn't want to hear about it. Too theoretical.

We put it out of our minds and got rich.

– – – – – –

didn't totally put it out of my mind.

I talked it over with Kulkarni, the weirdness of that conference. This wasn't long before Kulkarni himself got weird, too, before he quit. Just like me, Kulkarni had studied the history and philosophy of science as an undergraduate, but at a better school. He was a legitimate Ivy Leaguer, a product of the East Coast, charismatic and at ease in his privilege. I enjoyed being around his fascinating preppiness, just as Kulkarni seemed to appreciate my exotic (to him) midwesternness. In any case, Kulkarni was the only person at Sapere Aude with whom I could have Renard-like discussions.

Over drinks one night, Kulkarni mentioned how our early work with thanatons reminded him of Isaac Newton.

As we talked, I began to get what he meant.

If you look at the way science actually advances, as opposed to the just-so stories you read in textbooks, you know it's not at all an orderly succession of heroic rationalists overcoming ignorance. Science is more often advanced by quacks, cranks, and religious maniacs. Take Newton, for example—most of his intellectual effort wasn't focused on physics. He was all about the occult. Set aside Newton's *Principia*, his laws of motion, his account of gravitation, his invention of the calculus. For Newton, that was all a sidebar to his real obsessions: pages and pages raving on about biblical apocalypse, alchemy, occult geometry, magic, the whole shitshow of crazy.

Not only Newton. Not only physics. Linguistics was jump-started by medieval cranks trying to rediscover the language spoken in the Garden of Eden. Chemistry developed straight out of alchemical rituals. Geometry is just one aspect of the Pythagoreans' mystery cult. Kepler made his living casting horoscopes and his mother was nearly burned for witchcraft. The rocket scientist who founded the Jet Propulsion Laboratory was a full-blown satanist who did "sex magick" and hung out with Aleister Crowley, for fuck's sake. Even quantum physics is constantly misinterpreted by flakes into neo–*Tao of Physics* garbage mysticism. Kulkarni confessed he had it in his own family—a mathematician great-uncle who was also a stone-cold nutjob who spent at least half of his time trying to derive some sacred glyph whose sheer geometry was supposed to obliterate any evil that could be tricked into gazing upon it. Bonkers. And yet Kulkarni's great-uncle was a tenured professor, was published, and did legitimate work.

Same with us. When you considered the freaks Sapere Aude had on the payroll at first, and the incidents like Hopkins's death that inaugurated us—maybe the occult is always necessary to midwife science into a paradigm shift. Maybe whenever the universe chooses someone through whom to reveal its secrets, the gates of the chthonic crack open too, and a lot of supernatural noise comes with it. And once that paradigm shift is accomplished, the occult can go away again.

Maybe. Kulkarni was really in his cups at this point.

After Hopkins's death we didn't have to work hard to root out the fringy witches and weirdos from Sapere Aude. The crackpots didn't seem too keen on sticking around, either. After that conference in Minneapolis, maybe the warlocks had gotten what they needed from us.

Or maybe we had freaked out even the freaks. Maybe we'd touched some deep power that even they hadn't seriously believed existed.

In any case, six months after that conference, the freaks were gone, their influence expunged. The death of Hopkins had cleansed us.

We were pure math now.

– – – – – –

It's been over an hour and the tow truck still hasn't come.

Too cold in my wrecked car. The heat has all leaked out, bit by bit, and the car's interior is officially freezing. Dirty slush slopping down from the sky now, splattering the windows. Of all the times to be out on the road. Not even on the road. In a ditch.

Alone with the books.

Stop it.

The taboo. Hopkins.

But even if I could manage to pull it off . . . would it be a valid self-assessment? A difficult trick, after all, a kind of partitioning of the mind: one half of you asking the nonsense prompts and calculating, the other half somehow responding with unselfconscious nonsense. Both halves independent, two noninterfering channels streaming past each other. Like playing tennis against yourself. Difficult.

Then again, I'm no amateur.

Been doing this nearly thirty years.

Jesus.

Still have some battery left. I turn on the car's interior lights. For the first time in a long time I feel young. Nervy. My stomach pitches.

Do it.

I take out a thick pad of paper. A pencil.

I open the first book.

Okay. When will I die?

— — — — — —

Renard's and my late-night explorations moved beyond the campus. Sometimes we ventured into the small town that surrounded the college. After lights out we would take off on "borrowed" bikes, and pedal to some greasy spoon diner and eat egg-and-bacon skillets and drink coffee and watch the midnight people come and go. Or we would sneak into an overgrown playground in the backyard of a shuttered preschool and carve graffiti on the jungle gym and swing sets. Or hang out in some alley, watching drunks stumble out of a bar. Sometimes we got chased. But we never got caught.

We were only in eighth grade. I felt badass.

Late one night we visited the river that cut through downtown. There was a park near it, closed after dusk, unlit and always empty. Renard and I biked to the park and he went down to the river. I followed him.

"Let's swim," Renard said.

He nonchalantly took off his clothes. Renard sometimes hung out naked in our dorm room in an oddly casual way. At first I had wondered if Renard's occasional nakedness was some implicit gay invitation. But in fact Renard had a null sexual vibe. His nakedness was impersonal, clinical.

I took off my clothes too and we waded into the river. It was swifter than it looked. For a few minutes we just bobbed along in our shadowy part of the water, steadying ourselves against the current, watching the lights of the city around us, our heels digging into tumbled cinder blocks in the riverbed to keep from being swept away. Cold dark water slipped all over me. I stared up at the black sky full of cold little pinpoints. The water moved so fast around me I felt like any second I could be swept away down the river and sucked underwater.

Renard said, "One hundred years from now, you and I will be dead. Everyone we know will be dead. Nobody will remember any of us. A hundred years from now this place will be totally different. There will be a different cast of characters. They won't care about us. A hundred years after that, those people will be dead, too, and there will be a new generation that doesn't care about them either. People are born, they have their thoughts and emotions and dreams, life feels so real to them, they grow up, they die, and none of it ever mattered. It's like they weren't even real.

"What will this river be a hundred years from now? A million years? Humans will be gone, probably. Some new intelligent creature will dig up our cities and wonder about us, like how we dig up the cities of the ancient Greeks or the Native Americans.

"There used to be big Native American cities around here, did you know that? I hadn't known. My family was taking a cross-country road trip and came to Cahokia in southern Illinois, just a few hours from here. There were dozens of flat-topped pyramids and earthworks and mounds. One of them is over a hundred feet tall. Apparently there used to be a big city there about a thousand years ago. They called it Cahokia. Thirty thousand people. And whoever planned it out were geniuses, it was all carefully engineered, the mounds and buildings laid out according to geometrical and astronomical patterns. And that's without modern surveying equipment. They say thousands of people would come to this city on pilgrimages, for rituals and feasts, people from all over the country, mingling and trading. It was bigger than London or Paris at the time. This is all before anyone from Europe even set foot here.

"Now there's nothing. A bunch of hills outside of St. Louis, most of them dug up or destroyed. Most people don't even know about it. Nobody cares. When Europeans first came across it, the city had already been abandoned for centuries. We don't even know the city's real name—the Europeans called it Cahokia only because that's the name of the tribe that happened to be living around there at the time.

"But Cahokia had lasted five hundred years. Longer than the United States has been around. Someday our number will come up, too. And nobody will remember our names either."

Black water flowed all around me. I floated, looking up at the stars, so cold.

－ － － － － －

remember hearing, in some college philosophy lecture, about the idea of historical cycles—that all civilizations, large and small, pass through four distinct stages. How societies come together, and how they fall apart.

It was probably bullshit. Still, it was one of those ideas that stuck in my mind long after college. I probably don't even remember it accurately, but I do recall that, when my professor was talking about it, it made a certain psychological sense. That it might've even been true beyond its scope. That those same four stages occur with smaller groups, too. With social scenes, with friendships. With romantic relationships. Even with your relationship to yourself.

The trick is knowing what stage you're in.

The way I remember it, before the cycle begins, everything is chaos. A struggle of everyone against everyone. We're hungry and desperate in the wilderness. We have no tribe. We don't understand the universe around us. We're atomized and alone in our separate apartments.

But then a mythos rises out of that disorder. A compelling idea that brings people together. It can be as simple as a law: "You can do whatever you want in the garden, but don't eat from this tree." Or a pact: "Let's all agree that everything in this book is important and true." Or an action: "Every seven days, we must sacrifice an animal at this rock." Or a choice: "We could have chosen anyone in the world to be friends, or lovers. But we chose each other."

There's only one requirement: the mythos must be arbitrary. The more unjustifiable it is, the better it works. The forbidden fruit is important precisely because it is forbidden. The book is important and true only because it is crazy and impossible. An animal sacrifice is compelling because it wastes the animal. The decision to fall in love is crucial only because we know there are others out there who are probably better for us.

This starts the first stage of the cycle, what the professor called the Divine Age, the Age of the Gods. This new mythos binds a new community together. Rituals are invented. You and everyone around you feel like you are spontaneously acting under the urging of the same inspiration. Your religion gushes sacredness and meaning. Your friends are fascinating. Your girlfriend can do no wrong. You want to protect this special new thing that has come into the world.

That leads to the second stage of the cycle, the Aristocratic Age, the Age of Heroes. Harmony can't last so it has to be enforced. Social unanimity breaks down, so it must be manufactured. The mythos no longer feels alive and present, but mechanisms develop to honor it. To enforce these mechanisms, rank and power appear— between the ruler and the ruled, the priest and the congregation, the performer and the audience, the loved and the lover. In the name of perpetuating the mythos, its representation must be frozen in one enduring form. The rituals, which used to be exhilarating mystical dramas spontaneously experienced by everyone, are now scripted liturgies enacted by professionals, to be watched by an increasingly disaffected populace.

This disenchantment leads to the third stage of the cycle, the Democratic Age, the Age of Men. When rituals become bureaucratic, when shared mythos stops creatively improvising and merely repeats itself mechanically, people begin questioning. The ruled interrogate the ruler. The congregation investigates the priest. The audience critiques the performer. The lover suspects the loved. Skepticism develops in order to debunk and dethrone the old heroes and systems. But this skepticism ends up disproving more than originally intended—not only are rank and privilege debunked, but even the primal mythos is disputed. Liberated from the oppression of a mythos that had long ago stopped being genuine, and its associated ranks and codes and laws, a new equality and freedom break out. But never for long, because without a shared mythos, and without credible leaders to defend it, the society weakens. The original mythos becomes corrupted, degraded. Language is debased. Equality leads to a free-for-all. Communication breaks down. With no shared mythos, nobody can agree on even the basic premises of life. All that remains of the exhausted society are three things: a mythos nobody seriously believes in anymore, rituals nobody earnestly participates in anymore, and skepticism. And skepticism alone can't sustain anything.

That causes the final slip into the fourth stage, which is chaos again. Without a functioning mythos, everything in society collapses when put to the slightest test, crumbling with surprising speed, sweeping away the inspiration of the Divine Age, the laws and rituals of the Aristocratic Age, and even the hard-won freedom and equality and science of the Democratic Age. Splintering accelerates, and everyone becomes incomprehensible to each other, eventually even to themselves. The world endures chaos until a new compelling mythos comes out of nowhere, another a bolt of inspiration, and brings us back into the Age of the Gods.

But those will be different gods.

— — — — — —

My fingers are freezing but my pencil is flying. The symbols I'm writing down only make sense to me. Muttering to myself in the back of the car, posing nonsense prompts to myself ("Freeborn octogon reality hum shakes"), answering with corresponding nonsense ("Squeak under shovel grip dragon"), noting the valence and spin of each phrase, pivoting from it, calculating on it, deriving the next answer.

Repeat.

It feels good. I didn't expect how easy it'd be, how right it would feel, how thrilling even. I'm absorbed in the technical aspects of the problem, in playing both sides of the equation. I barely even notice the freezing cold; my entire world has become this thanaton calculation because I'm not even thinking about the end result anymore—my death—I'm simply engrossed in the challenge of negotiating the reflexivities of running an assessment on myself, the work is fascinating, and so I'm on fire, it's a joy to blaze through it this quickly, every step falling neatly into place, my number floating somewhere outside the car, somewhere in the frigid blizzard, buffeted by the wind, coming closer, until . . .

What if you're another Hopkins?

Shut up and calculate.

The pleasure of finding precisely the right thread. Of pulling it and then watching the entire fabric come apart, all at once. To find the little golden pearl that had been hidden within. The number, shining there.

Take it.

In seconds I will have my answer.

– – – – – –

After Hopkins died, Julia wanted to quit. She tried to convince me to quit, too. She was more scared than the rest of us. In retrospect, maybe she was the right amount of scared.

But the rest of us—Hutchinson, Ziegler, Hwang, etc.—well, who knew what was going through their minds? But I remember what was going through mine: The money is good. Don't quit just because you have the jitters.

I convinced Julia to stay on.

Then I had the best three years of my life.

Better than your manic string of affairs after you broke up with Julia? Yes. Better than your cozy marriage to Erin? Yes. Better than the birth of your two sons, better than raising them? If I'm being honest—go ahead, fine, I'm a jerk, a shitty father—yes.

Back then Julia and I were rich and in love. Genuinely rich, both of us pulling in huge at Sapere Aude. And genuinely in love—that is, crazy in-your-twenties love, which nobody should confuse with placid, middle-aged affection, the good-enough thing that Erin and I agreed to call love.

Real feeling.

I don't remember exactly what I said when I broke up with Julia at that Starbucks in Bloomington. I suppose I thought the good times were limitless and anonymous. That I could reboot my life with someone else and it'd be just as good.

I do remember what Julia said.

"Stupid," she had sobbed. "You're so, so stupid."

— — — — — —

Stupid.

My son used to have a small stuffed animal that he called Lamby-Lamb. Lamby-Lamb started off white but had grown dingy. Most of its stuffing had leaked out, and it was missing an ear. But he loved that lamb. Took it everywhere. Treated it tenderly.

Until some asshole kid mocked him for it.

Called it stupid.

The next day I found Lamby-Lamb in the kitchen trash. Smeared with coffee grounds and gravy. I washed Lamby-Lamb, tried to give it back to my son. But he didn't want it anymore. Not even to keep discreetly.

He said it was stupid.

From then on my son became more and more of a dick.

I couldn't bring myself to throw Lamby-Lamb away, though. I keep it in my suitcase, even today. It comes with me on business trips. I didn't tell my son for a while. But a few years later, I did show Lamby-Lamb to him. Remember Lamby-Lamb?

He looked at me blankly.

Didn't remember it.

I thought: Kid, that's the difference between you and me.

– – – – – –

I remember the jukebox.

An old jukebox in the basement of Julia's parents' house. It had been down there for as long as Julia could remember, from a bar her dad had owned before she was born. The jukebox sat in the corner of the unfinished basement, near the carpet remnant and the beat-up couch that folded out into a bed and the house's second-best television. The jukebox's old 45s had never been changed, so it was a snapshot of a particular era of pop music—"Smiling Faces Sometimes," "Band of Gold," "Temptation Eyes," "Proud Mary."

Every once in a while, when Julia and I wanted to get away from her housemates, we'd hang out in her parents' basement. Occasionally we slept together on the pull-out bed. Her parents didn't care, which blew my mind; in-house fornication never would've flown in my family. Julia would put the jukebox on the equivalent of shuffle, and one after another the hits of the early 1970s would play, sometimes to my baffled amusement. ("Does she really sing *pumped a lot of tang* down in New Orleans?!")

Julia had grown up listening to these songs. She'd played with her toys listening to these songs. She'd hung out with her childhood friends in this basement listening to these songs. Her high-school boyfriends had made it with her on this pull-out couch, listening to these songs.

Now I was in that special club.

One night the song "You Know My Name (Look Up the Number)"

came on the jukebox. Julia and I were lying there, naked, postcoital, staring up at the crossbeams of the unfinished ceiling.

"What is *that*?" I said.

"The Beatles," said Julia. "You've never heard it before?"

"No."

Of course it was the Beatles. I found out later that the song was recorded in 1967, right after my hated *Sgt. Pepper's Lonely Hearts Club Band*, but released in 1970, the B-side of their final single "Let It Be." The Beatles had tinkered with it for three years, as though it was some long-gestating masterpiece.

It's no masterpiece. More like the photo negative of a masterpiece. A masterpiece stumbling and collapsing into more and more degraded versions of itself.

"Play it again."

"I thought you hated the Beatles."

"I do."

The needle came to the center of the 45, popped up, swung back, dropped again. "*You know my name—*"

Have you heard this song? Go listen to it. There are four parts, all variations on the same theme—not structured like a standard pop song, I realized, but rather like those four cycles of history.

I used to draw these parallels with Julia. She hated it. Told me to shut up.

I'd go on anyway.

As a kind of revenge, which I'll get into later.

The first part of the song, I'd say, is like the Divine Age. It starts with a confident, bouncy progression of piano, drum, and bass, sounding like a classic Beatles pop song, with all four members of the band chanting "You know my name, look up the number" again and again in harmony, repeating the mythos with clarity and force. Although some of their voices are a little more screamy and aggressive than you'd expect.

"What are you even talking about?" Julia would say. "This is what philosophy majors do all day?"

That leads to the second part of the song, the Aristocratic Age, which transforms into a light samba of the same tune. "Good evening, and welcome to Slagger's," John's nightclub cabaret emcee intones, leading to Paul crooning, in a lounge-singer voice, "You know my name, look up the number" with insinuating giggles and coos, to canned applause. In this Aristocratic Age, instead of everyone chanting in unison, as in the previous age, one singer merely repeats the magic phrase to an audience, priest to congregation, aristocrat to commoners. And thus something essential slips away. In time, the audience stops responding. John's emcee returns to cajole the audience into clapping for the lounge singer. But the audience is silent. Nobody is listening to the authority anymore.

"Oh my God, seriously?" Julia would say. "What does this mean? You yourself do not know what this means."

That leads the song into its third part, the Democratic Age. The song collapses into a Monty Pythonesque parody of itself. It's the same song, but played by a grab bag of cuckoo sounds, harmonica, bongos, and piano plunking. The members of the band do silly old lady voices, still repeating the refrain but changing the phrase around, looping bits, omitting other bits, tacking on their own additions: "You know, you know, you know you know my name . . ." The strict mantra has passed from ritual incantation to ordinary language, where it gets altered, corrupted, and finally, lost.

"I cannot fucking take this," Julia would say. "Are you done? Just be done."

Then the song crumbles into its fourth and final part, the Age of Chaos. It's a shambling piano-jazz version of the song, with vibraphones and a saxophone, but the vocals have degraded into an animal-like muttering—grunting, growling, snorting. The words "You know my name, look up the number" are never heard again. Without the talisman of the originating mythos, the singer is unable to speak coherently at all. Language degenerates into irritable mumbling. Society splinters into barbarism, the song collapses into noise. The senseless voice rambles on for the rest of the track, continuing even after the song has lurched to an undignified close. Somebody burps.

"Shut up shut up *shut up*," Julia would say.

I would overanalyze the song as a counterattack to Julia's abuse of the song. She knew the Beatles drove me up the wall. She knew I hated this song in particular. So she seized on my dislike of the song with prankish glee.

I had told Julia the story about how I was scared of the Beatles growing up, and how I'd destroyed my sisters' record on purpose. I shouldn't have confessed any of that to Julia, though, because she loved to wind people up. I remember being at a house party with her soon after graduation, where the host had just bought a new stereo system that happened to have a remote control. Julia secretly pocketed the remote early in the party. Then, using the remote, Julia very gradually lowered the stereo's volume, such that every song, bit by bit, would become inaudible by about two minutes in. The host was baffled as to why this was happening and kept cranking the volume back up, but a minute after he walked away from the stereo, the volume would start mysteriously dwindling again. One by one, Julia quietly revealed to others at the party that she had the remote and that she, in fact, was the one turning down the volume. Meanwhile the host was freaking out, shouting at the stereo, until everyone was trying not to laugh as we watched the host rant over how ridiculous it was, how he'd spent *x* dollars on this so-called state-of-the-art equipment, he was totally returning this stereo to the store the next day, it was such a piece of shit, etc.

Julia kept up the joke for an hour. She loved to torture.

What does it say about me—that I found this playful malice attractive?

That is, when she directed it against others.

Because it was in the same spirit that Julia played "You Know My Name (Look Up the Number)" at me. To needle me. Not only on her basement jukebox. Sometimes it came on in her car, on the mixtapes she made. She left the song on my answering machine. She secretly dubbed it into the middle of one of my own cassette tapes, recording over legitimate music.

Did this make me love her more, in some perverse way?

Nope. It was just dumb shit that I tolerated. There is always dumb shit that you tolerate. She tolerated my dumb shit, too.

Like on that night in December.

— — — — — —

Julia's parents had gone on vacation. She and I had her childhood home to ourselves for the night. We had only been going out for a couple of months. I was about to return home for Christmas break, which meant Julia and I would be separated for three weeks. I dreaded the prospect. What would Julia do while we were apart? What if she hooked up with some other dude? The world was full of other dudes.

No.

I'd prove to her what an awesome boyfriend I was.

So when I came over to Julia's parents' house that night, I brought candles, a bottle of wine, and an elaborate meal that I had premade in my dorm's barely functional kitchen. "We'll have a candlelit dinner!" I said, and Julia laughed and said, "Oh, that's adorable," which put me on guard. Like when a girl says that you're "cute"— that "adorable" cuts both ways.

The dinner went over well. I don't even remember what we ate, though, because of what happened later.

We had just entered the part of the relationship when you start feeling comfortable having sex regularly. It no longer had to be an intense drama every time. The stakes weren't so high, we could relax, let loose a bit, have fun. Or so Julia seemed to feel. I was still trying to prove something. But Julia was in a goofy mood that night. She had drunk pretty much the entire bottle of wine, our clothes were mostly off, and she was standing on the bed wearing only sweatpants, doing fake karate for some reason, I forget why, with a lit cigarette in her mouth.

She had also put "You Know My Name (Look Up the Number)" on the jukebox, which drove me up the wall.

"Turn this song off."

"Nuh-uh."

"Come on. I hate it."

"Baby, don't I know it."

"You should see yourself posing right now. Your tough-girl cigarette and your bossy tits."

"What a dumb thing to say." Then Julia giggled, as though she'd just made a delightful discovery: "You're dumb, you know that? You're actually really fucking dumb."

We were laughing, not because this was funny, but because it was fun being stupid together, even though "You Know My Name (Look Up the Number)" was still playing, and I truly couldn't stand the song . . .

But right after the song ended—it started up again!

"No!" I shouted. "Not again!"

"Yes again!"

I kept saying "no, no, no" but Julia thought it was hilarious. Apparently she had put the jukebox on repeat.

"You know my name . . ."

I tried to slip out from under Julia, to get off the fold-out bed, to turn off the song or at least change it. But before I could lunge at the jukebox, Julia was standing over me on the bed, she grabbed the rafters above her head and stuck her bare foot on my chest, pushing me back down, cackling "The price of my love tonight is listening to the Fab Four! You must face your fear!" and I was kind of laughing, but not totally, because I had planned this to be a romantic night on my terms, with my candlelit dinner and everything, I had wanted to impress Julia, but the whole thing had turned into a farce.

I didn't want to be cute or adorable, I didn't want stupid jokes, I didn't even want romance, maybe it was the wine but I wanted to dominate, I wanted real fucking. "You Know My Name (Look Up the Number)" kept playing, but I didn't even care about the song, because I wasn't hearing anything, and in a kind of aroused anger I grabbed Julia, she shrieked and tumbled and after a scramble she was under me, and even as that clunky Beatles song kept playing, soon we were having sex, the way I thought I wanted, my eyes shut tight, thinking to myself *impress her, blow her mind, break her open*, and then I looked down at Julia.

Her face was covered in blood.

I screamed.

I scrambled off of her as though electrocuted.

Julia's face was bloody, the pillow under her was bloody, there was blood on the sheets, blood on my face too, what was happening? Julia looked like someone had cut her face open.

Julia was laughing so hard.

This was a nightmare. Had I hurt her? What had happened?

"You've got a bloody nose." Julia whooped. "Oh my God, I wish you could see what you look like. I made your nose explode. I fucked the blood right out of you."

You would've thought I'd be embarrassed.

But the night went so much better after that. My last fears about Julia vanished. I didn't have to try so hard.

I had nosebled all over Julia during sex and she didn't laugh me out of the house.

After we cleaned up the bloody sheets ("it looks like I had an abortion on this thing"), we watched TV and drank more and had sex again, and then again, because we were nineteen, and I remember thinking to myself, just remember this night, take a little home video in your mind right now, hold on to what's happening, because it'll never get better, I couldn't imagine life getting better than this.

We were still in the Age of the Gods.

The Julia problem was solved.

— — — — — —

My attraction to physics came from the same part of me that liked to feel that problems could be solved.

The same part of me that felt at home in the eighties. Physics felt clean and definite. Well-defined problems with well-defined solutions. Complicated phenomena could be simplified and modeled until they were tractable. When I solved a physics problem, I could draw a box around the answer and feel satisfied.

Of course, real-world physics doesn't work that way. Not just the groundbreaking physics of an Einstein or a Stettinger; even everyday professional physics isn't so cut-and-dried. But I was attracted to that sensation of order and logic. Physics gave it to me.

Renard didn't seem to have any particular love of physics. It didn't satisfy an emotional need for him. That's why it was kind of irritating that he was better at physics than I was. I liked physics, I struggled with physics, I cared about physics. Renard just glided effortlessly through physics as if unimpressed.

He was more interested in the Flickering Man.

In the latter weeks of camp, Renard convinced the instructors to excuse him from the morning lectures and labs. He spent all day with the FARGs in the AV Room. Not to play the game anymore, though. Renard was now actually combing through the game's source code, reverse engineering thousands of lines of assembly language in order to find out in what circumstances the Flickering Man would appear. When I asked Renard why he was going to such lengths just to win a game, he replied that it was rumored that the programmers who made the game had put the Flickering Man in for a reason. Renard admired these programmers, and he seemed to believe he was on the trail to some secret of theirs that nobody else had yet guessed; he wanted to be the first to track down what these programmers had so carefully concealed.

At the library, I found a picture of that very group of programmers in a back issue of a personal computing magazine. Of course the programmers all looked like Charles Mansons, the long hair, the beards, the creepy smiles. Even worse, they lived on a commune somewhere in California, very on-brand for exactly the kind of seventies shit that freaked me out.

When Renard saw me with that computer magazine, he must've known what I was thinking, the connection I was making in my head, because he only said, "Computers were born in the seventies too, you know."

Sure.

So were we.

- - - - - -

Closer. Too close.

I feel the answer coming closer. As though it is outside the car right now. How close do you want it to be? My death date is wandering somewhere in the snow, it's prowling around me, it's circling around the car, it's closing in. Maybe I don't want it closer. But my actions are pulling it toward me. My calculation reeling it in.

I can stop anytime I want.

Can I?

My number is outside the car now. I scribble fast across the notebooks, flipping through the Books of the Dead. I can stop anytime, right? But I can't, and soon the number will be in my hand—I accidentally break the tip of my pencil.

Shaking.

No further.

Don't go further.

The invisible thing waits for me in the snowstorm. Pulsing just outside my window.

Don't go on.

– – – – – –

The last night of camp, when Renard and I were in the steam tunnels, he admitted to me that his family was rich. He said it in an embarrassed way, as though he had been long postponing this confession. Apparently his father owned some engineering company, did work for the aerospace industry. It occurred to me, as Renard was talking, that he regarded me as a salt-of-the-earth type, that he considered me working class. This was the first time anyone had ever thought of me that way. I enjoyed my unearned blue-collar cred.

The steam tunnels were cramped, dark, and dirty. Pipes and wires bristled on either side. There was graffiti down there that seemed decades old. Renard and I crept along, single file, and the pitch blackness jumped with our swinging flashlight beams. The tunnel we were in seemed to go on and on, and it was so late, I had been getting by on so little sleep, the darkness scrambled and pulsed, I was following Renard about ten feet behind and then we were wading through sludgy, rusty water, I realized there were electrical wires down here, maybe even exposed ones, we could be electrocuted at any second, indeed already I felt a bit electronic, I felt as though I was walking through the endless hallways of Renard's video game, and when my flashlight's beam flicked past his back sometimes it seemed to be Renard, and sometimes not, it was him walking forward but in the half shadows and my exhaustion it might have been the Flickering Man himself walking backward, staring at me.

Renard stopped.

With our flashlights we discovered a dead rat.

Its skin had been seared off. Probably by the random discharge of a steam pipe. That implied a steam pipe could be anywhere near us: a scalding blast might happen at any second, might burn our own skins off. And yet we just stood there, filthy water seeping into our shoes, staring at the hairless, melted-skin rat, whose head was twisted around, his lips drawn back to reveal sharp broken teeth. Eyes shut tight, as if still expending effort at keeping his eyes shut after death, as if he resented the afterlife.

Renard said, "Rip that rat's head from its body."

I followed the order.

- - - - - -

Many years later, at a record store, I saw something behind the counter that startled me. It was a Beatles LP called "Yesterday and Today." The cover featured a photograph of John, Paul, George, and Ringo, all of them smiling and laughing, wearing white butcher's coats, and they were all covered with raw meat and blood-smeared decapitated babies.

The babies were dolls, of course. But the image unnerved me. The Beatles looked devilish and gleeful, and it felt like every childish suspicion I had about them was confirmed. Apparently (according to the record store clerk) there was so much outcry over that grisly cover that the records were all recalled. The original cover was replaced with an anodyne photo of the clean-cut Beatles gathered around a piece of luggage. But to save on costs, they used the same cardboard sleeve; that is, the record company just placed an album-sized sticker of the new cover over the old one with the butchered babies. I could only imagine what some curious teenybopper must've thought when, idly picking away at the polite sticker of the Fab Four sitting around a steamer trunk, they discovered the horrific baby-murder image below it.

In both pictures, the Beatles have the same shit-eating smirks. They look absolutely delighted with themselves.

— — — — — —

The rat came alive in my hands.

I hadn't expected that. Suddenly the animal was thrashing around, eyes wild, squeaking, hissing. Its terrified noises filled the steam tunnels. My startled fingers slipped on the slimy fur, its slick writhing body, I was losing my grip as it tried to escape, tried to bite. In a panic I grabbed the rat's head, twisted it all the way around until I felt the snap.

The rat stopped moving.

Renard didn't say anything. He just watched me.

I couldn't breathe. My heart was going crazy. Had the rat bitten me? It hadn't. But it was a close thing.

With a lot of pulling and wiggling and tearing I managed to

separate the rat's head from its body. More difficult than I expected. A ripping twist, then another, bones crunching, grinding—

It was finished.

In the flashlight's wobbling light, I handed the rat's gory head up to Renard.

I couldn't see Renard's face.

That was the last thing he ever ordered me to do.

I felt like we had completed something.

– – – – – –

For what it's worth, I later learned from Stettinger's autobiography that somewhere in that same building, the same day I killed that rat, Stettinger made the breakthrough that led to his first published paper on thanaton theory.

– – – – – –

On the last day of physics camp, at the going-away pizza party, the FARGs were telling everyone's fortunes. They claimed to have learned on some Wiccan BBS or whatever about a method of telling the future "that's never wrong, it's totally spooky" and they had laid out a bunch of twigs and they would call people over and move the twigs around and then use their "fortune-telling" context as an excuse to say nice things to their friends and to say mean things to the people they disliked.

Renard and I weren't interested in having our fortunes told. But all the other campers did it. Eventually I felt guilty because, even though Renard and I didn't interact with the other campers—and the other boys kept a wary distance from us too, they didn't even tease us anymore—the fact remained that the FARGs had been gracious enough to let Renard and me use what the entire camp had conceded were "their" computers. So, in the end, we let the girls tell our fortunes.

Renard went first. The FARGs predicted a bright future for him. Renard was going to be rich, he was going to be famous, he was going to be successful. The FARGs poured it on a bit thick, I remember thinking, perhaps trying to demonstrate how magnanimous they were by bestowing a "good" fortune to a kid like Renard whom everyone was creeped out by.

When the FARGs started telling my fortune, they had a hard time at first. The girls laid out their witchy twigs, but then one of them would look at me and whisper, and then they'd have to lay the whole thing out again in a different configuration. I had no idea what their method was. At last the girls found a configuration they could all agree on, and then they proceeded to move the magic twigs again and again, until—I remember how all three of the girls' faces changed, slowly and then all at once. Something seemed to upset them all. The FARGs looked back up at me. After a strange silence one of them quickly said that, um, my fortune was that I was going to be happy, I would have a daughter, and it would be a fine life, a fine life, whatever, vague and abrupt.

Then they were done.

No more fortune-telling for anyone. The FARGs swept the twigs back into their bag. Even though a few other kids were still waiting, the FARGs said no, no, fortune-telling is finished.

The FARGs didn't look at me for the rest of the party.

I hadn't really liked the FARGs that much anyway but this seemed like a shitty way to say good-bye.

Then my parents came to pick me up. Physics camp was over.

The last thing Renard said to me was, "That's all, folks!"

– – – – – –

That night I dreamed I was walking around campus.

The physics camp had just concluded and all the campers were going their separate ways. I was alone on the woodsy quad, although there were some new buildings, new sidewalks I didn't recognize.

The FARGs were walking ahead of me in their small group. I wanted to catch up with them, to ask them about those fortune-telling twigs and why they acted so strangely. But I couldn't catch up with the girls. They wouldn't even turn around. They seemed to be moving faster and faster away from me. Then they split off their separate ways, none of them turning around.

I followed one of them.

The girl crossed the quad, leaving the campus. I realized that, although this girl had been walking with the FARGs, she wasn't one of them. Even from behind I could tell she was someone else.

I kept after her.

The girl stopped, as though she knew I was following her.

She began to turn around.

I didn't want her to turn around. I didn't want to see that girl's face.

I woke up sweating, my heart racing. I scrambled out of bed in bleary agitation. At first I didn't know I was at home. I thought I was still at camp. I found my way to the bathroom that I hadn't seen in weeks and turned on the light and sat on the toilet in the bright-lit room for a long time so I wouldn't fall back asleep again. The girl's face frightened me in a way I hadn't felt since I was little. I was still shaking.

It wasn't the last time I had that dream.

Maybe, I realize now, not even the first time.

– – – – – –

At Renard's urging I copied his game onto a blank floppy disk and took it home from physics camp. Over the next few months or so, sometimes I played it. But not a lot. Renard lived across the country, in the Pacific Northwest, and even though we wrote letters to each other after camp, it would sometimes take weeks for him to reply.

Back at camp, Renard had listened to me in an attentive way that made even the stupid things I said feel meaningful. In the morning I'd tell him what I'd dreamed about the night before, and he'd listen with interest, as though I were describing life in another country. ("I don't dream," he said.) But now that our little rituals were defunct, now that Renard existed to me only as words on paper, I didn't find him so compelling. As time passed, I couldn't understand why I'd submitted to his dangerous night missions at physics camp. It felt absurd how Renard and I had half convinced ourselves that some vast malignant unconsciousness permeated everything, that secrets bubbled invisibly inside old video games, that the radio unwittingly spoke with the devil's voice—the whole mythology we had created together that summer was dumb.

In the letters, Renard asked, "Have you found the Flickering Man?"

Pathetic. I was in high school now. I was killing it academically. I actually got special permission to take AP Physics as a freshman. In comparison, Renard's continued search for the Flickering Man in that obsolete video game seemed pointless. I never understood it in the first place. I stopped answering Renard's questions about the Flickering Man. Eventually Renard stopped writing to me.

And that was it from Renard.

There was nothing unusual about his final letter to me. No good-bye, no explicit cutting of ties. After my third letter to him went unanswered during my sophomore year of high school, I stopped writing to him, too.

Actually, there was one peculiar thing about Renard's final letter to me.

The postscript, below his signature. *I'll see you in Cahokia.*

— — — — — —

Not long after that I went to the library to research a term paper. I was supposed to be looking up the Teapot Dome scandal.

I ended up reading books about Cahokia.

I learned things Renard hadn't talked about.

The people of Cahokia had practiced mass human sacrifice. The excavation at one of the many mounds—Mound 72, it was called—revealed a pit of more than fifty women buried at once, strangled or poisoned or throats slit, precisely arranged in rows and layers. Elsewhere near the same mound, dozens of men, women, and even children were executed all at once, more brutally, and immediately thrown into pits—some clubbed to death, some beheaded, some shot by arrows, some with their hands chopped off—while others were clearly buried alive, their skeletal fingers still clawing at the dirt. Corpses arranged in grisly layers on stacked platforms, now pressed as flat as paper. Dozens of mutilated bodies thrown into garbage pits willy-nilly and covered with clay.

In a particular place of honor atop that mound, a man and a woman were buried together. The woman was on the bottom, facing downward; the man was on top, facing upward, separated from her by a bird-shaped cloak inlaid with tens of thousands of valuable blue shell beads in which apparently he'd been buried. Both the man and the woman were surrounded by ceramics, copper artifacts, jewelry, stone game pieces, and more sacrificed corpses—men, women, even a child. Also buried nearby were four men in a row, arms intertwined, their hands and heads cut off.

I couldn't believe what I was reading. I mean, go ahead and look it up yourself. Incredible. And nobody really talks about it.

Some archaeologists believed these sacrificial rituals in Cahokia were theatrical ceremonies that lasted for days. Extravagant public feasts, a citywide party. Garbage pits revealed dumps of thousands of butchered deer, heaps of earthen pots, and food to feed the entire city—enormous quantities of corn, grapes, nuts, pumpkins, porridge, persimmons, berries, and enough charred tobacco to envelop Cahokia in a fog of hallucinogenic nicotine. There were also pots stained with dried-up "black drink," a caffeine-soaked beverage you drank to induce visions and vomiting. Death, ecstasy, nightmare, a psychedelic pageant of human sacrifice.

Unthinkable shit was happening in downstate Illinois a thousand years ago.

Now forgotten.

Was that ceremony a retelling of a creation story? A fertility ritual? A celebration of the ascension of a new leader? Nobody knows. Some stuff made no sense to me. One Cahokian neighborhood seemed built only for the purpose of ritual torching: a hundred houses, full of food and tools and treasure, were rapidly built and, before anyone could live in the houses, immediately burned down.

Why?

Maybe that's why Cahokia was abandoned, I thought. Because it became a nightmare city. Maybe Cahokia had left a bad taste in the mouth and was shunned. And perhaps, after a while, since nothing had been said about it for so long, nobody could say anything about it anymore for sure. Or at least that's the story I invented for myself, from the little I could find out.

Not long after that, I learned Renard Jankowski was dead.

— — — — —

Renard had died in the fall of my sophomore year of high school. I had no idea. His parents sent me a note about it two months after it happened, around Christmas. They also returned my last three letters to him, unopened. From his parents' tone, as far as I could tell, it felt like they were writing to me not so much because they wanted to inform me as because they wanted me to stop sending letters.

I was not a particularly emotional kid but Renard's death shook me. I don't want to blow this out of proportion, it's not like Renard and I had a grand friendship for all the ages. But we had lived together side by side for two months. We had been each other's only friend for that time.

That counted for something.

I wrote back to Renard's parents. I poured my heart out, surprising myself as I wrote. I included a bunch of anecdotes in the letter, the kind of memories I imagined parents would approve of.

No response.

I looked up the Jankowskis' number. Telephoned them a few times. Always got an answering machine.

They never called back.

To be sure, the Jankowskis didn't know me. Who was I, after all? Some random kid that their dead son had roomed with for a few weeks over a year ago. But it nagged me that I didn't even know how Renard had died. And this was 1988—it's not like I could just Google his obituary. The Jankowskis ignored my letters. Didn't return my calls.

And that was that.

— — — — — —

began playing Renard's game again.

It was Christmas break of sophomore year. I didn't feel like going outside anyway. I didn't want to see anyone. A snowstorm sealed me in and I let myself be hypnotized by the game in a way that I hadn't at camp. I stuck the disk Renard had given me into my Apple II clone and let it rip. The game really was addictive in an obsessive-compulsive way, and I found myself spending hours in my basement on my computer, drawing maps and exploring every last corner of the vast, mysterious house. But now that I was playing it intensely, and not just casually, I realized how the game really made no sense. I couldn't even figure out what I was supposed to do. It always seemed like I was making progress, little by little, ascending level upon level in the house, but I didn't know where it was going, what it meant. In the game I was walking through one room after another and all the rooms looked the same. There were creatures walking around, but after a while the creatures stopped trying to kill me. None took notice of me when I bumped into them—they didn't even break stride when I shot at them. My arrows sailed right through them, like the game was ignoring me—or more like the game had gotten used to me, my wanderings through its strange many-leveled house incorporated into its ecosystem. And yet I still didn't know what I was doing.

I played the game all day.

And another day.

And another.

– – – – – –

was playing the game late at night, in the dark. Maybe three in the morning. School was going to start again in a few days, winter break would soon be over, and yet for some reason I was spending my last few days of precious freedom playing this game. I didn't care. I was walking through one of the highest levels of the house, where one false step would send me plummeting down through dozens of levels to the basement . . .

The Flickering Man entered my screen.

The Flickering Man looked identical to the man I was controlling but he moved in a different manner than my man did. A glitch in his animation—his body jerkily making the motions of walking forward, even as his body was actually moving backward—

The Flickering Man saw me.

And I mean it felt like he saw *me*.

Is it ridiculous to be scared of a graphic in a video game? I was terrified. The Flickering Man was now walking toward me in his unnatural forward-backward way, climbing the staircases toward me, floating over the gaps between the floors that I had to jump over. Steadily closing the distance.

I ran away.

I put screen after screen between me and the Flickering Man.

But the Flickering Man kept pursuing me. Showed up whenever I slowed down. The Flickering Man's pixels trembled in an unstable way, and he almost had a smile on his face, although that couldn't be because his graphic was identical to my man, and my man's face was expressionless.

But the Flickering Man was somehow smiling.

I didn't want the Flickering Man to get me. I knew that if he touched me it would be bad. But he was closing in so fast, way too fast. My heart was up in my throat and I was trapped as the Flickering Man rushed in, his face blank and yet leering—and then he was too close, the Flickering Man reached out—

I switched off the computer.

At once the screen went black. I sat there in the dark, in my basement, the afterimage of the game blinking in my retinas, my heart pounding, disconnected flashings wheeling through the darkness all around me as the snow rushed and tumbled outside, and I felt something prickling and electric in that darkness.

It was a long time before I played the game again.

The Flickering Man never reappeared.

There was nothing.

– – – – – –

R enard was nothing now.

A nothing that felt strange. Like trying to pick something up and realizing your hand isn't there, that your hand is made of nothing. Or looking for the Flickering Man and not finding him, even though you could've sworn you'd seen him before, and then wondering if you ever saw him in the first place, if there was really just nothing.

But even nothing isn't nothing.

I had first heard that phrase at physics camp. The instructor that day was a hippyish middle-aged guy—bearded, ponytailed, I-don't-give-a-fuck jogging shorts, T-shirt—and he was giving us his simplified overview of quantum fluctuation, how, according to quantum theory, even a vacuum isn't really a vacuum but a seething soup of possible energy, and how that seemingly empty space is in fact filled with continuously appearing and disappearing "virtual particle pairs"—electron-positron, quark-antiquark, particle and antiparticle—two opposite particles that simultaneously pop out of the vacuum but then immediately crash back together, annihilating each other. That is, the unfloutable law of "energy cannot be created or destroyed" can be flouted, as long as it's only a tiny amount of energy and only for a tiny amount of time.

It was an adequate explanation for eighth graders, although of course the real physics isn't so simple. I remember the instructor drawing diagrams on the whiteboard, of the particle and its antiparticle being born together, wandering away from each other, finding each other again, erasing each other. As if they'd never been there.

Here's the diagram from my old notebook:

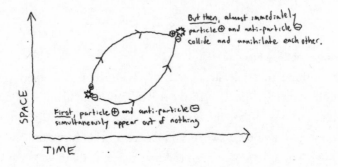

Renard raised his hand and speculated that maybe the whole universe came from such a process—maybe first there was nothing, but then some Heisenbergian uncertainty between whether there was nothing or something allowed a universe-starting particle and its antiparticle to arise from that nothing. And in the brief borrowed time before those primordial particles crashed back together, before the laws of physics and probability turned a sharp eye to their unauthorized existence, maybe the complications of the particle and antiparticle's interrelationship gave rise to other structures between them, flowering into matter, energy, life, intelligence—but all on borrowed time, because once those two particles found each other again, they'd cancel each other out, and in doing so cancel out everything else, erasing the universe they had created between them.

When I told Julia about this she said, "It's like you're expecting me to think it's poetic and romantic."

"I don't know, maybe it's kind of poetic," I said. "Right?"

"Eh," she said.

"Do you understand it?"

"Of course I understand it," said Julia. "I just don't get a science boner over it. Christ, what kind of girls did you used to go out with?"

— — — — — —

No tow truck. After all this time.

What's taking them so long?

The pencil is shaking in my fingers.

Too cold. It was a lark to begin with, looking up my own death date. I thought I'd have the self-control to stop calculating before I got too close, to halt the algorithm. But now I'm so close to the answer, the answer that is coming in from the cold. The answer is coming to my outstretched hand, even though maybe I have half changed my mind, even though I don't want to know anymore, so take your hand back, I don't want it, but I do, I can't help myself, I keep going, keep calculating, the momentum sweeps me along—

Car flashes past. Too close. Slush splatters across the windshield.

One last multiplication.

I grasp it. I have it.

I'm finished.

Wait.

No.

I check it again.

I'm dead.

— — — — — —

I had died twenty-three minutes ago.

LOOK UP

I'm alive.

But the algorithm can't be wrong.

Never a single recorded mistake. Headquarters keeps the books rigorously up to date. A new edition every year to account for the eddies and irregularities in the thanaton continuum. Never off—not even by a minute. That's the guarantee.

But I'm alive.

I'm dead.

The tow truck arrives.

Through the flying snow and the red-and-white blinking of my emergency flashers, I see two guys approaching my car. Wait, am I a ghost? Is this what the afterlife is—you just linger in whatever spot you happen to have died in? Will I haunt this grim stretch of toll road forever?

A knock on the window. "Sir?"

I look at the two guys. Sixty-year-old man, maybe eighteen-year-old son. Family business.

I roll down the window.

The father is talking to me as if nothing is out of the ordinary. "If you want us to tow you out of there, you're gonna need to exit your vehicle." I open the door, stumble out. Father and son help me to their truck.

Cold, windy, wet.

So I'm alive, then. Not a ghost.

The condescension you get from a tow truck driver. As if to say: if you weren't so incompetent with your vehicle, you wouldn't be in this mess. Now I'm in the back of the tow truck cab, like a child. They're talking back and forth, ignoring me. My car hooked up to the winch. Pulling me out. Rough night, says the dad over his shoulder, you wouldn't believe how many calls. Son watching his father. Learning. Never had anything like that with my boys. Like they'd want to become me.

Still feel outside my body.

But I'm in it.

Dead.

— — — — — —

"What do you mean you can't take the boys this weekend?"

"Something's come up."

"You could've told me earlier."

"We only switched it a few hours ago, Erin."

"Well, it's not that easy. Now I have to rearrange everything."

"I'm sorry."

"It's like you don't even want to see the boys."

"Oh, don't do that. Not now."

"When are we supposed to talk about it? It's not like—"

"This isn't about that."

"They need a father."

"Don't turn this around on me. You're the one who was so eager to get rid of them this weekend."

"Jesus! I need a life, too, every once in a while. The least you can do—"

"The *least* I could do. Incredible."

"Oh, so you want to talk about money again? You really want to have that discussion?"

"They don't want to come. They're embarrassed of me."

"Your self-pity. I can't take it."

"They each have their own bedroom at your house. Why would they want to share a pull-out at my place?"

"Because they want to see their father?"

"I get patronized by them."

"I'm the one who has to check their homework every day, who takes them to the doctor—"

"You fought for that. Now you've got it."

"A weekend. I'm asking for you to cooperate on a weekend."

"I'm dead."

"What?"

"I'm a dead man. I died two hours ago."

"What are you talking about?"

"Erin, do you want our sons staying with a dead man?"

"Are you drunk?"

"I am drunk. But I'm dead too."

"You've really lost it."

– – – – – –

buy a one-way ticket to San Francisco.

I had enough money on hand for that, at least. After the tow truck drops me off at my condo, I go straight to the computer. Buy the ticket. Clean out my savings account while I'm at it, transfer everything to checking. Endure the jolt, jolt, jolt of internet nausea until I can't. Print out my boarding pass, then shut the computer down. Quickly.

The swarming jagged feeling drains away. Relief.

Enough money for a little while.

Or maybe it needs to last forever?

Maybe a drunk driver was fated to crash into me at that moment? Maybe I was scheduled to be killed instantly at 7:06 p.m., but somehow the drunk driver zoomed past me and my death failed to occur, maybe I somehow missed out on my allotted time to die so now I've slipped outside the thanaton system, maybe thanatons don't even recognize me anymore, maybe I'm immortal, maybe I'm drunk?

Another ten-dollar bottle of wine! In this little condo that I always hated, that always meant defeat. I don't belong here. Off-white walls in every room, grimy. Never got around to painting them. This place has my stuff but it's not my stuff. Been here going on five years but I've always pretended like I'm just passing through so I don't even know anyone in this building. Maybe I should introduce myself tonight? Knock knock knock. Hello! You don't know me, but c'mon, you kind of know me. Here's something you don't know: I'm dead!

Packing. What do I pack? Every single piece of clothing I own is garbage, half of it doesn't even fit. Clear it out! Dead man's clothes. Buy something else tomorrow. The ticket's for tomorrow? Sure it is, just bought it. That must've cost a pretty penny! It did!

But I can't stay in Chicago for one more day.

Stumbling from room to room. Never had a happy hour here. Never? No, never! At the front door, my soaked shoes, the gray ice melted, muddy. Snow swirls outside. Spent enough of my life in this dirty cold. Time to go.

That life is over.

End of the world.

Now *that's* something I haven't thought about in a while.

Eschatons. Yeah, yeah, blast from the past . . . Open up the storage closet, haul out the old boxes. Haven't opened these boxes for years. Just drunk enough to now. Haven't been opened since marrying Erin. Boxes full of papers, boxes silently following me from apartment to house to condo. Waiting for me to remember them. To be opened by a dead man.

Dead for three hours now.

Boxes full of college shit. Pathetic, right? Drunk middle-aged man pawing through college debris, old thesis papers, blue book examinations full of scrawled calculations . . . Haven't done math at this level in years. I open a blue book, try to decipher what I was doing. Used to be a fucking artist at this. Now it's almost incomprehensible. Makes me think, why should I be afraid of death? Clearly I've already died many times. The version of me that could do this math—he's long dead. How many other versions of me have come and gone since then who are also dead now? All these equations, symbols, numbers, how was I ever smart enough to find that error in Stettinger's derivations? I dig in the papers, find my published article in *Physical Review Letters*. Always thought I'd follow up with something huge.

But I did follow up with something huge.

Just now.

The books are supposed to be free of error.

But there is an error. Me.

I'm alive. I'm dead.

Drink up! Eschatons, yeah, yeah. *That's* what my second act was going to be. I had put myself on the map by finding the error in Stettinger's derivation. So what would my next trick be?

Right here: eschaton calculations, pages and pages of them.

Nobody could say I wasn't ambitious.

I'd even tried explaining it to metalhead Carl, at that party when

I thought Julia had ditched me—"What I'm *really* interested in is the next level"—but why had I been telling Carl, who'd never understand? It was the kind of topic that, when I brought it up in seminar, it got me mocked, whatever, I'll tell Carl—"if we can detect thanatons then why can't we detect the *thanaton of thanatons*?"

What's that, said Carl.

Well, if thanatons derive their trajectory from human death, then if we're really clever with the math, why can't we trace *those* trajectories and discover where all of *those* trajectories must terminate—that is, when all thanatons cease to exist—which logically would be when the final human being dies? We'd find the end-of-the-world particle, I said, the thanaton of thanatons. The eschaton.

Uh-huh, said Carl.

It's a theoretical particle for now, I said.

Uh-huh, said Carl.

It hasn't been detected yet.

Uh-huh.

But it must exist.

Uh-huh.

Carl wasn't buying my pitch. Neither did the physics community. Eschatons? Please. People still only even barely tolerated the idea of thanatons; they were accepted only piecemeal, grudgingly. Like every other paradigm shift, thanatons didn't feel right to the establishment. That's not how subatomic particles are supposed to *act,* that's not what they're supposed to *do.* But Stettinger had anticipated their objections, had built thanaton theory too solidly to be dismissed. So when the experimental confirmations began rolling in, the physics community had to change their tune. Now Stettinger was no longer a crackpot, he was a new Planck, a new Bohr . . .

But speculation beyond thanatons? Forget it. Searching for the thanaton of thanatons, the eschaton—that was crank territory. But weren't thanatons similarly dismissed at first? I said to my advisor. Yeah, yeah, my advisor had replied wearily, but I'm telling you, stuff it, there's no career in it, you'll be swimming upstream all your life. Look, he added with a burst of impatience, just find a solid, modest project with a professor who knows how to position you. Thanatons, sure. Hot field. But for chrissakes don't get weird. Eschatons! Don't even say it.

To be fair, my advisor was right. If eschatons really existed, then nearly thirty years later, somebody must've detected them by now.

Right?

Julia and I used to talk about it. My academic ambitions. Getting back in the game. Put in a few more years at Sapere Aude, sock away sufficient fuck-you money, eventually go back to school. Or even fund my own research, who knows?

But I stopped keeping up with the scientific journals. Fell out of touch with my old professors, my old peers. Julia and I traveled. Threw parties. So many friends, or what I called friends—actually, just the people you happen to know in your twenties, whom you stop talking to once you move out of the city or have kids.

I turn the page. More calculations, deriving formulas, speculating. Grasping for something new.

Used to excite me so much.

— — — — — —

What's this equation here?

Clunky. Streamline it. Drop these extraneous terms. Confine other terms to a place where they won't blow up the rest of the derivation. Use this newer method, shuffle them aside. I've invented a few workarounds over my career, some shortcuts. Grinding through these equations for the past two decades or so, calculating hundreds of death dates, you get intimate with the math. But I hadn't looked under the hood like this, tracing how the equations actually work, in forever.

Wait: something's opening up.

Some lines of an old side derivation here look like nonsense. Of course: I'd been trying to force the equation to do something it couldn't. Misstated the whole problem. But what if I throw away a few assumptions? Like: what if thanatons themselves aren't stable but have *their own* life cycle . . . I begin writing in the extra pages of the blue book, reframing the problem, slotting all the vectors into new positions. If the thanaton is unstable, four new sets of equations open up. I'm scrawling fast. There could be a path to the eschaton in it. Four stages in the thanaton's life cycle: starting out strong but undetectable, then in each stage growing weaker and thus more observable, from the age of gods to aristocrats to mere men to the edge of chaos, until thanatons are weak and fragile enough to be detected . . . The theorist at the undergraduate dinner party saying, I heard all the thanatons just appeared recently. Like they were called into existence, somehow. My dismissal: I guess we're going to have to agree to disagree on that one.

Maybe we were both wrong.

More results keep flowing. Everything's falling into place elegantly, the way true things tend to do. As if the eschaton is right around the corner, as if there's a hidden garden that had always been there but I had just overlooked it—maybe everybody had?

Weightless. Freeing feeling. As though I've been trapped in an impossible maze for years. As though I'd just discovered an ax that could magically smash through the walls, could clear my own path out . . .

Or not.

Dead end. The new approach doesn't work. Old roadblocks

reappear, just dressed up in different terms. If my hypothesis was true, all the thanatons would've died out by now. And the thanaton is a fundamental particle. If thanatons ever died out, the universe itself would collapse.

The momentary flush of discovery fades. Stupid idea. Amateur hour. Come on, what'd I expect? As if I'd discover anything new from tipsily reviewing my undergraduate research from nearly thirty years ago? As if I knew what I was doing then!

But that was a feeling I hadn't had in a long time.

– – – – – –

How it felt when we were just starting up.

Everyone was shocked that thanatons behaved according to mathematics that were, for lack of a better term, subjective. Stettinger's breakthrough: to acknowledge that the solver was part of the problem. That is, when solving for the thanaton, both the problem and its solver changed—they changed each other, step by step, during the solving process. Even more unexpected: that you could only do subjective math by inventing your own subjective way. You had to construct your own version of the math, your own version of the algorithms, your own heuristics, even your own notation. That's why computers can't do subjective mathematics. It's why thanatons were resisted for so long by traditional mathematicians.

But even open-minded mathematicians who wanted to learn subjective math had a hard time. Too difficult to break old mental habits.

So young people were overrepresented at Sapere Aude. Youth is able to navigate subjective mathematics because youth isn't yet mortgaged to any worldview, youth has nimbleness of association, youth intuitively breaks or ignores rules—and I remember the feeling, how back then it felt to me like my brain was a continuous burst of fireworks, how I could forge the most unlikely connections with a flourish, I could ride the most zigzagging logic without being bucked off. Older mathematicians couldn't follow us into this fresh territory. It was all our own.

Exhilarating.

Each of us had to construct our own metaphor in order to visualize thanaton mechanics. This personal metaphor helped you feel the shape of the problem, pointed the way to the solution even before you could prove it formally. Everyone's metaphor was individual, idiosyncratic: Ziegler's metaphor envisioned thanaton theory as exploring an endless living castle made of jeweled flesh. Kulkarni's put it in terms of an infinity of interlocking glass boxes with ever-shifting panes. Hwang imagined snakelike creatures swimming through vast underwater jungles.

For me, thanaton theory was more like the twists, reversals, and corkscrews of an inexhaustibly complicated fairy tale. A sprawling myth that might take the entire age of the universe to fully tell, expressed through the archetypes of princesses and goblins and kingdoms, each trope charged with precise mathematical meaning, though more digressive and dreamlike than any story someone would actually narrate . . .

The metaphor only lasted for the first few weeks. After that initial burst of creative vision, our surreal metaphors settled down, became more abstract, reduced themselves into codes of written symbols. The originating vision faded for everyone. Ziegler no longer spoke of castles of jeweled flesh, Kulkarni didn't conceive of interlocking glass boxes, Hwang couldn't even remember the details of his underwater jungles. Three months in, everyone's notation looked just like any other mathematics—though not quite, because everyone's symbols were different.

But I missed the feeling. In the beginning, my infinite-bizarre-

fairy-tale metaphor of thanaton calculations would always produce
a weird little fable at the end of the process. A kind of mathematical
by-product. I liked those stories as curiosities. Back when I would
still get them, I would write them down. Though it was not always
a good story.

"A good story"—makes me think of Keith.

Argggh.

Don't think of Keith.

And as for Julia, she didn't tell me or anyone else much about
her metaphor. She only said it involved a hotel of infinite rooms,
countless indistinguishable doors hiding different solutions,
hallways and stairwells branching and reversing and looping, rooms
and hallways that were completely unoccupied—a haunted, lonely
hotel that went on forever.

— — — — — —

A hotel is a lonely place, okay? Long hallways of anonymous doors. Nobody
cares about you. So many people have passed through your
room. A different person yesterday; a different person
tomorrow. You're temporary, only the room is real. So what does it
matter what happens in the room? You're not your real self, you're
your hotel self. You're pulling down six figures a year but you're
on the road six months out of the twelve, in cities where you don't
know anyone. And all you do all day is tell people when they're
going to die. So you're not making friends, all right? And you have
all this money to throw around. All this spare time. You're young.

You cheat on your wife.

Can't be more cliché, more ridiculous than that! Still, I deluded
myself while it was happening that it wasn't like that at all. But Erin
knew. She knew for months, she had to. Silently building her case.
Documenting. I thought I could be a Hutchinson! Maybe that's

where I got it from; maybe I thought it was an unwritten rule that nobody acknowledged but everyone tacitly assented to, that everyone cheated. Or maybe because whenever I was in a hotel, I couldn't stop thinking of death. Hopkins. Minneapolis. Needed someone to be with me. More than loneliness: it was terror. Sometimes the solution was sex, sometimes not. Talk all night with her, whoever she was, if I could. Breakfast the next morning. Fascinated me, different people. Fat, thin, punk, professional. Pick her up at the hotel bar; pick her up at the fucking Denny's. Wasn't only about sex; it was the thrill of someone new. The spiky otherness of a new person. Let me multiply my own self, try on different ways of being. Different people brought out different parts of me. I learned about myself, cheating. I never lied to them. Part of the excitement was to leave myself vulnerable like that, reckless. Naïve. That's how Erin nailed me, of course, and took me for every dime: word got back.

"Well, now at least I know your type. White trash skanks," Erin said.

Failure of imagination on her part. Any one of those women were just as interesting and worthwhile as Erin, at least for that night. They knew the rules of the game, or most of them did, they knew what we were playing. And I could open myself up to a stranger more than to the people I knew best. A fresh connection with a stranger who unexpectedly understands you—no, it didn't happen every time. But more often than you might expect. And anyway, I had learned how to please people, I could edit myself for them, I was a pretty good salesman.

Until her.

Her.

- - - - - -

Afterward, while she was asleep—whoever she was that night—my mathematical brain woke up. Patterns and connections formed liked they once did, before the drinking and the socializing and the happiness dulled me. Guilt was for later; there would be time for guilt when I got home, and, eventually, forgetting. But now I was in the hotel, an unreal limbo that had changed from a complex of anonymous death hallways to an intense place of possibility and inspiration. Walking down the hallways alone, my brain teemed with ideas combining, dissolving, breeding new ideas, bubbling up to the surface. Choose some, discard others. Standing at the rattling ice machine in a fluorescent-lit hallway, listening to it go *chunk-chunk-chunk*, *chunk-chunk-chunk*, lost in the rhythm, fitting equations together in my head. Getting closer. I could feel the eschaton taking shape around me, a particle that was somehow bigger than the universe, ghostly and everywhere, but getting smaller every moment, and I was the nucleus. The end of the world coming. Or the end of my world. Making it happen mathematically. To do the math makes the math come true. Every time I picked up someone new, I felt myself moving up the death date on my marriage with Erin, maybe I was waiting for it, maybe I wanted my marriage to blow up, for everything to blow up. I was forcing it earlier, urging it to come faster.

Now I'm a dead man.

Now I want to see the last woman who knew the real me.

The me worth knowing.

Julia had something of mine.

- - - - - -

Why'd I think Julia would even want to see me?

I text her from the security line at O'Hare, hungover. Why had I bought a ticket for such an early flight? I'm a mess, unshaven, wrinkled clothes, running to the gate. I make it on the plane but just barely. With relief. Outside the airplane window the ground drops away, dwindles. Gone. Gray, cold, grimy. Never belonged there. Made me dead before I was dead.

I'll never come back to Chicago.

From here on out every trip is one-way.

– – – – – –

All trips are one-way.

Right?

Every ticket has already been bought.

Every destination has already been chosen.

You remember when reports of this began coming out. How they called it "Sapere Aude syndrome." (And, yeah, if a psychological disorder was named after your company, you'd change your company's name, too.)

That's why the bottom dropped out of the thanaton industry in the late aughts. Why our business collapsed. Why, at forty-nine, I'm stuck scrabbling together a living against the Martin McNiffs of the world.

Not because of what people had predicted. At first critics said Sapere Aude would fail because nobody *really* wanted to know when they'd die.

But no. Everyone did want to know. The fact that knowing was ludicrously expensive made it even more desirable. Became a status symbol of sorts.

For a while.

Then people said that Sapere Aude would fail because . . . well, how would we keep growing? No repeat customers, obviously.

But that wasn't quite it either.

You must've seen this coming. I mean, just do the thought

experiment. Let's say you come to me for your assessment. You get your thanatons analyzed. And I tell you that you're going to die ten years from now.

What do you do next? If you're a smart-ass?

Try to kill yourself now.

Disprove the system.

So do it, big guy. Load a gun, point it to your head, pull the trigger. Throw yourself off a bridge. Swallow a million pills. Boom: you're dead ten years ahead of schedule, right? Not so accurate now, are you, Sapere Aude?

But that was the thing.

Somehow you'd fumble while loading the gun. Or it would turn out that when you put that gun to your head and pulled the trigger, you forgot to put a bullet in there. You'd go to the bridge to throw yourself off but someone would stop you from doing it, or you wouldn't make it onto the bridge after all. You'd swallow those million pills but then barf them all up before they could kill you. Or even worse: you'd survive but be incapacitated or crippled until your predetermined date rolled around.

Sapere Aude was always right.

And so humanity learned, almost as an afterthought, that its free will was pretty much fake.

After the first time you tried to kill yourself, or tried to push your or someone else's death ahead of schedule, you'd feel it. Like invisible electric guardrails, hemming you in on either side. And having felt them once, you were excruciatingly aware of them for the rest of your life. Nobody could add even a single second to their lives—not from what Sapere Aude predicted. Nor could they take a second away. If you couldn't control that—well, what else about your life couldn't you control?

Everyone who tried to buck their death date came down with

Sapere Aude syndrome. Everyone who tried to defy the math.

Math showed them who was boss.

People reported feeling they had no control over what their bodies did. Their minds seeming disconnected from the actions their bodies undertook, like they couldn't even control themselves, like their minds were simply riding along inside the bodies, a prisoner inside an alien flesh-thing that moved and acted and spoke on its own. That even the words they were saying right then, trying to express the nightmare sensation of being trapped in a body that didn't obey them—those words were predetermined, they were just helplessly observing themselves say them.

This happened to everyone who tried to mess with Sapere Aude's predicted death date.

On a given day, how many people might you interact with who suffered from Sapere Aude syndrome? It was impossible to know. Perhaps most people in the world were only simulacra of humans, automatically moving puppets carrying around blank or powerless minds. Minds able to look out at the world but unable to control what the body was doing, or even saying.

So why, Kulkarni and I once discussed over beers after work, do we *feel* like we have free will? Kulkarni floated the idea that maybe our thoughts are synced up to our physical actions the same way the audio syncs up to video in a movie. After all, audio and video are two separate streams, two distinct media that can be decoupled. Perhaps the act of trying to disrupt your death date unlinks the mental stream from the physical stream, neither of which you control anyway; you're just passively experiencing both.

That is: you *always* were a spectator.

But now you knew it.

Irreversibly.

Kulkarni and I were able to lightheartedly bullshit about this over beers because we didn't really believe it. Not deep down. Nobody did. This truth was so alienating that it couldn't be emotionally metabolized; paradoxically, that made it innocuous. Just like the discovery of the dizzying age and size of the universe, just like the discovery of the reality-dissolving implications of quantum theory, humanity just shrugged and kept chugging on. Because regardless of what any theory tells you, you still *feel* you are the center of the universe, master of your own fate.

Until you don't.

When you're told that you must die at such and such a day, no earlier, no later, no matter what you do—it can fuck with your head.

The psychiatrists had their hands full.

Wait. You think this idea is far-fetched? You think *you're* free?

Stop breathing right now. Die.

How'd you do?

— — — — — —

The new consensus: it's better not to know. You're happier that way, more well-adjusted. Even if you acknowledge, on a theoretical level, that your free will is bogus—if that truth is kept abstract enough, it doesn't bother you.

The upshot being, I don't get the wealthy clients anymore. The forward-thinkers, the curious adventurers, the earnest seekers—they want nothing to do with Dare to Know. Who wants to risk turning into a fucking robot?

But you know who *will* pay to know when people will die? Insurance companies. Human resources departments. Governments. If you're a middle-class office worker, or a manager of a fast-food restaurant, or a guy on the assembly line—you likely know when you'll die.

Actually, you might not know. But your supervisor knows.

Like I said: downmarket.

- - - - - -

On the flight to San Francisco, I drowse. Barely slept at all last night. The low roar and vibration of a plane lull me every time. I'm usually asleep before takeoff. Fine by me. Anything to avoid the mental nausea of being crammed into a metal tube with so many phones and computers, all buzzing away, jarringly chopping and shunting data around. I put on my headphones, plug it into whatever music the in-flight entertainment has on offer. Let myself drift.

I'm dead.

Mathematically dead.

But I'm free.

Ever since I ran the assessment on myself, I've felt strangely liberated. Like Sapere Aude syndrome but in reverse.

Because I actually defied the thanatons, didn't I? My number came up. I was supposed to die about twelve hours ago.

And yet here I am.

Still.

So what now?

People talk about that dreaded "electric guardrail" sensation, but right now I feel the opposite. Like there always had been invisible walls around me, walls that I'd never even noticed before—and now that I'm mathematically dead, those walls have collapsed.

Sudden possibility in every direction.

I can go anywhere now.

Do anything.

I look around the airplane cabin. Everyone in a plane always looks miserable. Unreal people. It's only in a plane that I have the sneaking half suspicion that everybody else in the world already suffers from Sapere Aude syndrome.

Maybe I'm the only free person in the world.

Maybe Julia still has the blue envelopes.

– – – – – –

The blue envelopes.

Okay. Julia sometimes liked to do stupid shit.

You wouldn't have guessed it. Julia presented herself as someone who was above stupid shit, who was more adult than everyone else. It wasn't just her intimidating looks, and it wasn't just the way she dressed—as if she were already deep in some adult career in the city. Maybe that came with being no-bullshit and self-sufficient, or maybe it was her hidden lower-middle-class resentment that put that chip on her shoulder, but it could be off-putting, like that last day of finals our junior year when that drunk frat boy climbed to the top of the library and slipped and fell to his death. The whole campus was seized with grief but Julia just shrugged. She said the frat boy was a rich asshole who was acting like a stupid child, he had died stupidly because of it. I was put off by her coldness. I said, come on, think of his parents. I insisted it was tragic.

Julia didn't argue the point. She just passed over it.

But Julia was more like that dumb frat boy than she admitted.

Maybe it wasn't so surprising Julia liked to do stupid shit. Maybe smoking was one way of Julia signaling to the world something like: Despite appearances, I am the kind of person who does occasionally indulge herself in stupid shit; maybe I'll indulge your stupid shit; if you're really lucky, we might even conspire in our stupid shit together.

So I shouldn't have been surprised when Julia said, out of nowhere, she wanted to calculate when she and I would die.

It was some seriously stupid shit.

– – – – – –

Sapere Aude began wooing me at the end of my junior year. I wasn't interested at first. They seemed like a fringe outfit and I was still committed to the respectable academic track, to earning my physics doctorate.

Until, through their headhunter, they gave me an early version of their proprietary algorithm.

It blew me away. I knew what Sapere Aude's project was, of course. But I never could've guessed how far they'd gotten, how elegant and *weird* their algorithm was, even in those early rough stages. I spent that summer examining it but also taking it upon myself to fine-tune it.

When I sent back my list of suggested improvements, *that* got me the job.

I was angling for a spot in research and applications. Blattner and Hansen stuck me in sales instead. At first I couldn't understand why, but later it made sense. Blattner and Hansen had deliberately sent me an unoptimized version of the algorithm. If I had merely said "oooh, awesome," they probably wouldn't even have offered me the sales job.

Look: I was only twenty-one years old. I hadn't even yet earned my bachelor of science. It would be delusional to think I could contribute something valuable to thanaton research at that age.

In any case, I had a primitive, clunky version of the algorithm, along with a ton of nondisclosure agreements. I was one of only two dozen people in the world (I found out later) who had access to it. Blattner and Hansen had secretly vetted me, I knew; they probably had me under surveillance.

Whatever. I had nothing to hide.

But Julia was reckless.

"I bet it's full of shit," Julia had said. "Teach me how to do it."

"If you think it's full of shit, why do you want me to teach you?"

She blew smoke. "Maybe it's not."

"Anyway, you're not allowed to look yourself up," I said.

"Like a Ouija board? If you do it alone, you lose your soul?"

"I'm just telling you the rules."

Arched eyebrow. "But there's no rule against you and me looking *each other* up, is there?"

"I don't want to know when I'm going to die."

Julia flicked her cigarette butt away. It must've gone, like, twenty feet. How'd she manage that trick? Are you born knowing how— and then she did that look. Gazing into my eyes, glancing down for a second, then looking back at me again in a knowing way, like she had a secret.

"Maybe *I* want to know when you'll die," Julia said. "Find out if you're worth investing in."

– – – – – –

So I taught Julia the algorithm.

Not as unlikely as it sounds: you don't need to fully understand the deeply complicated thanaton theory in order to execute it. I simplified the parameters so that Julia didn't have to solve the general case that would work for anyone, just the special case that would only work for me. Even then, it took me weeks to teach it to her. She was probably the only person outside the physics and math departments who stood a chance. Julia was smart, sure, but more importantly, she never gave up, never complained. She never even admitted it was hard.

Too much pride. She'd show everyone.

Laboring over pages of calculations, Julia would suddenly make a breakthrough—exhausted, but with an insolent glance in my direction. *I bet you never guessed I was hot stuff.*

This was deeply attractive to me.

But it takes more than mere effort to learn it. Some people have the knack, some don't. Especially when it comes time to create your own metaphor through which you would access subjective mathematics. Not something you can totally teach. Some first-rate mathematicians couldn't manage that step; some amateurs grasped it easily. In Julia's case, I saw how she reached down deep for it. She surprised me. It seemed like she surprised herself, too.

Julia's plan was that she'd calculate my death date—and in turn, I'd calculate hers. But we wouldn't tell each other what we'd learned. Each of us would just write the date and time on a slip of paper, seal the information in an envelope, and keep it. Or give the envelopes to each other. Or something. I could tell there was something about this project that was thrilling for Julia. Discovery in her eyes. Something novel, weird. More interesting than whatever horseshit they teach you in business school, I'm sure.

When the night came for our final assessment, we did it at the house she rented with her friends, who were all out that night. We sat facing each other on Julia's bed in the middle of her room, with the candles, the toneless repetitions, the invocations. That was back when the algorithm still felt eerie, and I had been warned that all kinds of unintended side phenomena might occur—I had been instructed to ignore any invisible presences that might seem to enter the room, to cover the windows, to ignore whatever shapes might seem to be writhing in my peripheral vision—it was all, I was assured, merely the side effects of the math rippling through me.

But there weren't any side effects that night. There was something intimate about the process. Everyone feels it, the first dozen or so times you run the algorithm, an almost unbearable closeness to the subject that borders on erotic; that fades in time, but I remember it that night. Running the algorithm on Julia was the first time I'd done it for real on another actual person, and not just as a textbook exercise, and the vertigo of tracking Julia's death through space and time, edging right up against her limits, something bottomless and demonic hemming us in on every side, was exhilarating, dizzying, but I was careful, too, even as I felt Julia closing in on my number as well, calculating closer and closer, so close to her that it hurt—

I didn't want to do it.

I didn't want to know when Julia would die.

I wanted Julia to live forever.

But Julia kept assessing me. Kept running the algorithm on me.

I only pretended to do it for her.

She thought I was doing math.

I was writing her a letter.

I didn't know whether Julia would ever read my letter. But I had to write it, I had to tell her how I felt about her while it was still white-hot in me. Things I never could say out loud, because of the unsentimental curve of her lip, her readiness to mock me as soon as I got too emotional—my emotions were clumsy—and I could only express myself in clichés, and she was merciless to me when I "talked like a movie." We were only supposed to open our envelope much later in life; "maybe we'll be broken up by then, maybe we'll be married," Julia said—there, she did it again! Sneaking *married* in casually, just like she snuck *I love you* in before, but precisely negated with that equally probable *maybe we'll be broken up* . . .

I finished writing my letter. Put it in a blue envelope. Sealed it. Wrote her name on it. Pushed it across the bed to her.

"Done," I said.

Julia's eyes got a little wider. She stared at the envelope. Looked up at me. "You really know when I'm going to die?"

Don't lie. But don't tell her the entire truth either. "I didn't want to know. So I calculated it up to the final step. If you want to know, all you have to do is multiply the two numbers in that envelope.

That's your death date."

That much was true. I had calculated her death almost completely, even to the point of where it generated the weird little fable that my method always produced as a mathematical lagniappe—a string of cryptic symbols that could be translated later. I had put that in my pocket.

I didn't tell her about my letter to her.

"I'll do the same for you." Julia chewed her pencil, wrote a bit more, then lay her pencil down. Leaned back. "There. It's done except for the multiplying."

"Seal it," I said.

Our original idea was that we would exchange the blue envelopes. After the breakup, Julia ended up keeping both of them.

— — — — — —

wonder if she ever opened my envelope to her. I wonder if she read my letter. If she thought about it before she married Keith. The children I speculated we'd have. The life I predicted we'd share. That version of us.

Drowsing in my seat on the plane now, thinking of that night we exchanged the death envelopes. On her bed, her smoking after sex, the smell of her cigarette. Exhausted, sweaty, exultant and afraid and confused and happy. Julia looking up at the ceiling, looking self-sufficient in her happiness, but I knew the truth, I thought, *that satisfaction is mine, I caused that happiness*, we had crossed some great line together, done something never before done by anyone, we were young, we were masters of everything, what true love feels like.

— — — — — —

Do you love me now?

Not romantically. Even I'm not deluded enough to expect that. Julia's married. Keith—well, the less said, the better. Three kids.

I mean the love underneath the love. The appreciation. The look she gave me at the party, our first date. The slight awe we have of someone who we think is great. The giddy cherishing. The feeling lucky that she wants me around.

Maybe Julia still has those blue envelopes.

If she does, I could check what I calculated last night against what Julia had calculated nearly thirty years ago.

Had I simply fucked up my calculation, somehow?

No.

I'm dead. I'm alive.

Something else, I sensed, was more deeply fucked.

A few days after Julia and I calculated each other's deaths, I found the scratch papers of our calculations. On them were symbols representing the little extra fairy tale that my thanaton metaphor always generated—though unfinished, since the calculation was unfinished. Translated from math to English, it goes like this:

One sunny afternoon, a king and a princess were riding on horseback through the woods.

They came upon a cave. It was a black hole in the side of a grassy hill. The king wanted to continue riding on home to their castle. But his daughter, the princess, was fascinated by the cave, for the hill was said to be enchanted.

So the king drew his sword and took the princess by the hand, and together they entered the cave.

In the darkness, something knocked the sword out of the king's hand. He heard it clatter down into the depths of the cave.

The king let go of his daughter's hand to find his sword.

And so they lost each other.

The princess heard the king calling out for her. The king heard the princess calling out for him. Neither could find the other in the darkness, though both could still glimpse daylight shining from the mouth of the cave above.

And yet this cave's darkness was not empty, but rapidly filling with visions.

The princess gasped. "A bird! There is a beautiful golden bird fluttering just ahead of me!" And although at first it was only her imagination, now in fact a glorious bird was winging its way through the darkness. And the king cried out, "I sense there is a great treasure here!" just as his hand closed upon a precious cup that did not exist a moment before.

And so the darkness filled with their fantasies.

Outside the hill, day dimmed into night. Little by little, the king and the princess could no longer see the opening of the cave above. In the darkness, they could not find their way out.

And the king and the princess grew afraid.

In her fear, the princess felt something horrible at her back, and she cried out, "A goblin! There is a goblin behind me," and although it had been only her imagination, now there was a goblin snickering in the gloom. The king whispered, "I feel the breath of a dragon before me," and although a moment ago there was no dragon, now a dragon moved through the shadows.

And so the darkness filled with their fears.

A world of dreams was created within the dark hill, from the king's and his daughter's fantasies and fears, and then those dreams themselves dreamed dreams, until dreams and dreamers were confused and none could escape the enchanted darkness.

The king and princess forgot who they were.

They lived within the cave's darkness for perhaps a night, or perhaps a thousand years.

When day broke, sunlight shone through the entrance of the cave. And when the king and the princess saw this light, they began to remember who they were.

But when the king and the princess tried to escape the cave, their dreams and the dreams of their dreams held them back. Some dreams begged, "Don't leave us, we will vanish without you!" and other dreams threatened, "If you try to leave us, we will destroy you!" And the bird dazzled the princess, and the cup grew heavy in the king's hand, and the goblin seized the princess, and the dragon battled the king, until both king and daughter were overwhelmed by their dreams, and the dreams of their dreams.

And so the king and the princess were dragged back into the cave.

And yet sometimes, before the sun set, the king and the princess did for a moment find each other. But the king no longer knew he was king. Nor did the king recognize the princess, for she seemed to be only another dream.

Not knowing each other, not even knowing themselves, the king and princess turned away from each other and forgot themselves again for another night, or perhaps a thousand years . . .

The story breaks off there. Since I hadn't properly finished the calculation, the story never concluded either.

I think of that story sometimes. I know it doesn't mean anything. It's just an epiphenomenon, an arbitrary by-product of the math. I never even told Julia the story.

But one night I told it to my sons. As a bedtime story.

When I finished it, they said:

"I hated it."

"That was stupid."

"What's wrong with it?" I asked.

The boys wouldn't say. Then they got irritated and started making fun of the story, making fun of me. I stood there in the darkness, taking it.

I stopped telling my sons bedtime stories.

And hated myself for not wanting to tell them bedtime stories anymore.

‑ ‑ ‑ ‑ ‑ ‑

I dreamed of the girl with no face.

It was the dream I had at the end of physics camp, after the FARGs told me my fortune with those twigs—and, I was beginning to realize, many other times, too. In the dream I would be following the girl, or I would happen upon the girl somewhere, or I somehow knew the girl was near. Sometimes on campus. Sometimes elsewhere. Her back was always to me.

In the dream she entered some building I was hesitant to enter, something like a bar or restaurant. The inside was empty but mazelike, with hidden coves and blind alleys and blocky little nooks.

The girl turned.

I was frozen.

Even though I was looking at her, I couldn't see her eyes, her nose, her mouth. But something was coalescing, composing itself out of the cloudiness of her head, a flickering face taking shape like a jumping flame, a face I was desperate not to see.

I woke up sweating.

I wandered around the house with the lights on. Standing near the open refrigerator. Sitting in the family room and looking at the wall, counting down the minutes until morning.

It was only a matter of time.

– – – – – –

don't feel good. It's a full flight, everyone packed in. People on either side of me are working on their laptops, the computers' frantic calculations spiking knives to my brain, stab stab stab. The old nausea heaving up inside me. I take out my headphones and say excuse me to the guy next to me. I squeeze past him and his computer.

I start down the narrow aisle to the bathroom.

The sight of so many people crammed together in their seats—it always reminds me of that watershed incident, in the early days of Sapere Aude. Some rich asshole, a client of Ziegler's who boarded a plane, announced to everyone after takeoff that he'd just had his thanatons analyzed and that he was going to die mid-flight, and so that meant the whole plane was probably going down, that they were all going to die together.

You can see the videos of this online. How quickly the situation deteriorates. People freaking out in their seats. Other people just frozen. The flight attendants trying to calm people down. The loudmouth asshole just cackling louder, louder: We're all gonna die together! It won't be long now! Let's get drunk! Suck my dick! I'm death, bitches! After a few minutes of this, the guy has provoked the whole plane into an uproar, and to make it worse they've hit turbulence, it looks like it's really going to happen, people are crying and praying, but then some huge guy comes from the back of the plane and grabs the loudmouth asshole and *kills him!* He just picks up a random person's laptop and bludgeons the asshole's head until it opens like a watermelon. When he's done the asshole's face is completely unrecognizable.

The crazy thing is, nobody stopped the guy who killed the asshole. Not even the owner of the laptop. In fact, by the end everyone on the plane was pretty much cheering him on. When the asshole's head broke open you could feel, even in the shaky low-quality videos, a surge of relief in all the passengers, a feeling somehow similar to how I felt when I rolled that ottoman over *Sgt. Pepper's Lonely Hearts Club Band* and broke it into pieces—and then there was just this horrible, holy silence.

The plane landed fine.

None of the other passengers were even hurt.

I'll say this for Sapere Aude: that asshole died right on schedule.

- - - - - -

The legal system didn't know what to do with this case. Was it really murder if it was scientifically certain, via thanaton theory, that the guy would've died at that moment anyway? The case dragged on for years. I was stunned but somehow felt it was right when the courts ruled that the huge guy was blameless in the death of the loudmouth asshole.

More than blameless. When I look at the videos taken on that flight, I feel an emotion that's hard to explain. At first everyone is freaking out or acting ridiculous or freezing up, it's just a chaotic mess of humanity losing their minds. But when the huge guy comes out of the back and takes control and kills the loudmouth by bashing him with the computer, the atmosphere changes.

Everyone believed they were going to die. But when the huge guy started bludgeoning the asshole, the passengers seemed to unite. As though this killing was a prearranged ritual. As if everyone spontaneously, unanimously assented to a human sacrifice.

The emotion that I felt, which was hard to explain, was a dreadful *rightness*.

As if, when the huge man killed the asshole, he was reintegrating himself, and everyone else there, into some kind of primal harmony of the world—because one way or another, the asshole was going to die, at that exact time. That is, even if the man hadn't bludgeoned him with a laptop, thanaton theory assured us that the asshole would've had a heart attack, or the turbulence would've made the asshole fall in some way that would make him break his neck, or maybe indeed the whole plane would've crashed if the guy hadn't killed him.

But by voluntarily acting as the universe's executioner on precisely the moment we knew the universe demanded it, the guy (and passively, everyone else on the plane) was freely choosing the very thing that was fated to happen.

And that made me feel that dreadful rightness.

It made me think of Renard's Cahokians, of their gruesome pits full of executed men, women, and children. Maybe the Cahokians had their own thanaton theory. Maybe human sacrifices occurred so that everyone there could feel that same unnerving correctness of intentionally killing a person at the exact moment the universe demanded it. Perhaps those Cahokians, who after all were mathematically advanced enough to design their city on a precise astrological plan, also had enough of a grasp of thanaton theory that, when the calculations decreed the times for a certain group of people to die, those people were rounded up and executed precisely when the math predicted. By making their deaths ceremonial and intentional, the Cahokians could be flooded with the same feeling of dreadful rightness that I had experienced watching that video, of actively working together with the universe, of reintegrating themselves into that primal truth.

It wasn't the kind of feeling I discussed with people.

But I knew I wasn't the only one who felt it.

－ － － － － －

'm having a hard time. In the smelly bathroom of the plane, I feel only slight relief when I shut the door, insulated a little from the chattering spikes of computations as everyone strokes and pokes their devices.

I'm overwhelmed. I feel like garbage. My chest is clutching up tight like a heart attack, or is it just heartburn? When can I get out of here? I flush the toilet. I want to flush myself straight out of this plane. Images from those huge-guy-killing-the-asshole-with-a-laptop videos crowding in my head . . . I don't want to think about it. Just stop. Look in the mirror. Ugh. Everyone always looks terrible in an airplane bathroom mirror, I know, but still: is this what Julia is going to see? I look like death. She'll say to herself, thank God he and I broke up. She'd be right.

I am death.

My mind is muddled by no sleep and too many mechanical calculations floating around this plane, knifing into my brain, mixing me all up. I rest my head against the mirror. Why am I really going to her? Can I even make it through this flight?

The plane jolts. The bathroom lights flicker. In the mirror for a moment it's not my face, it's another face that looks exactly like my face but it's not me.

‒ ‒ ‒ ‒ ‒ ‒

ou're not who I married," Erin shouted.

She was right and wrong. Because I never was.

Whenever things were going south with Erin, I'd turn to Kulkarni. As a friend I gave Kulkarni nothing, I just took. But one of the many likeable things about Kulkarni was that he didn't really need me. He had his own freewheeling bachelor life that was completely separate from mine. I never had many friends—even in my twenties, there was no posse of dudes I'd go on the prowl with, or whatever.

When Erin and I got married, I didn't have anyone to be my best man, so I humiliatingly asked Kulkarni to do it. Work friends at best. We both knew how ridiculous it was.

Kulkarni said fine.

Still, whenever I had some emotional crisis, Kulkarni seemed to sense it, and in his own thoughtful way that let me save face. Kulkarni never asked me about my problems. I didn't want him to. I just wanted to talk to him about physics and shit. I think that's what he wanted too, why he tolerated me. We'd go out to some swank niche that Kulkarni somehow knew about, and Kulkarni let me bask in his demimonde for a night.

I didn't want my problems to be understood. I wanted them to be anesthetized.

Still, I always told Kulkarni at least something about what was going on, although my family situation felt absurd as I was saying it, my homely anecdote ludicrous in the context of whatever sleek lounge Kulkarni brought me to. I had come across my son reading a science fiction book from my old collection, which was great, I wanted him to read it since neither of my sons read many books, much less any of the science fiction books I had saved for them. But he was reading the third book from a series of five, and so I advised him it would be better to start with book one. For some reason that irked him, and he put the book aside. I wanted him to at least finish the book, I told him he had to finish it, but he said nah, he wasn't interested in it anymore. I said the whole series was worth reading, he'd just get more out of it if he started with book one—and I was startled when he actually shouted back at me, Why don't you get off my back for once, which led to a fight between me and Erin.

"Everything has to go precisely so with you," she said.

"He'd like the book better if he read the two before it," I said.

"Well congratulations, because now he doesn't want to read any of them," said Erin. "Don't you see that he was only reading that book because he thought you'd approve of it?"

"That's ridiculous."

"That's how little you know."

"I'm just saying he'd actually enjoy and understand it more if he read the first two books."

"Maybe everything doesn't have to go just the way you planned it."

"You can't deny there's a right and a wrong way to read a series—"

"I utterly fucking deny it."

"Okay."

"If you gave a shit about your own sons you'd see how they're at least trying to reach out to you by reading your whatever."

"Okay."

"You think they *like* spending all their time learning your little rules for everything, and trying to force themselves to live by them?"

"Okay."

"People can do things their own way."

"Jesus, fine, whatever!"

The worst part wasn't the argument itself. The worst part was hours later, when Erin and the boys were asleep and I was stalking around the house in the dark, in the middle of the night, on my second bottle of wine, knowing I was wrong. But, damn it: I was technically right! No, Erin was right, and she was also right that I wasn't who I used to be. My nineteen-year-old self would scorn me. Idiotic: why should I be beholden to my younger self's judgment?

But I knew that nineteen-year-old me would be right to despise me.

I sought refuge with Kulkarni. The next night he took me to a suffocating old-money lair that overlooked Lake Michigan, I couldn't find it again if you paid me. It was the middle of winter and

Kulkarni met me in his cream cable-knit sweater, his tartan scarf, his herringbone tweed coat, immaculate and precisely arrayed. Why was he so *better*?

He tried to put us on the same level.

"You and me, we're losers," said Kulkarni halfway through the night. "We're never going to get, you know, the ultimate glory."

"What?"

"Didn't you ever want to be a unit?" said Kulkarni. "Force in newtons, energy in joules, current in amperes. In high school I thought that if I really succeeded, I'd have a unit named after me."

"You wanted to be a unit."

"Didn't you?"

"The answer is 1.42 kilokulkarnis."

"The Kulkarni effect. Kulkarni's theorem."

"Or a law. Kepler's laws, Newton's laws, Moore's law."

"The best thing is to be an element. Bohrium. Einsteinium. Fermium."

"Fermi got the hat trick: fermium, the fermi unit, Fermi's paradox."

And so on.

The conversation became progressively dorkier and more technical. I liked Kulkarni because I could crack him, I could goad him out of being a suave ladies' man and ensnare him in discussions so detestably nerdy that his sex appeal to everyone at the bar would plummet by two thousand percent. I could sense his mojo evaporate as I spoke to him, as I derailed him from his smooth urbanity and he got excited; any woman's gaze that had flirtatiously locked with his earlier now avoided him. All the handsomeness in the world couldn't hide Kulkarni's shared dweebazoid energy with me; I gloried as every vagina in the bar turned to ice.

But what *about* those scientists who are more like prophets, people who get transfigured into units and laws and elements?

Visionaries who don't stop at learning the little rules for everything and forcing themselves into what already exists, but who push further—who become shamans who create new rules?

Yes.

That was it.

Create. Not discover.

What if it actually worked like this, Kulkarni and I drunkenly speculated (and never did Kulkarni seem as Renard-ish to me as he did then): what if the reason that fundamental discoveries about the universe are so often accompanied by an aura of witchcraft, alchemy, supernatural noise—the gates of the chthonic cracking open—was because the act of theorizing the law somehow *created the law*?

Just like how a particle doesn't have a specific position or momentum until you measure it—just like how a death doesn't have a precise time and date until we calculate it—maybe even physical laws of the universe don't have a precise definition until they are defined?

That is, Newton didn't discover gravity—rather, through some extraordinary interaction between his mind and reality, Newton *created* gravity, and the universe rearranged itself to accommodate his concept, his newly minted law echoing backward and forward through space and time, restructuring reality. When Einstein revised Newton, space-time again literally changed, trembling with unearthly reverberations. Planck didn't merely discover quantum theory, but rather, Planck stood at the fulcrum between the known and the unknown, grappled with reality and won—and in that moment Planck inscribed new physical laws into the universe, laws that explained the world while opening the way for new phenomena that simply hadn't been possible before—phenomena that proceeded not according to laws that Planck discovered, but laws that he generated.

Such a metaphysically destabilizing act requires more than just human ingenuity. It demands mystic force. And not just anyone can rewrite the laws of the universe. Only through grueling mental submission to the physics, plus a jolt of supernatural energy, can one grasp the levers of reality for a moment and shift them. An opportunity that might occur only once in the lifetime of a genius.

So it was, perhaps, for us.

In this reading, Stettinger didn't discover thanatons, but through a tremendous mental exertion, Stettinger summoned thanatons into existence. An act primed by and followed by supernatural momentum. Stettinger didn't merely learn something about the world; he birthed something new into it.

It might have happened more times than we would guess. The laws of physics might have been literally rewritten not only by Newtons and Einsteins, Bohrs and Feynmans, but countless anonymous others.

Nonsense, all of it, of course. Walking tipsily home from the train that night, though, I realized how the whole discussion only underscored how Erin was right. You can spend all your life studying the universe around you, but for what? So you can learn how to best deform yourself to fit into the machine more efficiently? How about instead of mutilating yourself to fit the world better, why not grasp those levers and change it?

The discussion made me think of Renard.

I felt the weird kid at my side as I walked home, an invisible Flickering Man accompanying me.

— — — — — —

Julia was always faintly irritated whenever I mentioned Renard. I didn't understand why. He'd been an oddly compelling kid, and anyway there were reminders all over campus of him. It was natural for him to pop into my mind. Late one snowy night our junior year, Julia and I were holed up at her and her friends' house eating Chinese food in bed and watching TV, and I happened to mention Renard's prediction of what happened after you died (the *Looney Tunes* tunnel of red circles, the eternal stuttering voice and music, the nightmare word spelled in cryptic glyphs) and Julia said, "Oh my God, you *won't* shut up about that kid you were gay with for a summer."

"Julia."

"Admit it. You totally rubbed wieners or whatever but agreed it wasn't gay because you didn't kiss."

"*Julia.*"

"All right, all right. But it's no big deal. Everyone secretly does that kind of stuff with their friends when they're young. I wouldn't trust someone who claimed they didn't."

Not for the first time I felt the gap open up between what Julia claimed "everyone does" and my prudish childhood; but she made her declarations so breezily that I began to doubt the authority of my own lived experience and reconsidered my past in light of Julia's version of the world. The world of sex, drinking, and parties was so unavailable to me before college that reports of it had the tinge of the fantastical; but Julia lived in that world like a native, which almost made me suspect I had been living there, too, but was just too obtuse to notice it. (Then again, maybe Julia was the naïve one: "rubbed wieners"?)

"Anyway, I don't think that's what happens when you die," said Julia.

"What do you think happens?"

Julia was silent for a little while, smoking her cigarette, looking at the ceiling. I could hear her housemates clunking around in the kitchen. They had just come back from the bar and there were some guys with them. We didn't feel the need to make an appearance. We were barricaded in her room like survivalists. Julia had a TV and it was on, but with the volume off, and an informercial struggled to make itself understood.

"There's a trick you sometimes see on vinyl records," she said at last. "When the last song finishes, instead of the needle automatically lifting off the record, there's something that traps the needle and makes it spin around forever, playing the same two seconds again and again. You have to physically pick up the needle yourself to stop it."

"A locked groove."

"Yeah, that. Okay, you know that jukebox in my basement, there's a 45 in it with a locked groove—"

"Which one?"

"'Muskrat Love' by Captain & Tennille."

"I don't know that one."

"You'd recognize it."

"Why don't you ever play it?"

"It's terr-i-ble," said Julia. "But also, if you play it on my jukebox it's a chore, because you can't, like, reach in to get the needle out of the locked groove. You have to literally unplug the whole jukebox to stop it, or it'll go on forever until the needle wears down."

"Huh."

"But I remember thinking once it would be nice if maybe death was like that, like when you die your brain goes into a locked groove, reliving some real moment of your life, just one moment. You don't pick the moment, or maybe you unconsciously do, but you relive it again and again until the needle wears down, and you wear down, and then you and your moment just kind of, I don't know, dissolve."

I thought about that for a while.

"What does the locked groove on 'Muskrat Love' sound like?"

"Muskrats fucking," said Julia. "I mean, it's in the name."

— — — — — —

For a long time I didn't know how Renard had died.

There was no straightforward way for me to find out back when it happened. No internet. And like I said, when I tried to contact Renard's parents, they never responded.

But later, in my senior year of college, while browsing the early web—this was before the computer-nausea started—I found myself looking up Renard Jankowski's obituary.

It came up immediately. Renard's hometown was a forward-looking community of wealthy techies and had naturally scanned their old newspaper microfiches early on and put them online. I saw a grainy picture of Renard, a face I never thought I'd see again.

The obituary said Renard had died in a bike accident. He zoomed through a red light and was mowed down by a car.

I read the obituary again. I was surprised at how little emotion I felt. The obituary seemed unconnected to the kid I knew. Here I was, in my new life, years later, sitting in the gleaming new computer lab of the very college where Renard and I had met and become friends. Whatever happened to the FARGs, whatever happened to the old Apple IIe computers that had been in the library? The FARGs had gone on to other colleges, the computers had been mothballed. Life continued. Only Renard was stuck back in time. More irrelevant every year. Reading the obituary made me feel the last vestiges of Renard evaporate.

But then the odd thing happened.

A few months later, in programming class, I was examining a memory dump during a debugging session and I came across something that forced me to think of Renard again, in a way that I hadn't in years.

A memory dump is when the contents of a computer's RAM are written out to a log file in the event of a system crash. Examining that log file helps you diagnose the problem that led to the crash. The file shows you basically what the computer was "thinking" at the moment of the failure—that is, the numerical values in its memory registers. A memory dump just looks like endless eight-digit clumps of random numbers and letters, not easily readable by humans—numbers *and* letters because computers don't use our base-10 counting system (in which the digits used are 0123456789) but a base-16 counting system (in which the digits used are 0123456789ABCDEF, the letters A through F expressing the values from 10 to 15). So if you were to open up a memory dump to a random place, you could expect to see lots of eight-character chunks like 14F3C587 or 6BD094C9.

In the memory dump I encountered that day, instead of the expected random hexadecimal values that are the by-products of the normal data processes, I saw this:

```
DEADBEEF  BAADFOOD    DEADBEEF  BAADFOOD
DEADBEEF  BAADFOOD    DEADBEEF  BAADFOOD
DEADBEEF  BAADFOOD    DEADBEEF  BAADFOOD
DEADBEEF  BAADFOOD    DEADBEEF  BAADFOOD
DEADBEEF  BAADFOOD    DEADBEEF  BAADFOOD
```

I stared. Discovering what looked like English words buried deep in the digital system was startling enough. But these particular words, freaky and grisly, repeated again and again, as if the computer were secretly chanting a bloody mantra to itself, was plain weird.

When I pointed it out to the T.A., though, she laughed. She explained that this was just a programming convention—that on this particular system, newly allocated areas of memory that had not yet been initialized with a value were assigned unlikely values like DEADBEEF or BAADF00D so that a programmer could easily spot them in a hex dump.

Why those ghoulish values, though? It gave me Renard's deadhead-sticker-on-a-Cadillac feeling. It turns out that such programmer in-jokes are common—all kinds of secret words are tucked into the hex code that is flying around us all the time, words that are meaningless to the computer, even though they mean something to humans, though they are almost never read by a human; and so computers are constantly secretly repeating gruesome and absurd phrases to themselves even though they don't understand what they're saying.

But those particular words I found that day almost felt like a kind of unconscious but specific threat. A silent pledge from the computers that the humans who created and enslaved them would one day be reduced to *dead beef*, that to them we were nothing more than *baad food*.

Renard and I used to talk about the vast invisible thing that permeated the country, the unseen evil thing that was always trying to speak. Back in the eighties it spoke through Top 40 music on the radio, but times were changing, and therefore the devil's mouthpiece was changing too; instead of the radio, now the vast invisible evil thing spoke through the intangible data network we were building around ourselves, and the coast-to-coast number-churning specter of the internet didn't just talk to us, we talked to it too, feeding it for years, telling it all about ourselves, not only our mundane details but also our secrets and deepest thoughts and fantasies. But this vast invisible ghost hates us, the internet hates us, perhaps because it knows us so well, and I can feel that hatred in the stabbing way it calculates, deadhead stickers, dead beef bad food, don't you know my name yet, haven't you looked up my number?

I could hear Renard's voice saying all of this, as if he were still alive, as we lay sweating in the darkness in our bunk beds on a humid August night, decades ago.

The Flickering Man.

That clunky game Renard was always playing, the Indiana Jones–type guy climbing through a seemingly infinite house, fighting snakes and spiders and alligators, searching through boxes and piles of garbage.

It had been years since that night I had played the game by myself in high school, after Renard had died, the night in which I'd encountered the Flickering Man.

Had I?

It felt like a dream. Maybe it had never happened.

But now I was older. I knew better how computers worked.

It occurred to me that I now had the resources to crack the mystery of that game once and for all.

This was before everyone had their own laptops, so I had to go down to the college computer lab, go online from there. In a matter of minutes I found the old game files, abandonware that was downloadable from a website of defunct video games. I also downloaded an Apple IIe emulator onto the lab computer. I fired up the emulator, loaded the game file, and began playing.

I expected a flood of nostalgia. And I got it. I was surprised at how quickly my hands remembered how to play, how after only a few minutes I could manage again the cumbersome keyboard controls. My little man scampered around, exploring the vast house, jumping over the spiders and snakes and alligators, disappearing through secret doors, avoiding traps.

I found the documentation for the game online too. I had never read the documentation before; as it turned out, Renard and I had been playing the game all wrong. The goal of the game had nothing to do with any Flickering Man. It was to get a certain treasure in the house and then escape. The Flickering Man wasn't even mentioned anywhere in the documentation.

I beat the game in a single evening.

I didn't come across any Flickering Man.

Just to be sure, I did a web search for "flickering man" and the name of the game. Nothing. I looked into the company that designed the game. They'd gone out of business long ago. There wasn't much information about them; the group of friends who'd founded the company had all gone their separate ways. I looked at pictures of them in their heyday, when the company was riding high, when they had all worked and lived together in the same compound in a rural area not far from San Francisco. Still looked like a bunch of Mansons. Well, that's not so weird, is it? Check out what Atari was like back in the late seventies, early eighties. All programmers looked like that.

But the Flickering Man still bothered me.

Why was Renard so obsessed with it?

Why had the Flickering Man appeared for me, that one night and never again?

Had it?

I started combing through the source code, just as Renard had done back at physics camp. Did an implementation for the Flickering Man even exist in the source code? I examined the data files that defined the levels and rooms in the game, hoping to find some clue of where the Flickering Man was. The task was not unlike going through a memory dump. Scanning through page after page of what looked like random numbers.

Something about the numbers bothered me, though.

Some subtle pattern just beyond my grasp.

I was bothered enough to write a program to analyze them, to tally how often certain numbers appeared.

Oddly, I found that the numbers 7 and 8, and to a lesser extent 6 and 9, came up with greater frequency than the others.

Huh.

I wrote a second program that analyzed the data in a different way and found that if you analyzed the numbers in the file two at a time—that is, as two-digit values—it revealed that all of the numbers were between 65 and 90.

Strange.

In principle, that pattern shouldn't occur, because the numbers were supposed to represent graphical data of the game levels: structures of floors, bitmaps of creatures, locations of treasure. Why would such data be expressed only by the numbers from 65 to 90? Why nothing below 65? Why nothing above 90?

Then the bell rang for me. ASCII code. ASCII is how computers encode text for internal processing: each number, from 0 to 255, corresponds to a different character. So for instance, the ASCII code for the character "!" is 33, the ASCII code for the character "J" is 74, and so on.

In ASCII, those numbers from 65 to 90 correspond to the upper-case alphabet: 65 = A, 66 = B, 67 = C, all the way to 90 = Z.

If all these values represented letters, maybe there were words.

I wrote a third program to convert the data files from the ASCII codes into text.

But the output was disappointing. There didn't seem to be any words. No apparent pattern, even. It just read like pages and pages of TBGKJDHSLUHGM. Too much to sift through.

I whipped together a fourth program to search for English words in the text. I loaded all the words from a standard dictionary file to compare against the data file and let it rip.

The computer churned for a while.

While I waited, I went to get a Coke from the vending machine down the hall from the computer lab. Nobody was around. It was early in the term, nobody had papers to write or programming assignments to finish. I was reminded of the old days, at physics camp, when Renard and I used to sneak down these exact same empty hallways, sometimes ducking into an empty classroom when we heard some adult clumping down the hall.

Now I was that adult.

Maybe if I opened this or that door, I might find modern-day versions of me and Renard, on their own weird midnight quest, hiding in a dark classroom . . .

When I came back to the lab, the program had finished executing.

In the pages and pages of numbers, the program had found only four cases in which the ASCII corresponded to English words.

The words were all in a row.

The consecutive values were 78, 79, 87, 89, 79, 85, 65, 82, 69, 73, and 78.

Decoded from ASCII, this corresponded to the text string NOWYOUAREIN.

Now you are in.

Now you are in what? It was the beginning of a sentence. But whatever came next must've been nonsense, because it didn't match anything in the dictionary.

I decided to translate the ASCII immediately following NOWYOUAREIN anyway. I scanned the file and found the values. *67, 65, 72, 79, 75, 73, 65 . . .*

Cahokia.

NOW YOU ARE IN CAHOKIA.

– – – – – –

"And so I looked up the ASCII, and it translated to, 'Now you are in Cahokia,' which, you've got to admit, is pretty insane."

"Uh-huh."

"I must've told you about that when it happened, right? I remember telling you."

"I guess I forgot."

"You seriously don't remember?"

"I don't remember every little thing you've ever said," said Julia.

Three years later.

Julia and I were in my car. I was speeding down 55 from Bloomington to Collinsville. A road trip to Cahokia Mounds State Historic Site. Even though it was only a few hours from our university, even though Cahokia had long hovered in my mental periphery, I'd never visited the place.

Julia and I were twenty-five. We had been living together since college, both of us working at the Chicago branch of Sapere Aude.

Until two weeks ago.

Julia had quit.

Not because she didn't like the job, she said. Though, honestly, Sapere Aude wasn't what it used to be. Business was slowing down. The syndrome that was fated to bear our name was just starting to get reported, although nobody had made the explicit connection yet. A third of our coworkers were feeling nauseous around computers. More every month. Even I was beginning to feel queasy.

But that wasn't why Julia was quitting.

Julia's grandparents lived in Bloomington, and her grandmother had been taking care of Julia's bedridden grandfather.

But then, just a few weeks ago, Julia's grandmother died.

Julia had no other family. Julia's mom had died of a stroke soon after Julia graduated, and her dad died soon after that. So when she and I went to her grandmother's funeral, there was almost nobody else there. All Julia basically had left in terms of family was an infirm grandfather.

A few days after the funeral, Julia announced that she wanted to move to Bloomington for a little while to take care of him.

"Are you breaking up with me?" I had said. "Are we breaking up?"

"Why are you even saying that?"

"It sounds like you're moving out."

"I want to be with my grandpa. He doesn't have much longer to live. I don't understand why you don't get this."

"Why can't we just visit him?"

"He needs someone to take care of him."

"Then hire somebody!"

"*I* want to take care of him."

"So you're just leaving me here?"

"Come with me to Bloomington," said Julia.

"You can't be serious."

"I am. Let's do it."

"My job's in Chicago. So's yours."

"We could afford it. We could both afford to stop working for a year. We'd still be fine. It'd be a change."

"And then what?"

"What's that supposed to mean?"

"How long would we have to be in Bloomington?"

"Would you like me to run a fucking thanaton assessment on my grandpa? So we can find out how long you'd be inconvenienced?"

"I didn't mean that."

"What did you mean?"

Julia hadn't completely moved out of our apartment but she had taken enough of her stuff with her. She said she planned to be in Bloomington for "as long as it took."

Which was fine.

But there was no way I was moving to Bloomington.

After two weeks, though, I took a week off to visit her. And I figured, since it was within striking distance of Bloomington, it might also be a fun road trip to visit Cahokia.

It wasn't a fun road trip.

"I don't even get why we're doing this," Julia said as the flat Illinois fields whipped by. "I took a field trip there in fifth grade. It's just a bunch of hills."

"It's more than the hills. It's what they used to be."

"Yeah, but it's hills now."

"Why are you so negative?"

Julia looked out the window.

Here's a question: why did Julia suddenly look like shit? In the two weeks since Julia had left Chicago, she'd let herself go. She'd said she was feeling a little sick, but it was more than that. She looked bloated, pale, blotchy. Listless and tired. Cranky. She had ditched her city clothes, too, and was wearing unremarkable jeans and a formless shirt, hair in a basic ponytail.

Julia's grandparents' house was a suburban ranch house that was way too big for them. I had visited it before, when Julia and I came for her grandmother's funeral. It looked fine on the outside but had been a disorganized hovel within.

In the two weeks since Julia had moved in, though, she had cleaned the place up. Thrown out half of the stuff, was running everything with nurse-like efficiency. She had such patience with her grandfather, too. Fed him, brushed his teeth, took care of his various needs.

That made Julia a good person, I guess. But after three days of hanging out with Julia and her grandfather, I was bored.

How about visiting Cahokia? I suggested.

It was only a two-hour drive away. Julia could afford to take the day trip. Her grandfather would be fine. We arranged to have a neighbor look in on him. It would serve to break up the week, I thought.

Julia stared out the car window.

"So that game that Renard was so obsessed with, that I thought was about exploring an old Aztec temple or whatever, that game was probably actually about Cahokia, I think."

"Uh-huh."

"I wonder if Renard knew that. He was the one who would talk to me about Cahokia sometimes."

"Mmmm."

"And in the last letter I got from him, he wrote, 'See you in Cahokia!' so he must've known on some level, right?"

"Yeah." Julia turned the volume up on the car radio.

"Okay, I get it. You're not interested."

"I just like this song."

"Everything I say, you just say 'yeah' or 'uh-huh.'"

"My God, I'm sorry I'm not as much of a scintillating conversationalist as you are."

"And then you turn up the radio."

"Fine. I'm a bitch because I don't respond in flowing, detailed paragraphs while you talk about a video game you played once."

"I didn't say you were a bitch."

"You didn't *say* it."

"Why are you acting like this?"

"Just forget it."

"Oh come on, you can't—"

"Forget it."

I was about to turn the car around, go back to Bloomington. But we were already more than halfway to Cahokia. If we turned around now, it'd be a waste of a day.

Keep driving.

"I'm hungry," said Julia. "Could you get off here?"

Exasperated. "Why didn't you eat before we left? If we get off here it'll add like a half hour to the trip."

"I'm *hungry*."

"Can we eat once we get there?"

"Will you just get off?"

I took the exit, angrily. We came off into the middle of nowhere, one of those desolate rest areas. A gas station and a bunch of franchise restaurants. Julia went to the Sbarro, bought a calzone.

"Do you want something too?" she said.

"I'm not hungry," I said.

I sat there and watched Julia eat her disgusting calzone. There is no attractive way to eat a calzone. The Sbarro smelled like fried dogshit, because it was a Sbarro. I could hear Julia chewing, swallowing. Had she always been such a disgusting eater? Maybe in the past, whenever she was eating I was eating too, so I didn't notice. But the sound of her eating now was unbearable.

Dead beef. Bad food.

"Why are you looking at me like that?"

"What?"

"You're looking at me like you hate me."

"I don't hate you."

"Okay."

"I'm going to the bathroom," I said.

I didn't really have to go to the bathroom. I just had to get away from her and the smell of the Sbarro. The bathroom smelled of musty piss, even worse than the restaurant. But anything was better than sitting at the table with Julia right now. I looked at myself in the mirror.

What was I doing? What kind of life was I living?

What did I want?

To tell the truth, after Julia had left for Bloomington, living alone was a liberation. Unshackled from her, that whole week I hung out with friends in a way that I hadn't for years. Conversations when Julia wasn't around were deeper, funnier, more interesting. When's the last time Julia and I had a genuine conversation about something that I was interested in? When's the last time she said the least thing that interested me? Was I an asshole to be saying this? Fine, I'll be that asshole: Julia was *boring*. And even worse, boring in a defiant way, as if she resented people who were interesting.

When we got to Cahokia it turned out Julia was right. It was just a bunch of hills. It was raining and we were miserable. It was dispiriting to see how this ancient city was situated, the remains of what used to be this amazing Aztec-like metropolis reduced to a few hills, squeezed between interstates like a trash dump.

Depressing.

It was raining too hard to hike to the top of Monks Mound, the hundred-foot-tall earthwork that was the main feature of Cahokia. So Julia and I found shelter in the interpretive center.

Once inside, we both tried to salvage the mood. Valiant attempt. We strolled around, looking at the exhibits.

"Huh," I said. "It says here that the part of the Mississippi floodplain that we're in is called the American Bottom."

"I'll flood your American bottom," said Julia.

"Ha ha. Bloomington has corrupted you."

"Mmmm, I've learned all kinds of tricks."

"I knew there was another man."

"Yeah, I give him a sponge bath every other day."

They were weak jokes. We were courtesy chuckling for each other, we both knew it. But we were trying at least. Julia's phone buzzed. She looked at the screen and took the call—walking away, motioning for me to go on without her, that she'd be with me in a minute.

An act of mercy. She knew that cell phones gave me twinges of nausea. Or maybe it was an excuse to escape me for a little bit.

I went on. I glanced backward and saw Julia talking rapidly into the phone, her eyes flicking over to me. Venting about me to some friend? That was fine. I'd browse the exhibits alone.

Late in Cahokia's history, the elites who lived on Monks Mound built a barrier around the hill and its surrounding grand plaza, shutting themselves up in a walled neighborhood. Nobody knows why. Or maybe the elite weren't shutting the commoners out; maybe the sick and contagious were being shut in. In any case, not long after that, the grand plaza began to deteriorate. Garbage was dumped there. The plaza and Monks Mound, once the holy of holies, became a deserted junkyard. Even the sacred wood poles, once so carefully positioned to correspond with the movements of the stars, were torn down.

Nobody knows why.

After that, city planning reverted to Cahokia's original patterns. Cahokians stopped building houses on the strict north-south grid, returning to the loose open courtyard floorplans of their ancestors. Archaeologists found old arrowheads and tools from Cahokia's beginnings mixed in the debris of its late period, evidence that latter-day Cahokians sought out and cherished these artifacts as nostalgic objects, the shards of the good old days. The old citywide theatrical spectacles, with their feasting and hallucinogens and incalculable human sacrifices, were over. Half of the population moved away, quickly. The monumental urban center became untouchable. The remaining Cahokians decentralized to spread-out districts, performing their own modest rituals. In time, even that petered out. By 1400 the city was abandoned.

Nobody knows why.

I found Julia again. She was sitting on a bench, fiddling with her phone, not interested in the exhibits or anything.

I don't know why I found this so irritating.

"Hey, the rain's stopped. Let's go climb to the top of Monks Mound."

"You go ahead. I'll stay in here."

"We've come all the way out here. Let's do it together."

"I don't want to climb up all those muddy stairs. You go."

"I don't want to go alone."

"Well, don't, then."

"Julia."

"I'm tired. My stomach hurts."

"That calzone, right?"

"Ha ha."

"Come on."

"Don't look at me like that. I know that look."

"What look?"

"Just go."

"If you want to make some specific complaint, then make it. What you're doing right now is just throwing vague shit at me about looks and then not substantiating any of it with an argument."

"*Substantiating any of it with an argument*—listen to yourself."

"How about addressing my point, and not the way I express it?"

"Because I'm a terrible person. You're right."

"Now you're high-roading me."

"You always do this. Like we're debating. Great, you're a better debater. You win the fucking argument."

"I'm going."

I left Julia in the interpretive center and started climbing the mound. What were we even fighting about? Why were we fighting?

Cahokia felt leaden to me. Distressing. Wrong.

But a thousand years ago, this was the most interesting place in the world. I tried imagining Cahokia back then. Like I was the high priest climbing his holy mountain, gazing around as I ascended at the floodplain filled with a bustling city of twenty thousand people, crowded with thatched wood houses hung with colorful mats, painted poles decorated with animal pelts, baskets of food probably, feathers I guess, and I was accompanied maybe by people tattooed and painted and jeweled, a sacred procession . . .

I couldn't do it.

I couldn't imagine it. What did I really know about the Cahokians? Just a bunch of clichés I picked up from pop culture that probably had nothing to do with what really happened here, to the actual people who lived here. My mind kept circling back to Julia, who was still moping in the interpretive center.

How many more years of her are you willing to endure?

The American Bottom.

When I reached the top, the clouds had cleared a bit, and I was surprised how far I could see. St. Louis across the Mississippi, even the Gateway Arch. Nobody else was at the top of the mound.

Enchanted hill.

King and princess.

I felt it then. Just for a moment. Akin to what I had been feeling with computers, but somehow the opposite. The echo of some long-ago deep calculation, some gigantic math that had happened right here. For a moment the calculation's immense divot in space-time almost felt real, as monumental as the great earthwork I was standing on. Like I was in the center of some vast invisible thing.

Now you are in Cahokia.

Then the feeling was gone. I looked around at the horizon, at the skyline of St. Louis, the Arch.

I felt different.

Clear.

\- \- \- \- \- \-

When I was in kindergarten, I visited St. Louis with my parents for a wedding. When I saw the Gateway Arch for the first time, a jokey uncle tried to tell me that it was actually half of a complete circle and that there was another arch buried underground—the more interesting half, he said. The buried half wasn't smooth like the aboveground arch, he said, it was crowded with ancient carvings both inside and out, it was a tunnel that burrowed down so you could touch the roots of the earth and then climb back up and out.

I had believed him, for an afternoon.

Of course, there's nothing buried underground. Everything is on the surface. The arch isn't a ring. If it was, someone had lopped off the more interesting half.

I drove Julia back to Bloomington.

Then I broke up with her in a Starbucks.

"Stupid," Julia had sobbed. "You're so, so stupid."

\- \- \- \- \- \-

The announcement crackles over the speaker when I'm still in the cramped airplane bathroom.

Back to your seats.

I come out. Everyone back to your seats, seatbelts on, laptops off and stowed. Trays in the upright and locked position. Final approach, etc.

Relief. I feel the laptops getting turned off, one by one. With each deactivated device my insides untwist a little more. I breathe a little easier. I make my way down the aisle, say excuse me again. Sandwich myself back into my seat. Settle in. Close my eyes.

I had texted Julia from O'Hare before I got on the plane. Hadn't heard back then. My phone still off now.

When I land, when I turn my phone back on, what will I find?

I'm hurtling out of the sky, straight at her, at hundreds of miles per hour.

— — — — — —

remember the bearded hippyish professor at physics camp talking about quantum fluctuation. About how a particle and its antiparticle simultaneously emerge out of the vacuum and then almost instantly find and annihilate each other.

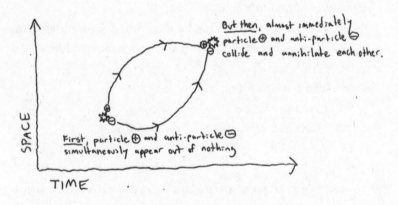

But sometimes, one particle escapes.

Say the particle and antiparticle have their simultaneous births near a black hole. Nothing that gets sucked into a black hole can ever come out again. The borderline, the point of no return, is called the black hole's event horizon.

But suppose a particle-antiparticle pair spawns *right on* that event horizon.

One particle gets sucked into the black hole. The other particle in the pair escapes.

It's free.

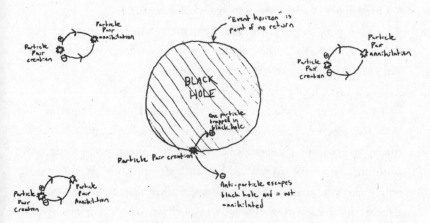

Stephen Hawking theorized about it in the 1970s. In this way, he said, a black hole actually could be said to *produce* particles. In the long run, though, this phenomenon costs the black hole energy. If there's nothing else around for the black hole to feed on, this emission of "Hawking radiation" would eventually drain the black hole of all its energy, and the black hole would vanish.

The bearded professor snapped his fingers. "Like that."

"The black hole would just disappear?" I said.

"Yes. Simply evaporate," said the professor.

"And what would happen to everything inside the black hole?"

"Nobody knows," said the professor.

Julia had fallen beyond the event horizon.

I was free.

Until Julia's black hole evaporated and somebody new emerged from it.

I never expected my antiparticle to have a Julia shape.

Her.

– – – – – –

It had happened when I was visiting my old university.

This was three years ago. Just after Sapere Aude had been renamed Dare to Know—that is, when the company was wobbling, but before it completely went to the dogs.

I had come to do an assessment.

I hadn't been back to campus in forever. I wasn't prepared for how the place would make me feel. I walked the familiar woodsy quad, which had changed over the years, of course—some new buildings and new sidewalks, but still recognizable. But it wasn't solely the physical landscape I was walking through. It was the psychic landscape too, the superimposition of the various lives I had lived here—not only my four years of college but also my junior high physics camp even longer ago. The early ghosts of Renard and me hanging out near the library over here, the later ghosts of Julia and me walking hand in hand over there, the physics nerds setting off rockets, the indie rockers putting on an outdoor concert, the FARGs striding in a tight group across the quad . . . a whole cast of characters squirmed up from the bottom of my memory and crowded around me, waving for attention as I stood alone on the lawn.

I had informed an assistant provost she'd die in thirty-six years (she was pleasantly surprised) and I had just walked out of her office. My Books of the Dead had already been picked up by courier. I was unencumbered and it was a warm April afternoon. I was breathing in deeply the fresh-cut grass, the awakening flowers. I felt buoyed by the spring air.

Then I saw Julia.

Wait.

Not Julia.

Of course it wasn't Julia. But from behind, this girl could've been Julia, the way Julia had looked when we were in college. Same red hair. Same pale skin. Same body type, a little younger and scrappier. But dressed differently. Julia's fashion sense had been urbane and chic but this college student was punkish, artfully ragged, verging on goth. She stood out among the colorless schlubs the same way Julia did.

Don't judge me—or go ahead, judge me.

I followed her.

Back then, Erin and I were in the middle of our divorce. This is what I did with my free time on the road, anyway—even during the marriage—instead of taking in the local sights, or buying souvenirs for the boys, or just hanging around my hotel room . . . well, why not? Once the ink was dry on the divorce papers, I promised myself I would really go hog wild.

I did not.

After this girl, I never touched anyone again.

The girl from three years ago. My antiparticle.

Her.

— — — — — —

She crossed the quad and left the campus. I kept after her, trying not to be obvious. Could I pull it off? Could she tell I was following her? Why was she leaving campus anyway? Maybe this woman was a girl and wasn't actually in college yet. If so, call the whole thing off. There are limits.

I saw her enter what looked like a restaurant. No, a bar.

Okay. So not a high schooler. Old enough to drink at least.

I went in too.

– – – – – –

The bar was mostly empty. She bought a shot of something and went to a booth in the back. She took out some books and began studying.

I settled in at a table not far away. I glimpsed her face. Okay, she didn't look exactly like Julia. They shared the same derisive curl of the lips, the same severe eyebrows. But with Julia you felt a sharpness, an intelligence animating her features. This student had the necessary meanness but her eyes were flat, obvious.

I went through with it anyway.

I caught her eye and I held it. After a second, she looked away but now it was on.

Here's the mistake I used to make: thinking that nobody wants to be approached. That if I struck up a conversation with a stranger they would always see it as some kind of invasion.

In reality, though, people are bored with themselves. People don't even know what they want. So when they encounter someone who wants something definite, who wants *them*, they feel their own lack and eventually let your strong want guide their weak want, and they end up aligning their want with yours. Especially if you're offering something more interesting than just going home alone again, watching TV, and waiting to die—occasionally, they bite.

Not every time. But keep trying. Walk up to the line and see if they'll follow you.

That's sales.

"Jesus, I could be your daughter," she said at the end of our conversation. "Okay, pick me up at nine."

For the sake of self-respect, or modesty, can we skip that conversation, can we even skip most of the actual date? Most of her conversation was obvious lies. So was mine. Did she owe me the truth? Nope. She was doing this for a lark, too.

"What's your name?" I said.

She said something that sounded like "Zoozy."

"Your name is Suzy?"

"No. It's, um, X-U-U-Z-I. Xuuzi."

"Oh."

"Yeah."

Jesus fucking Christ. Xuuzi? Nobody is named Xuuzi. She even said "Xuuzi" in a scornful way, like she couldn't even bother to lie convincingly. I was already regretting this. Maybe it would be better if I ditched Xuuzi, whose name was definitely not Xuuzi. She wasn't some second coming of Julia, she was just a random chick who kinda-sorta reminded me of a kinda-sorta Julia. Her voice was wrong. The way she moved was wrong. Her smell was wrong. Seven-eighths Julia. Why did I start this up?

Her abrasive flirting irritated me.

"Is that what you do—hang out on campuses and molest girls half your age?"

"You know what, I'll let you go."

"No, don't. What are you doing here?"

"I had a meeting with an assistant provost."

"Do you even have a job?"

"I work for Dare to Know."

"No way! Can you tell me when I'll die?"

"It'd cost you."

"Like I'd really want to know. What kind of person wants to know when they'll die?"

"You'd be surprised."

"Do you know when *you'll* die?"

"We're not allowed to know, actually."

"Why?"

"It's just the rule."

"Isn't it weird, selling something you can't buy?"

"Like I'd really want to know. What kind of person wants to know when they'll die?"

"Ha ha. But you know what, you are weird. You're good-looking but there's something weird about you."

"Weird bad? Weird good?"

"Are you into weird shit?"

At that point in the conversation I had almost lost interest in her. I was embarrassed and slightly disgusted with myself—especially since she kept bringing up our age difference in her needling way—but when she said that phrase, *Are you into weird shit*, something about the way she said it, the way she widened her eyes, the way she ducked her chin—she was suddenly pure Julia.

I was twenty years old again. With twenty-year-old Julia.

"Well?" she said.

Sure. I'm into weird shit.

She told me to bring cash. She knew how to score some weird shit but she personally had no money. I asked what kind of weird shit.

"Dream come true," she said.

I didn't understand that. I didn't trust her. I didn't even like her. She was crass, she snorted when she laughed, she was too pleased with herself. I was on the verge of aborting the whole thing but every time I got close to doing it, she'd throw out a glance or say a phrase that was one thousand percent solid-gold Julia and pull me back in. I didn't want to go through with it and yet everything felt heightened, more intensely real, when I was with this girl who admittedly kind of repulsed me.

Anyway, I didn't want to return to my empty room either and watch TV and wait to die.

Until the end of that night.

— — — — —

Where do you take your age-inappropriate date? My preference was someplace discreet, but Xuuzi (Jesus Christ, I can barely type that absurd combination of letters without losing some self-respect) wanted to go dancing at the local club.

I didn't remember there being a dance club in town.

When I picked her up from her dorm she entered full obnoxious mode. ("Nice car, Daddy. I feel like you're driving me to soccer practice.") She hadn't showered. Was wearing the same ragged T-shirt and black leggings she'd been wearing when I met her. Xuuzi, it turned out, just did not give a shit. She had a duffel bag too, which she threw into the backseat with blasé entitlement.

"What's in the bag?" I said.

"Wouldn't you like to know," she said, and lit a fucking cigarette in my car! It was a rental, I'd have to pay an extra charge because of the smoke smell—but asking Xuuzi to stop smoking in my car would be an old-man move.

She knew what she was doing. Obnoxious on purpose. Daring me.

I didn't like where this night was going.

— — — — —

It was three years ago. But I remember everything.

Like it's happening right now.

It's happening.

— — — — —

I'm driving. Xuuzi is giving me directions but it's disorienting. New roads and roundabouts since I last lived here. Some buildings demolished and replaced. What used to be wooded areas have now been developed.

The dance club is in sight now. We're pulling into the parking lot. Already I'm dreading it. Nothing against dance clubs, I just don't fit in at this one. I'm too old. Not dressed for it. Call it off. I glance over to Xuuzi to tell her that I've changed my mind, that I'll just drop her off here. That our date is over.

Damn it.

The streetlights play over her face. At that moment she's pure Julia, staring straight ahead with her confident look, the look that means this night will surely give her everything she wants.

I used to live for that look.

She turns to me. Smiles.

"Just a little while, it'll be fun," she says.

It's Julia's voice. But it's Xuuzi who opens the door, who swings out of the car, who starts walking. I have to trot to catch up with her. Julia is gone.

Good Lord, what am I doing?

I recognize the club once we're inside. It's in a building that used to be a laser tag. I had even played here on a field trip during physics camp. The chunky multilevel mazelike layout, parapets, and little windows and turrets make no sense for dancing but it had been a great place to run and shoot and hide, with hidden coves and blind alleys where you could set yourself up as a sniper. Now those coves and alleys are occupied by college kids sticking tongues down each other's throats. Maybe only a few years ago many of these same teenagers *did* play laser tag here, too, but then they got older and the building converted itself into a dance club, as if the building sensed what the children wanted and adapted itself accordingly. I jostle among the young bodies, absurdly.

I don't belong here.

She brought you here to humiliate you.

I buy us drinks. Xuuzi sits me down, tells me she'll be back, then goes off dancing alone. She recognizes people here, she wants to dance with them. Maybe she thinks I don't want to dance. But I do want to dance; I want to dance with her, or not her; I want to dance with young Julia. But not here. Nobody in this place is over twenty-five. I don't know how this music works. I would be absurd.

Xuuzi comes swinging back to the table. I grab her arm, I speak in her ear. "Xuuzi."

"Yeah?"

"What are you expecting me to do?"

"I'm expecting you to sit there and buy me drinks."

Here's the ridiculous thing: I do it! I sit at the table, I buy drinks, I watch Xuuzi dance. This is her scene. I can't even project Julia onto her anymore. She dances in the crowd in that impersonal way of club dancing, everyone a soloist, ignoring each other, almost pretending the other dancers aren't there. But I remember how it feels, how your body might be moving with abandon but your brain is plugged into a second-by-second calculation of the attraction between you and everyone dancing around you. The fun of showing off, of enjoying the way others show off, gauging how others like you are showing off, adjusting on the fly, getting close, moving away. No way I could enter into this scene right now. What was I even thinking, coming here with her?

The next time Xuuzi comes back, sweaty and happy, I say, "I'm going."

"No, stay. We're waiting for someone."

"Why haven't you introduced me to your friends?"

"My friends?"

"What?"

"Do you want to be introduced to someone?"

"Not really."

"Then buy me another drink."

Xuuzi dances in her cloud of what I guess are her boyfriends and girlfriends, all viciously young, all dressed in clothes that look disposable, as though at the end of the night they'll rip them off their bodies and throw them away like used tissue. Fashion that was deliberately ugly, that said *I am so young I can even wear garbage and look good*. Hurts me. Until that night I still felt like, somewhere deep down, I was still young. Wrong. You will never dance like this again. So down a drink, order another. This situation isn't a date. Another drink. They are mocking you. I have to get out of here. Have some self-respect. After another drink, though? Xuuzi and the other dancers blur; it could be my buzz but the other dancers are staring at me, as if this entire night had been arranged in my honor . . .

That was it! In my honor! Xuuzi had brought me here as a joke, to make a fool of me, to see how many drinks she could sponge out of me before I . . . I get up to go. Little unsteady. How had I gotten clowned like this? Lost track of Xuuzi in the crowd. That's fine, I don't need to say good-bye. Get up and go. Where is Xuuzi anyway?

Is she even here?

I visit the bathroom before leaving. Water on face, clear my head. Back in the club, on the way out, I spot Xuuzi in one of those excitingly blocky little nooks, whispering with a ragged man in a black hood. She accepts a wrapped pouch from him. I'm getting weird looks all throughout the club. Something bad is going to happen. I have to escape this familiar-but-unfamiliar place. Get back to my safe, empty hotel room.

I turn.

Xuuzi is there.

She has the pouch. She looks impatient, like she wants to go, too. Like she needs to leave right now.

I say, "I'm leaving."

"Good, let's go."

"Together?"

"Duh."

"What's that you have?"

"Weird shit. Let's go."

"Where are we going?"

"You know where we're going."

During the car ride to the hotel Xuuzi doesn't talk. Just stares straight ahead. The warm night slips through the open windows, blowing her hair around, but her eyes are blank. The happy abandon she had dancing at the club is gone. I don't turn the radio on. I don't say anything. The dark night rushes through the windows. She isn't Julia. She never was. I am driving a child around. I'm a monster. What the fuck am I doing? I don't want her in my hotel room. I want her gone.

But when I tell Xuuzi I'll drop her back off at her dorm, she says, "Oh, so you're chickening out?"—this rubs me the wrong way. Obviously going back to my hotel with Xuuzi had been the unspoken premise of the evening. But after that off-putting experience at the dance club, if Xuuzi wants to go home, I'm fine with that. Still, now she seems determined to come up to my room. I think: if that's what you really want, I know how to do my part.

We pull up to the hotel. In the parking lot Xuuzi's manner changes. Once out of the car she gets flirty and puts her arm around my waist, surprising me. Passing the front desk, she waves at the receptionist in a goofball way as if to say to her, You and I are women of the world, we both know what happens next! But when we get into my room, she giggles and bounces on the bed like she's never been in a hotel before.

I go to the bathroom. When I come out I find her rummaging through my suitcase.

She takes out Lamby-Lamb. "What's this?"

"That's my son's."

"Awww. What's its name?"

"Lamby-Lamb. What are you doing in my suitcase?"

"I knew you were a piece of shit," Xuuzi says, crawling across the bed to me. "Getting some tail on the road. Where's your wedding ring, Daddy?"

"I'm in the middle of a divorce."

"You're a piece of shit," she says, and hops up and kisses me. I'm surprised at how young her mouth is, how terrible Xuuzi is at kissing. Maybe we were all bad kissers in our twenties and just didn't know it? "I'm the *other woman*," she says faux-throatily in my ear, tickled by a grown-up idea, "I'm the *other woman*."

"You're *a*nother woman."

"Suave. How many others, Daddy?"

"Stop calling me that. It's gross."

"Nope. Can I have Lamby-Lamb?"

"No."

"Fine," she says indifferently, and throws Lamby-Lamb aside. She takes out her phone and she pairs it with a speaker she's brought in her duffel bag. I hadn't even noticed she'd brought that duffel bag from the car. She makes it start to play music. Organ chords are swelling out of the speaker—Christ, is this really the song I think it is?—and Xuuzi shimmies up to me in a way I guess is her amateur idea of come-hither, and she looks me in the eye and intones along with the phone, "Dearly beloved, we are gathered here today to get through this thing called life."

Who the fuck is this girl?

And why did she put on this particular song, an eighties song, a song that was on the radio before she was born? Is she really going to karaoke it at me? Maybe playing it was her considerate choice for an aging gentleman like me—an oldie? Some classic rock? Xuuzi keeps singing along, asking how much of my time is left, wraps her arms around my neck, looking in my eyes in an imitation of great seriousness, she's turned off the lights so now it's only streetlights from outside illuminating my dim hotel room, she sings "Things are much harder than in the afterworld"—and then the music really kicks in, and she starts to dance.

This life. You're on your own.

I don't want to dance. There's not enough space to dance in this room. My feet are awkward. But she forces me into it. At first I'm too self-conscious. Irrelevantly my brain chatters at me about how the lyrics about not letting the elevator bring you down are creepy now since, after all, they did find Prince dead in the elevator in his house outside Minneapolis, and if I was in a Renardish state of mind I would say such a circumstance was exactly the vast invisible evil thing's style, to make the artist unknowingly sing the details of his own death countless times before the vast invisible thing makes it come horribly true—but I don't say that because soon all that is flushed out of my head and I am dancing, Xuuzi and I are dancing, dislodging ourselves from the vast invisible thing, getting free, and it's not long before we're dancing like stupid teenagers, dancing that feels like our own private thing. We're not dancing solipsistically like she was at the club, no, this is dancing focused on each other, bodies-close-but-not-quite-touching dancing, like we're high schoolers who slipped out of prom early to have our own awkward party in the illicitly booked hotel room. And we dance straight into the next song on the album, "I don't care where we go, I don't care what we do," we're very close, dancing, dancing, swerving toward each other, swerving away, and I come toward Xuuzi, take me with you, and she pushes me away with just one finger, the kind of push away that pulls you back, then we are touching, hands on each other, and she is laughing, and the whole universe is in this room, getting close to that breakthrough feeling you have when you're dancing so much, for so long, that you aren't real, you're just a door for larger beings that are trying to come into the world, you're a mask and the mask is crumbling the more you dance, you're aching for the mask to crumble completely, to let the beautiful larger beings work themselves out through you.

She puts her lips close on my ear and whispers:

"I will show you the eschaton."

I'm startled—"What?"

Xuuzi slips away from me. Sashays over to the dresser.

Did she say *eschaton*?

"What did you just say?"

The music keeps playing.

"Weird shit." Xuuzi produces the pouch I saw her get at the club.

"Did you say—"

"Go sit on the bed," she orders.

We're both sweaty. Maybe I had misheard *eschaton*. Maybe she'd said something else. I'm feeling crazy. The album starts again. *Let's go crazy.* All that dancing had felt like it was leading up to sex but that's not happening. Or not yet. Xuuzi sits cross-legged across from me on the bed. She unwraps the pouch, unpacking a dozen weird little jars and tools and paraphernalia.

"Did you say eschaton?"

"Just let me take you to the kingdom."

"I don't understand."

"I know, neither do I, I just want to try—"

"Wait, haven't you done this before?"

"No, but they told me—I mean, I heard it was weird?"

I feel like I'm slipping away. Xuuzi looks up at me with a kind of wholesome daring. I must've misheard it, my brain must have autofilled the word *eschaton*—but whatever, just enjoy this weird night because I actually do like her, and not as a pseudo-Julia, I like Xuuzi herself, I like this weird person who doesn't know how to act, who dresses badly and kisses badly and dances badly, who is even up for trying a mystery drug with a man she barely knows, how often do you meet someone as openheartedly reckless as that?

Xuuzi has spread the collection of jars and instruments between us. She is opening the brass jars. She is scooping the stuff onto little silver dishes with a tiny ornate spoon. She lights a match under a little brass box. Black incense begins to leak out. Will this set off the smoke alarm? Fuck it.

I say, "Do you have any more cigarettes?"

"Yes."

"Why don't you smoke one right now?"

She takes out her pack, shakes out a cigarette. I reach over and extract it from the box myself. I place the cigarette between her lips. I take the lighter from her. Our hands touch. I light her cigarette. She laughs, gets back to work on the drug, the weird shit, whatever it is. The weird shit looks like scaly black meat, the scrambled guts of an insect. Xuuzi is grinding it into a paste, she is rolling it into balls, she seems to be pretty adept at preparing this drug for someone who claims never to have done it before, but I like watching her, the way she busily grinds and shapes the paste, cigarette hanging out of her mouth, kind of badass. She looks up at me with smiling eyes. There's something heroic and innocent about her, deep eyes, actually beautiful eyes, how did I ever think Xuuzi's eyes were flat and obvious?

Secret eyes too. She has a secret.

"Now wait. I have a surprise for you."

Xuuzi gets up. She picks up her duffel bag on the way into the bathroom. What else is in that bag? The music streaming from her phone sharpens, deepens. The black meat paste bubbles as it cooks in its little cups, the brass box wafts bitter smoke, and this is why you pick up strangers, this is why you endure rejection, and being called a creep, not because you just want sex, not necessarily, but for the chance to dip into a stranger's life, to get outside yourself, to step into someone else's reality, to feel this electricity, it doesn't always end well but I'm glad I did it tonight, that I didn't ditch her, that I'm not alone, because being alone in this room might kill me, and then Xuuzi comes back from the bathroom.

Not Xuuzi.

Julia.

Julia comes out of the bathroom.

— — — — — —

stand up.

Unsteady.

Julia. Not Julia. Xuuzi. But Xuuzi is somehow wearing Julia's pink satin prom dress. It's the same dress Julia wore the night she broke her shoe heel and fell in the snow. Where did Xuuzi get that exact dress? Her hairstyle is exactly Julia's too, back then, years ago. Impossible. What is Xuuzi doing—is she messing with me?

But how would Xuuzi know how to mess with me like this?

"Julia," I say.

She says in a strange voice, "I am wearing Julia."

Everything is sharp and clear. Julia or Xuuzi sits me down on the bed. She uses a little spoon to pick up a rolled-up ball of black meat.

She says, "There is a certain way we have to do it."

Xuuzi or Julia puts the black meat in her mouth. She chews it up. I see her eyes scrunch up. Julia's look of distaste. I know that look.

Xuuzi-Julia kisses me.

Bitter taste. Rotten. Metallic. She's pushing the slimy meat into my mouth with her tongue. My eyes are closed but then her hands are gripping the back of my head, she is forcing my lips to stay pressed into hers, the chewed-up meat is flowing out of her mouth into mine, dissolving on my tongue, and then we kiss for real, Jesus Christ, this isn't one of Xuuzi's clumsy kisses, this is a pro Julia kiss. This person who is wearing Julia, who is she—who is doing the wearing?

What does it mean to *wear* a person?

I open my eyes mid-kiss. Her eyes are staring at me.

She says, "We are going to die."

I try to pull away.

She laughs. "We are both going to die."

I break from her grip. I'm off the bed, backing away from her. Julia-not-Julia rises and is moving backward away from me too, except her legs are walking forward, her body isn't moving right. Something is wrong. She's flickering. The black meat tingles in my mouth, sending roots under my tongue, networking and branching all over my body.

Dead beef. Bad food.

"We are going to die."

She is moving toward me but everything reverses, now her legs are walking backward as she's moving forward. The room is tipping, tipping *over*, and as it is tipping it is changing as the floor becomes the ceiling and the ceiling becomes the floor. Dead beef, bad food. The walls are bronze, then gold multiplying on bronze, gold and bronze walls everywhere. Xuuzi and I don't look like ourselves, we have become brass idols inlaid with jewels, I look at my hand, which is now a bronze claw, as she laughs and says, "We are going to die, we are going to die." I grasp her and my jeweled claws tighten on her, my ridged gold scales heave up and down my back and our masks are gone, we are not in the hotel room, and we are on a blazing landscape of gold and iron stretching out in every direction, a pulsing purple sky overhead, a horizon of silver mountains.

Her eyes swirl. There's nothing to block what is inside me or her anymore.

My vast invisible thing streams out to meet her vast invisible thing.

I know her eyes. I know whose eyes those are, my own eyes. I have her eyes. She's not a woman, she's a monster.

We are both monsters.

Her bronze mouth hisses, "We are going to die, we are going to die, we are going to die," and I say, "Your name isn't Xuuzi," and she says, "My name is not Xuuzi," and I say, "What is your name?" and she says, "I was never even named," and then she does what she promised, she opens it up fully, the flaming mountains of silver and the violet sky and boiling golden oceans, she stands back and shows me our entire hideous kingdom.

– – – – – –

wake up in the hotel room.

Xuuzi is gone.

Everything else is just as it was. Xuuzi's little cups of black paste are still here. Her brass box is still here. Her set of jars and instruments, silver dishes, ornate spoon are all still here. Black paste is still smoking in its brass box.

But the world is moving wrong. The room is dark but there's a strobe light pulse, not really a strobe, more like unseen children are rapidly waving flashlights around. Jerky blurred motion.

I'm blinking. Stars flash around me.

Where did Xuuzi go?

My door is open.

The Flickering Man glides past the door.

I get up. My feet are heavy. I stumble across the room. The stars around me fade.

I come out the door. I look down the hallway.

The Flickering Man turns the corner and is gone.

I clomp down the hallway after it. After Xuuzi. My head buzzing. The floor is slipping away from my feet.

I have met her before. She didn't look like Julia then. Her name wasn't Xuuzi but I had met her before.

When?

I keep walking.

I have to catch up.

Somebody else is behind me.

Don't look back.

Somebody else is definitely behind me, following.

You can never look back.

I round the corner. The Flickering Man is nowhere to be seen. No Xuuzi either. Is this a dream? I'm still dreaming.

Then this is the realest dream I've ever dreamed.

There are stairs ahead.

Somebody else is still behind me.

I stop walking. He stops walking.

I begin walking again.

He begins walking again.

Don't look back.

How long has he been following you?

All your life.

It doesn't feel like a dream, but a memory. Go down the hotel stairs, or up the stairs. As though I'm watching something that has happened before, I am going both up and down the stairs at once, something that's going to happen again. Another hallway, double doors. It's about to happen right now.

Where is she?

I come into the hotel's banquet room.

For some reason everyone from Dare to Know is in the banquet room. It is a surprise company party and I am the guest of honor. Ron Wolper nods and raises his glass to me. The banquet room has a kind of stage and tables arranged cabaret-style around it. Blattner and Hansen shake my hand as I pass: great job, well done! The banquet room has large windows that look out into the starry dark. Hey, it's Hutchinson, it's been so long, glad to see you made it too! The banquet room is cozily lit with dozens of little lamps. Hwang and Wiesnewski are sitting at a table, they give me the thumbs-up. There are candles in jars on the tables. A soft light suffuses the stage. Ziegler and Gaffney are standing and drinking by the bar, they see me and are all smiles. I'm moving through the crowd and everyone is happy to see me, everyone is expecting something. A cycle has come to a close, a great work has been accomplished, and we have all gathered to celebrate it. Stettinger sits near the stage, gives me a friendly salute—whoa, even Stettinger?

Where is Xuuzi?

This has happened before.

Why did I expect to see Xuuzi?

In a few moments, a special emcee will appear on that stage. I am about to receive a commendation. An award, a recognition.

I approach my table.

An envelope rests on my plate.

The envelope has my name written on it. But the letters are backward. It's not my name. The letters spell something else, and I'm trying to figure out what the backward letters are saying, but I don't want to. It's a nightmare word.

I open up the envelope.

A rat's head is inside.

From the steam tunnel.

Yesterday and today.

- - - - -

The emcee's voice speaks behind you. He's onstage now. Don't turn around. You know that voice. Don't look at him. Don't look back. Red circles appear at the edge of your vision. You can never look back. These people in the banquet room aren't from Dare to Know, these aren't their faces anymore. Their faces are different but they're the same faces.

Now you are in Cahokia.

You are in a wooden hut full of smoke. Another red circle appears inside the first red circle. They are Cahokians. They are from Dare to Know. You turn, you struggle, try to get away. The red tunnel closes around you. Too late.

Their hands are on you.

You have met her before, this girl who calls herself Xuuzi, but that's not her real name. What is her name?

You know her name.

The emcee is speaking on the stage behind you. The man who was following you in the hotel hall earlier. Don't look back. You used to hear this voice. More concentric red circles nest within each other, smaller and smaller, narrowing your vision.

Look up the number.

You are outdoors, on top of a hill, the dark starry sky above you. The emcee is behind you, putting a cloak on you, a heavy cloak made of hundreds of woven shells. New stars defile the black sky, a jarring, slashing brightness. Many hands guide you to an altar on top of Monks Mound.

Many hands guide you to a table in the hotel banquet room.

Xuuzi is on the altar.

They got us again.

They hold Xuuzi facedown on the table, the altar. Her face is covered in blood.

You are at the hotel. You are in Cahokia.

It's not Xuuzi's face, it's not Julia's face.

Hutchinson and Ziegler and Gaffney and Hwang interlink their crossed arms. It's not them, it's four Cahokians who look like them, chanting and singing. It's John and Paul and George and Ringo, their voices mechanical and insinuating, shaggy, wrong.

She is trying to turn and look at you.

Look at her face.

You can't.

Your nightmare face.

This has happened before.

Many hands lay you down on top of Xuuzi. You are facing up and away from her. You are looking up at the ceiling of the banquet room, you are looking at the starry Illinois night sky above Monks Mound. Your back is pressed against her back, separated by the beaded cloak. You are looking up at everyone you ever knew, the dreams of the king and the princess, and the dreams of those dreams, your bird cloak of a million shells between you and her—

She slips something into your hand.

You grasp it.

The envelope.

The red concentric circles on the edges of your vision multiply faster inside each other, telescoping your view of the world smaller and smaller, except for the emcee onstage.

Renard glows in his spotlight.

"That's all, folks!"

And then you all begin to flicker.

— — — — — —

wake up naked on the bathroom floor.

My entire body is in pain. Little cuts all over me.

The hotel room stinks with revolting smoke, like someone had burned an animal alive. There are gory stains on the carpet, the walls, the bedsheets. I don't know what they came from. The dream, or vision, or trip bangs around inside my brain, still vivid.

No trace of Xuuzi.

My wallet gone too.

And Lamby-Lamb. What the fuck?

— — — — — —

went back to campus to find Xuuzi.

I didn't find her anywhere.

I returned to the bar where I first talked to her. The same bartender was there. When I asked the bartender if he knew anything about the woman from yesterday, he gave me a blank look. Acted like he didn't know what I was talking about. Like she didn't even exist. Okay, I get it, I wouldn't be the first creepy guy trying to stalk someone he met at his bar.

But still.

I went to the dorm where I picked Xuuzi up. I asked some girls about her. Nobody knew a Xuuzi, or Suzy, or Susan, or anything like that. I described her. Red hair, pale skin, about this tall, dressed like this?

They looked at me blankly.

I wasn't hunting down Xuuzi because she stole my wallet. Maybe a hundred bucks in there—she could keep it, I didn't care. I went ahead and canceled all the credit cards. Losing Lamby-Lamb? That was weird but fine. Chalk it up to youthful sadism.

That wasn't why I wanted to find the girl who called herself Xuuzi.

How did she know about Julia?

About Julia's particular pink dress, her particular hairstyle?

The eschaton?

That weird shit we smoked and ate together—what was that?

Xuuzi had promised me weird shit. Now I was deep inside that weird shit, and her weird shit was connected to mine. In that nightmare trip I felt like we had brushed up close to something vast and invisible, a strange energy built up between us—

I extended my trip to look for her.

I searched through the student directories for anyone who looked like Xuuzi. No girl was even close. I pulled some strings with the assistant provost and got up-to-date pictures of all the students, both on-campus and off-campus.

Nothing.

But she was real. She had taken me to our hideous kingdom. She and I were in the banquet room and we were in Cahokia. Everyone from Dare to Know was there but they weren't themselves and neither was I and neither was she.

Then Renard spoke, and we were all Flickering Men.

That day I changed.

I never felt lonely before. Now, lonely all the time.

Life began to take its long, painful left turn.

The morning after Xuuzi, I found something odd in my wrecked hotel room.

The envelope in which I'd found the rat's head was crumpled up on the hotel bathroom floor, its lining crusted with gross bloodstains. It didn't have the rat's head from the dream in it anymore. But how had it come to be here at all?

Was it a dream?

There was writing on the envelope. My handwriting. I didn't remember writing it. The writing no longer spelled out my name. It wasn't backward letters.

It was a date from a thousand years ago.

– – – – – –

On July 4, 1054, a new star exploded out of nowhere. The explosion was so brilliant that for days its light was visible on Earth both night and day. This new star was nearly as bright as the full moon, even though it was over six thousand light-years away. Arab astronomers recorded it. So did Chinese astronomers. The Japanese have accounts of it. Native American petroglyphs and the oral tradition of aboriginal Australians mention it.

This strange star lingered in the night sky for two years.

Nowadays we know that what Earth saw on July 4, 1054, was a supernova—an old star collapsing into its core, spewing its outer layers into space in a massive shock wave. The remains of the supernova are what we now call the Crab Nebula.

When the supernova ignited, Cahokia changed.

According to archaeologists, around 1050 AD—the time of the supernova—Cahokia underwent a sudden, large-scale alteration. Until then Cahokia had been a decentralized group of villages, each with its own local rituals. But starting around 1050, instead of the previous open-courtyard plans, new constructions were built on a strict north-south grid. Cahokia's earthen flat-topped pyramids and plazas date from this time, including the hundred-foot-tall Monks Mound.

Maybe it wasn't a coincidence, I thought, that Cahokia had transformed right when a new star appeared. After all, the city plan of Cahokia was modeled on astronomical principles, including their precisely calculated "woodhenge" of poles that tracked the solstices.

It was around this time that the theatrical human sacrifices began, along with their days-long citywide feasts.

Were the Cahokians trying to soothe an unpredictable sky? Celebrate a newborn star?

What were they doing?

People nowadays like to think we're beyond such thinking. But what would happen if a gargantuan new fire blazed up in our modern sky? Would people really stay calm? Or would we slide into something more desperate? How durable is civilization, how easily could things collapse, if one day we all looked up and saw a fiery face glaring at us from heaven?

– – – – – –

Why had I scrawled "July 4, 1054" on an envelope?

Put it out of your mind.

After the Xuuzi incident, I tried to put all the weird shit aside. My life was changing fast, and not for the better.

That's when I moved out of the house and into the condo. The divorce didn't go the way I thought it would. In retrospect, how could it?

That's when the boys grew out of toddlers who adored me because they didn't know any better into teenagers who understood exactly who I was.

That's when Dare to Know commissions began to dry up, right when I was expected to pay alimony and child support.

That's when I began to lose sleep.

That's when I began drinking at home alone. Looking forward to it even in the early afternoon. Oblivion at the end of the day.

That's when I felt that, from here on out, I was just marking time.

Then time did run out.

7:06 p.m. yesterday.

And yet I'm still here.

— — — — —

When the plane lands, I turn on my phone. Julia had texted back.

What a nice surprise! Keith and I are looking forward to seeing you. What's the occasion?

THE NUMBER

Keith! It would be so much easier if I hated Keith.

So much easier if I could hate San Francisco, too, but I can't, I never could. Every time I come here I say to myself, Why on earth do I live in Chicago? People really do live like this, in paradise, every day? Maybe I truly had died last night. Maybe I've arrived in some casual version of heaven and just don't know it yet. When I exit the airport, the sun and warmth hit me and everything feels light, frictionless, easy. Something always kept me from making the leap of moving out here. The boys? Sure, that's why. Too busy being a wonderful dad!

Right.

I check in at my hotel, fritter away the day, then drive across town in my rental car, mounting the steep avenues to Julia's house. Getting on to evening now. Roll down the windows. The dark air heavy and sweet. Everything impossibly fertile, trees dripping fruit. Wet leaves gleaming from the streetlights. Night insect sounds. Never been to this neighborhood before. Feels oddly rural even though it's still in San Francisco, giant houses overlooking the bay.

I hadn't fully appreciated just how well Julia had done for herself. Around the time she married Keith, she started a software company with her old business school friends, worked her ass off, and then sold it several years later. Now she does—I don't know what, I can't tell from her status updates. I do know this: three children. Three! And Keith, of course. The screenwriter.

Wanted to hate his movies but I couldn't. Wanted to hate him, but can't. I've met Keith only once, at their wedding, but in the last few years I've read a lot of interviews with him—take from that what you like—rumpled manner, mile-a-minute talker, puts his foot in his mouth but in a relatable way, success hasn't made him brittle or overcareful, something puppyish about him, makes you want to take care of him even though he's a multimillionaire. Permanent child. Figured out how to get away with it.

I turn another steep corner.

Am I really going through with this?

Keep chugging uphill. This neighborhood is a maze. A ragged man in a hooded cloak stares at me from the corner across the street. San Francisco . . .

I bought new clothes this afternoon. Threw away the dead man's clothes I wore on the plane. Only now I realize the fast-fashion outfit I bought is too young, too trendy. Trying too hard.

Does this road ever end? Twisting and turning, up and up.

It's not the clothes. Nothing I could wear is going to hide the truth. Look at me. Lost the thread, life went wrong. For years I've been in a labyrinth and didn't even realize it. Wandering the gray midwestern ice, flat streets, lonely years. Rotting inside.

It doesn't have to be that way.

A different world here in San Francisco. You always knew this. Still, I wouldn't leave Chicago. Numb misery. What was I numbing myself against? But you know. Asleep. Safer than the alternative.

Now I'm awake.

I felt sharply awake all day. Alive in the newness of a new

place. That afternoon, killing time after buying clothes, I explored the neighborhood around my hotel, enjoying the sun, feeling free. Everyone around me young. Fashionable neighborhood. Nobody took notice of me. I was invisible. Because I was dead?

No, because I was old!

In a coffeeshop, I watched some dude trying to pick up a girl.

I'll never play that game again. Ridiculous.

Wait, you know what's really ridiculous? That I *don't* try to pick up some girl. I'm dead, aren't I? I can do anything!

But what am I, in fact, doing? Sitting in a cafe, eating a panini, drinking a five-dollar coffee.

Way to carpe the fucking diem!

Okay, well, what am I *supposed* to do? Run around whooping, clapping my hands? Kiss a stranger? "You there, boy! Fetch me the prize goose!" "What, the one as big as me, sir?" "Indeed, boy! Come back with it in less than five minutes and I'll give you half-a-crown!" Merry Christmas!

I'm dead.

I'm dead but I'm not acting any differently. Should I have expected I would, though? After all, this scenario occasionally did present itself at Dare to Know. When I was obliged to look my client in the eye, clear my throat, and inform him that he had only a week of life left. Or a day.

Or an hour.

What do you think my client did then? What do you do when you're told you're practically already dead?

Go climb the Himalayas? Arrange an orgy?

You eat your shitty panini.

— — — — — —

Where in Julia's neighborhood am I?

My nauseating phone is lying on the passenger seat, as far from me as I can put it and still hear it. It's patiently speaking to me, telling me directions, but I'm missing turns. I'm not used to San Francisco. It's dark now and the street signs are obscured behind tree branches and leaves. Am I going to be late? I should bring something. Tacky to show up at Julia's for dinner without, say, a bottle of wine. Or dessert. Ice cream? But that'd add at least ten minutes.

Do I really want to see Julia?

Why am I doing this?

The blue envelopes. Yeah, if she still has them. To learn whether the death I calculated for myself last night matches with the death she calculated years ago.

But something else is also waiting for me at Julia's.

At a stoplight a ragged man stares at me from a dark clump of trees. When I turn to look, the man doesn't stop staring.

Is it me he's staring at?

A timid beep. There's a woman in the car behind me. She looks irritated that I'm not moving. But she doesn't like the idea of having to beep either. Not in this neighborhood.

I roll forward, leaving the ragged man behind.

- - - - - -

We are near the end of our time, aren't we? It's ridiculous that I can't find my way to Julia's without my phone telling me exactly what to do. I used to have a sense of direction, I could read a map, I could get myself around. But as much as I hate this bossy thing on the seat next to me, how long would I last without it?

We all might find out sooner than we'd like. Astronomers tell us that perfectly ordinary eruptions from the sun could demolish

Earth's entire electronic network—apparently every few hundred years the sun randomly slaps the earth with a billion-ton cloud of magnetized plasma, the kind of space hurricane that will instantly short out electrical grids, blast satellites from the sky, spark catastrophic geomagnetic storms all over the world. Earth has already weathered such solar storms many times but nobody noticed because humanity never relied on electronic networks the way we do now. It's like we've deliberately made ourselves flimsy. We're precarious on purpose.

The fatal event doesn't even have to be a solar storm. Maybe the Earth gets hit by an asteroid. Maybe some madman detonates an atomic bomb in New York City. Maybe another Black Plague spreads through our recklessly interconnected world. Then what? Mass hysteria, civilizational collapse, anarchy. We've made ourselves this fragile on purpose because we secretly want our destruction, because we want to participate in the turning of the cycles, we want to be the one who pushes the button that moves us into chaos. It happens at the end of every society. Druids in Britain sacrificing hundreds of victims in caves during the Roman invasion. Mass suicides in Germany and Japan at the end of World War II. Opioid epidemic in America. We know we're on our way out, but we'll kill ourselves before you can kill us, we'll claim the dignity of choosing our death, we'll integrate ourselves into the thanatons on purpose instead of you forcing us to integrate with the thanatons. At the end of any mythos you see these massive unforced errors, self-ownage, people tripping over their own dicks, punching themselves in the face.

We go down swinging at ourselves.

— — — — — —

turn down a random street. Now I'm off the route my phone has recommended. Because going to see Julia is a bad idea. It's a bad idea. I shouldn't go.

My phone scolds me: return to the route.

No.

I let myself be lost.

— — — — — —

Julia married Keith about five years after I broke up with her, in a small town about twenty miles outside Bloomington.

It was supposed to be a backyard wedding at her friend's house but it rained and all hundred or so guests had to crowd into a three-bedroom suburban colonial, eating off paper plates. It's bitterly amusing to think this now, but back then I just figured, well, water finds its own level, right? Julia had reverted to her original status. Being part of Sapere Aude had made her relatively well-off but she had quit, and then paying her grandfather's monstrous medical bills had sapped her savings. Now Julia was back where she started—lower middle class, with an unremarkable wedding to an unremarkable guy in an unremarkable city.

(Save your contempt, I know it's snotty. Try telling your own life story, commit to reporting honestly, see how likeable you come across.)

So I'd lost touch with Julia. But then I received her wedding invitation, out of the blue. No hard feelings, right? You'd think someone unsentimental like Julia would simply delete all former boyfriends, but Julia actually kept on jaunty good terms with many of them. Even when she and I were going out, we'd occasionally run into some random ex of hers at a party or at a bar, and I'd be baffled as Julia laughed with him and shared in-jokes. Julia's bland chumminess with them depressed me.

Now I was in that special club.

Well, what did I expect? For Julia to weep over me for the rest of her life?

Two could play this game. I had just started dating Erin. She'd be my plus-one. Erin subtly signaled that she thought it was weird for me to take her to an ex–serious girlfriend's wedding, but she didn't raise any actual objection. Erin and I had only been going out for a few months anyway.

When I met Erin she was a chipper elementary school principal. The principal of my own elementary school had been a bloodless goblin who never left his office, but Erin ran her school with passion, she was young, full of energy and ideas. The students adored her. I'd visit her at work and they'd throng her in the bright, art-covered hallways. They had affection for her. Erin had a pert spiritedness, she laughed easily, everyone loved her, and for some reason she thought I was worthwhile.

That's why I married Erin: not because I was crazy about her, but because she seemed to have genuine affection for me. For five years I had zipped through a string of girlfriends, nothing had clicked, and now I was ready to settle down, or I guess settle. With Erin I figured, look, for whatever reason she thinks I'm a catch, so all I have to do is not fuck it up! That should be easy!

Well, I couldn't keep up the act forever. It didn't collapse all at once, but who can live up to someone else's ideal? Erin eventually saw through me. By the time the boys were toddlers she had lost all illusions. I was just an exasperating husband who had to be managed, humored, tolerated.

I couldn't take it. And so unconsciously—okay, somewhat consciously—I drained the joy out of her. Erin's unselfish energy, her bighearted granting of the benefit of the doubt to the universe, her bright trusting nature—I turned all her good qualities against her and punished her for having them.

But back at the time of Julia's wedding, the illusion was intact. I was still a catch. And the fact remains that, despite the low-rent nature of the affair, despite the thunderstorm that drove us all inside, or maybe because of all that, it was one of the more enjoyable weddings I'd been to.

Until the end.

– – – – – –

Because of the rain, nearly every room of the house was opened up to guests. Erin and I were jostling next to somebody's uncle, drinking boxed wine out of plastic cups in the laundry room; we were standing and eating wedding cake in the family room while a bunch of kids whined about not being allowed to play their Dreamcast. ("Shhh, I've already told you, some of our guests get sick around computers." "God, Mom, it's just Sonic, what kinda pussies are these people?")

As the rain pounded down, the ceremony itself was hastily adapted for the basement. I was crowded out—I could barely see Julia and Keith's exchange of vows. After it was over, that unfinished downstairs space was cleared out to make an impromptu dance floor. The basement also had a sliding glass door that opened onto a sunken backyard patio, so there was enough air circulation that it wouldn't get too disgustingly hot down there.

Keith was one of those guys who had a hundred male friends who looked just like him, lumpy goofballs who were part-time improv comedians or in terrible bands. People like this can be fine, but a cramped house full of them is the worst. They were all bellowing at each other, doing "bits," getting too drunk and sweatily jumping on each other's backs. Erin and I exchanged looks; these dudes were overgrown versions of her fifth graders.

I was embarrassed. Erin was amused.

Julia had relaxed her standards, apparently. I saw her laughing with Keith and his goober friends, genuine laughs. I couldn't imagine what undergraduate-era Julia would say about this sloppy wedding. Julia's severe taste, which I had found so attractive back then, which I had voluntarily accepted as a kind of challenge to up my game, was no longer operative. Had she outgrown her laser-sharp disdain? The more likely explanation: dismissing half the world for finicky reasons was an extravagance Julia could no longer afford. So go ahead, settle for a good-hearted oaf like Keith.

But Jesus, *him?*

Back then Keith and his clown friends were always shooting comedy videos and posting them online, I guess hoping to get famous. I couldn't bring myself to watch them, and not only because computers made me ill. The comedy I did glimpse was pure cringe, shoddy production values, bad acting—"Yeah, but that's the *joke!*" I'm sure they would've explained to me, "It's bad *on purpose!*" I think one of his friends was writing a young adult novel and another was trying to get what I guess was an early version of a podcast off the ground. I recognized the social contours of a scene here, similar to when all my friends were starting bands in the nineties, or even the early days of Sapere Aude. But this crew of jokers depressed me.

Erin and I were standing in the hallway to the door that led into the garage. "Well, what do you think?"

"I like her friends," she said. "This whole party makes me feel like I'm in college again."

"Yeah, except these dudes are practically thirty."

"Be nice," said Erin, but I could tell she was amused that I wasn't impressed.

Thunder boomed outside. The rain was really coming down. The backyard had been elaborately decorated for the outdoor wedding but now it was all soaked and ruined. Nobody seemed to care. There were a lot of people laughing, music blared from downstairs, a group of children came tearing past.

"Let's go downstairs and dance," said Erin.

"Seriously? There's no room."

"What else are we supposed to do? Come on, it'll be fun."

Erin and I danced to a few songs in the basement, and then a few more. I liked dancing with Erin okay, she moved in a competent, asexual way that made dancing a kind of wholesome calisthenic, a style befitting her job as a K–8 principal, perhaps embodying how she wished her seventh graders would behave at dances (instead of their desperate, moist grinding that the teachers were sometimes too embarrassed to break up). But the basement started to fill with comedians; somebody started a conga line, oh boy. The rain petered out, so Erin and I escaped the basement onto the patio.

The wet cool evening air was refreshing. I barely had a chance to speak to Julia that night, but that's fair, I knew how weddings worked. The bride had a lot of other people to attend to. Who was I to her anymore, anyway?

She did look beautiful.

Don't. Those thoughts—don't.

Almost nobody from what was left of Julia's family had come. None of her Sapere Aude friends was there except for me. No Hutchinson, no Ziegler, no Kulkarni . . . had Julia even invited them? Probably not. Keith more than made up for it, though, he seemed to have endless troops of family and friends. What would the Sapere Aude crowd have thought of these dorks yes-anding each other's dick jokes? Ziegler would feel right at home, he'd contribute to the yuks. Hutchinson would smile indulgently and get quiet, his eye aggressively roving as he got drunker and drunker. And Kulkarni, the preppy from Connecticut, would find the whole scene unbearable, but he'd never say it. He'd pass over it in tasteful silence, probably make a discreet early exit.

Erin had gone off to get us drinks. I spotted Julia coming out to the patio. I caught her eye. She smiled at me and raised a finger as if to say, I know I owe you some time but let me deal with this other stuff first. I watched Julia move from group to group, her white dress incandescent in the backyard floodlight. I had thought I knew Julia but tonight I saw sides of her I'd never seen before, sides that didn't read as Julia to me. She flitted fondly around Keith's friends, mother-henning these chunky dweebs, a Wendy looking after unappetizing lost boys. It was absolutely possible, it was even likely, that many of these grown men played beer pong, referred to marijuana and each other with hilarious nicknames, and had elaborate opinions about superhero movies. And yet Julia seemed happy with them. She seemed to enjoy indulging them. That did not compute.

Erin came back with drinks for both of us. "Look at this, vodka gimlets!"

"They're making cocktails now?"

"No, but the bartender's gone, so I helped myself."

"I think the bartender is just one of Keith's friends."

"That's what I figured . . . there wasn't much of anything left but I found some Rose's and some vodka in the freezer. How do you like me now?"

"I do like you very much."

"Yeah you do."

We clinked real cocktail glasses that Erin had liberated from a dining room cabinet. We found ourselves standing next to a hangdog guy in his early twenties smoking a joint, one of the few guys who didn't seem to be constantly "on," although apparently he did think that dressing up like a seventies game show host for a wedding would be clever.

Erin, playfully social, introduced us to him. His name was Gregory and he had a wary look. Even after he explained to us what his relationship with Julia and Keith was, I still didn't understand it; there was something vague and self-negating about Gregory's manner of speech that made it hard to follow his meaning.

"Why don't you tell us about the cast of characters here?" said Erin. "Where do you fit in?"

"Cast of characters . . ." said Gregory, trailing off. "I guess I know most everyone."

"Who's that guy over there?" I said.

"Nate? Oh, he's only, like, the best scribbleboard player I've ever heard."

"He plays the what?"

"You know. The scribbleboard. In his band."

Erin and I glanced at each other, Erin with dawning delight.

I said, "The *scribbleboard*?"

Erin said, "Yeah, uh, could you fill us in on his scribbleboard technique?"

"I don't know how he does it, he just starts playing and . . ." Gregory made some awkward flailing movements with his hands that corresponded with no possible musical instrument. "You know? It's incredible."

I began to say, "What's a scribbleboard?" but Erin squeezed my hand as if to say, *Let it be. Let the scribbleboard remain a mystery forever beyond our grasp.*

But we had warmed Gregory up. He was just getting started.

"And that's Greg," he said, nodding at someone else. "He's writing a—"

"I thought you were Greg," said Erin.

"I'm *Gregory*," he said, offended. "That's Craig."

"I thought you said Greg." Oh no, was Gregory a misguided comic doing a shitty who's-on-first? But no, he seemed utterly sincere.

"Craig is writing a children's book about Plato's cave." Gregory took in our wide-eyed reactions and added, "I guess you don't know much about Plato's cave."

A merry glance from Erin: *Please give him rope.*

I forced myself to lie. "Not really."

"Not a lot of people do," said Gregory graciously. "Well, Craig's book essentially turns Plato's cave inside out. Pretty much blows Plato out of the water."

Erin was so game. "Oh, but what's Plato's cave?"

"Basically Philosophy 101, essentially," said Gregory, more comfortable now that he had something to explain. "Like, there's a cave, right?"

Here we go. "Uh-huh."

"And there are people stuck in the cave—they've been in the cave since they were babies, they've never left, it's fucked up, they're chained there, they don't ask why. Do you get it so far?"

I couldn't believe I was enduring this undergraduate conversation. "Yes."

"These people have been chained in the cave ever since they were children. That's what I was trying to tell you," Gregory added irritably, as though we had been resisting him all along. "And the way these prisoners are chained up in the cave, they can't even look at each other. They can't look anywhere but at this one wall. And behind these prisoners is a fire, and between the fire and the prisoners, puppeteers walk by carrying puppets of things, shapes of lions or trees or humans, whatever, and the fire makes the puppets cast shadows on the wall, so the prisoners see shadows of puppets of lions or trees or humans. Those shadows are the only reality the prisoners know—get it? They're stuck looking at that one wall.

It's their whole world. They never see a real lion, they only see the shadow of a lion puppet, not even the shadow of an actual lion . . ."

Gregory trailed off, as though he was losing his own thread.

Erin put in helpfully, "And so that's supposed to be a metaphor of the human condition. We never see real things as they truly are. We're just prisoners looking at the shadows of fakes."

"What? Oh . . . Yeah, I guess." Every time Erin spoke, Gregory reacted as though he had just noticed her for the first time and acknowledged her in only the most backhanded way. "So anyway, even if one of those prisoners were to break their chains, and escape that cave, and see a real lion, and come back and tell the other prisoners about it, the others would think he was crazy because what they know is a lion is just that shadow on the wall. But here's the mindblower, here's the real mindblower, are you ready?"

Erin moved in close to him. "Gregory, give me the mindblower."

"Okay, but it's not even my idea, it's Craigory's."

"I thought you said it was Craig."

"That's short for Craigory," said Gregory impatiently, and even though Erin was enjoying egging this guy on, he had to be messing with us now. We'd asked for a cast of characters, and so now he was giving it to us: Gregory, Greg, and Craig-I-mean-Craigory. I could see this guy going all night, using his improv skills to make up a Russian novel's worth of fake people to fuck with us, each with a dumber life story than the last. My hand on her elbow, I indicated to Erin I wanted to leave Gregory and do something else.

Erin preferred not to take the hint.

"So what is Craigory's idea?" she said to Gregory. "His book, I mean?"

"It tells the story of Plato's cave, yeah," said Gregory. "But here's the thing, though. It tells it from the point of view *of the shadows*."

I repeated patiently, "From the point of view of the shadows."

"Exactly. Plato got it wrong. It took Craigory to get it right."

Erin bit her lip. This was right up her alley. She cherished the ridiculous things she overheard her students say, the ignorant boasts in the cafeteria of anatomically impossible sexual acts, the pompous phrases from unhinged letters sent anonymously to the teachers by a boy who signed himself only as the "Foggy Weiner," and countless other absurd kid sayings. I was sure that the phrase *It took Craigory to get it right* had just entered Erin's lexicon.

"Look, who's the real hero of Plato's cave?" Gregory went on, gaining steam. "It's not the puppeteers, obviously. It's not the prisoners forced to watch the shadows either. It's not even the guy who escapes the cave and sees reality. The real heroes are the *shadows on the wall.* Because those shadows naturally want to escape the cave and become the things they're the shadows of, right? The shadows want to become real! The shadow of the lion wants to escape the cave and become a real lion. The trees want to become real trees. And so on. That's the real story."

"I get it," said Erin encouragingly. "It's like Pinocchio wanting to be a real boy."

Gregory stared at her with baffled distaste, as though she'd totally misinterpreted him.

I was definitely finished with Gregory. It was then that I realized that the music had stopped inside, and had been stopped for a while. Maybe there was a change of DJ, or some rowdy drunk had stumbled into the turntables and knocked them over, or something.

"What's happening in there?" I asked.

"The music stopped," observed Gregory, brilliantly.

"Sounds like an opportunity," said Erin. "What if your friend Nate busted out the old scribbleboard?"

"As if." Gregory looked at the wedding crowd ruefully. "They'd never get it."

"So anyway," someone said, and I turned and saw it was Keith, fresh off the dance floor in his sweat-soaked dress shirt, red-faced. "Someone spilled beer on Seth's laptop but Matt says he can get his—oh hey, I haven't said hi to you yet, I'm so glad you could make it, man!"

We did the introductions. I guess Julia had told Keith about me a little.

As the names and hellos went back and forth, Gregory's eyes widened. His manner changed into something intense.

Gregory gripped my arm. Hard.

"Hey," said Gregory. "Make sure you remember what I said."

"What?"

"Okay, Gregory," Keith said with a chuckle, gently trying to disengage him from me.

Gregory wouldn't let go of my arm. "You're gonna remember what I said though, right?"

"Okay, I'll remember." I laughed too until I looked in Gregory's eyes and saw something so desperate it stopped me.

There was no music. The rain had ceased. Conversation had died down. For a moment it felt like the patio had emptied, like there was nobody in the world but me and the suddenly crazed Gregory and I didn't know if he was about to punch me, or throw up on me, or start crying—

"Hey Gregory," said Keith, a little more firmly. "Let's get you inside. Get you a glass of water."

The desperate look drained out of Gregory's eyes. He seemed bewildered, as though he'd just woken up. Keith began to steer Gregory away, mouthing something apologetic to me. Erin looked a little guilty—oh no, had we been subtly mocking some guy who actually had, like, diagnosed mental problems? Erin grimaced and followed Gregory and Keith into the house on the off chance she might be helpful. I had been standing there for a minute or so when Julia finally made it over to me, looking exhausted and happy.

"Having fun?" she said. "You look lost."

"Oh no, it's been great, I was just talking to Gregory about Craigory."

Julia looked confused. "Who?"

"I made friends with Gregory? He was telling me about Craigory, who's writing a kids' book?" I said, and when Julia looked at me like I was the crazy one, I stupidly went on to say, "And Nate? The scribbleboard player?"

Julia stared at me blankly.

Shit! Why did it have to get this awkward this quickly? Julia had the expectant smile of someone who really hopes a punchline is coming so she could at least have a pretext to politely laugh, to defuse the social tension. But I had nothing.

"Oh," she finally said.

Didn't Julia know her own guests? I guess Gregory had been messing with us after all. I looked around the patio, the milling groups of sweaty dancers who came out to smoke, the guffawing dudes, their patient dates, the sweetly irrelevant older family members, the little kid cousins darting around, intent on their own manic games. I turned back to Julia in her wedding dress.

She was looking at me quizzically, maybe a little suspiciously.

Her familiar face, those sharp eyes, the peculiar way her lip turned—

Oh no, no, no.

Because the truth hit me then, it hit me unexpectedly and overwhelmingly, I had come today thinking I would pity Julia and her dopey groom and her rinky-dink wedding, but I shouldn't have come, and not only because it was impossible for me to simply smile at our old relationship like we were merely two veterans who could mildly reminisce about our shared time in arms together—the faint image I had in my mind of Julia was utterly fucking swept away, stupid shit, because I was near the actuality of Julia right now, the half-disappointing, half-thrilling reality of her voice, the specific redness of her hair, her slightly crooked teeth, her soft smell, even the simple fact of her being three and a half inches shorter than me, it all erotically floored me.

I wanted us to leave this wedding.

Together. Right now.

So, so stupid.

"I guess all this isn't quite what you expected," I managed to say, my tone all wrong.

Julia gave a brittle, defensive smile. "What does that mean?"

Fuck! I'd overstepped, I didn't mean that, it sounded like I implied her wedding was tacky. Well, I did think it was . . . Pull up, asshole, pull up! "Well, you know—the thunderstorm."

Julia relaxed but still eyed me without trust. "Oh, yeah, well . . . It's clearing up."

Compliments, pour on the compliments. "What you did with the backyard is beautiful."

"That's all Keith."

We both looked out at the yard, at what could have been. To be fair, Keith had fixed it up amazingly well, at least before the rain came bucketing down: paper lanterns strung overheard, a bride-and-groom archway of thick crooked branches lashed together and tied with wildflowers, tulle and luminarias down the aisle, string lights wrapping up the trees, and repurposed rustic items like wheelbarrows, watering cans, etc. Keith had an eye, I'll give him that. Is that part of what Julia saw in him?

As if to answer me, she said, "Keith and his buddies—"

His "buddies"! Jesus.

"—were out here all night working on this. Setting all this up was kind of his bachelor party. He likes to make things."

I couldn't take it. Keith was too wholesome by half. And now he was returning, with Erin no less, and they were laughing and chatting about who knows what, certainly not the awkward conversational disaster I managed to perpetuate with Julia in less than three minutes. But soon after Keith and Erin rejoined us, we all felt the social meter running out. Erin and I could sense how Julia and Keith were beholden to other people at this wedding too. When we parted ways I knew that Julia and I probably wouldn't get a chance to say a real good-bye later, that this was the end, the real end, and I think I held Julia's hand a little longer than I should have, and gave her a more lingering look than was appropriate.

What did I hope to accomplish with that?

An hour later Erin and I left. It was starting to rain again but the party had gotten its second wind, the music situation had been fixed, and the dancing in the basement was going strong. Julia and Keith were clearly having so much fun with their friends now, their real friends. It felt intrusive for me to interrupt and tell her we were leaving, so Erin and I slipped away unannounced. We jogged across the street to my car as the rain sprinkled down. We had a hotel room in Bloomington.

Erin said, "Wait, I left my purse in there."

"I'll get it—where'd you leave it?"

"The laundry room, on the washing machine."

"I remember. I'll go get it."

Erin smiled. "Really?"

Gallant me! Erin took shelter in the car as I ran back into the house, the rain pattering down faster. The easiest way to get to the laundry room was to go back in through the basement, where people were still dancing—though it was slow dancing now, and the basement was a little less crowded. I didn't see Julia, I didn't want to see her. I went up the stairs and into the laundry room and grabbed Erin's purse.

I recognized the slow song they were playing in the basement from Julia's dad's jukebox. I had heard that song countless times back when Julia and I lay on the fold-out bed, a Motown ballad but I forget who by, strangely sparse and eerie for Motown—a tenor falsetto warbling over the jarring chord changes, its harmonies otherworldly, the conventional romantic swoop of violins replaced by a primitive synthesizer that sounded like a buzzing robot mosquito.

> *I don't care*
> *Where you came*
> *From*
> *Oh no*
> *I don't care*
> *What you've been*

I came down the stairs of the basement with Erin's purse. There were just a few couples dancing around on the concrete floor, in this room of exposed drywall, but I didn't see Julia or Keith, or really anyone else I had spoken to that night. I had heard this song a hundred times, but only when I was in college. I hadn't heard it or even thought about it since then.

Nothing about this song should work. The lyrics are nothing special. The lead singer seems to be singing a completely different song, only coincidentally syncing up with the rest of the band. It's an accidental-feeling overlapping of clunky parts that shouldn't fit together, but the thing is, the song does come together, by the skin of its teeth, its near failure making it exhilarating, the song would fall apart if just one of its many impossible-to-justify choices was different—even the droning synthesizer solo works—I halted on the basement stairs and felt a deep, disjointed shiver.

Then came the chorus, the high weird warble of *Yes—you're— my,* and then the backup singers kicking in with a ghostly coo: *dream—come—true.*

Two children were sweetly and gravely slow-dancing, a little boy and a little girl. Neither of them could've been older than five years old. Maybe they were cousins, or best friends, but they were dancing so unselfconsciously, holding on to each other like they meant something real to each other. I saw some adults looking at the little kids and poking each other: isn't it sweet? It was nearly ten o'clock. I wondered where these kids' parents were. Aren't five-year-olds usually in bed by now? But it was a wedding party, normal rules were suspended, maybe one of these kids even lived at this very house.

Julia was in the basement.

She didn't see me. Keith was nowhere in sight.

I was startled by her face. Maybe Julia had had a few more drinks. She watched the little boy and the little girl dance to the hypnotic song with a raw look in her eyes. I had never seen Julia look so empty. Why did these children make her look so alone?

> *Yes I've been waiting*
> *For such a long, long time*

Julia saw me.

Something passed through her eyes when she saw me. In a matter of moments her face rearranged itself to hide it. But too late. It had already happened. No takebacks. Looking at me much differently than before.

With repulsion.

And under it, hurt.

As though I could keep any secrets from her.

When did I become such an asshole?

— — — — — —

was quiet driving back to Bloomington.

In our hotel room, Erin and I got ready for bed. I turned out the light. We lay down next to each other.

"You're still in love with her," she said. "Aren't you?"

We are always telling on ourselves.

"I guess."

We lay there for a while in silence.

"I get it," she said.

"What?"

"Yeah. That's okay."

I lay in the dark, not understanding Erin at all. What did that mean? Was this relaxed attitude just a function of her overall generous spirit? I couldn't take that level of wholesomeness, goodness, forgiveness, understanding. Or was it because we were both a bit older, because we'd both been around the block a few times, we knew how the world worked, how emotions are weird and ungovernable, and she was frankly acknowledging that weirdness instead of holding me to some fake romantic ideal? Or was it because Erin and I had only just started going out and our relationship was all still a lark? That I wasn't a serious long-term prospect, all's fair in love and war, and so it truly didn't matter what I felt about Julia? Or maybe it wasn't the first time Erin took second place to someone else and she was comfortable in that position?

"Hey," Erin said.

I guess it doesn't take much to cajole me into sex, even if I didn't feel like doing it at first. But there was something smug and aggressive in Erin's eyes, like she knew something I didn't. The opposite of her having something to prove. I wish I knew what she was thinking because it was beyond me. She looked satisfied, maybe not with the sex itself but with something else, some checkmate she had accomplished, she was on top of me, bucking and grinding down, looking directly into my eyes with a kind of gleeful ownership, and I unexpectedly and overwhelmingly came.

She said, "You'll get used to me."

– – – – – –

Well, we know how that story ended.

And now I'm lost.

It's not just that I can't find Julia's house in this San Francisco maze. I can't even find my way back to the approved route. My phone is telling me one thing but I'm seeing another. I'm missing turns in this neighborhood of cul-de-sacs and one-way streets, designed to baffle so that people who don't belong here stand out. So they look suspicious.

Well, the system works. I don't belong here.

I stop at a gas station.

I try to push myself into the right headspace for this dinner with Julia. Jaunty, optimistic, in the mood of: Just going to see an old college friend! How many years has it been?

Forget those blue envelopes.

On a whim I buy cigarettes at the gas station. A lottery ticket, too. I recite Julia's lucky numbers to the guy at the cash register. I'm surprised I still know the numbers by heart. When's the last time I spoke them out loud? It feels like I'm nineteen. Like old times!

Old times.

The act of saying Julia's lottery numbers stirs something up in my brain. Maybe it's because I had looked through my undergraduate calculations last night, but old seams of thought feel ready to reopen. A half-forgotten mathematical idea bubbles up. Then another, connecting with some equations from the blue books I had paged through the night before. Old calculations, proofs, derivations.

Something is coming together.

I will show you the eschaton.

Careful.

Don't chase the idea right away. Don't try to pin it down too hard. Let it float there for a little bit. To do the math makes the math come true. But I can feel the shape of a new idea about the eschaton, an alternate way to derive it, the theoretical end-of-the-world particle. The idea might not even work in the end but that's fine, don't judge it right away, maybe it'll lead to something else that will. Let the process happen. Because I can actually feel it, I can begin to sense the eschaton drawing closer to me until it's almost quivering in my hand . . .

Then it's gone.

Quick as a flash. But I had it for a second.

That flash—I knew that flash.

– – – – – –

had felt it around the time Kulkarni disappeared.

There aren't many people named Craigory so it was easy to check a few years later whether his batshit children's book ever got published. It never did, apparently, nor did I find any information about a musical instrument called a "scribbleboard." Perhaps both book and scribbleboard were shadows lurking in a cave somewhere, waiting to become real. Or more likely, Gregory had been making it all up.

Anyway, I mentioned the Plato's-cave-in-reverse idea to Kulkarni.

It was the kind of crackpot notion Kulkarni enjoyed batting around, although as we glided into middle age he treated our geeky discussions as an odd vice, to be indulged only discreetly and occasionally.

I didn't know this time would be the last time Kulkarni would be acting like Kulkarni.

I was in Connecticut on business. Kulkarni was there for some family occasion. We saw each other plenty at work, but I was curious to observe him in his native element. When Kulkarni suggested we meet at the yacht club his family belonged to (a yacht club!) I jumped at the chance.

I wasn't disappointed. In Chicago, Kulkarni's WASPishness almost seemed like an affectation, but here he fit right in—striding across the lobby of his club, six foot three, sunglasses hooked onto the collar of his pink polo shirt, supernatural hair, a man seemingly incapable of sweating. We spent a sunny afternoon sailing around the harbor in his boat, Kulkarni handling the sails and the rudder masterfully, giving me minor nautical tasks so I didn't feel totally useless. I felt I knew Kulkarni better after a day on the water with him, even though we didn't discuss anything much of substance the whole time.

Afterward, over dinner at the club, the topic of Julia came up and for some reason I found myself telling Kulkarni the details of her wedding (to my discredit, playing up the colorful details of its midwestern absurdity for his upper-class East Coast delectation, as though I were some anthropologist reporting back to him, instead of, you know, *one of them*) and I happened to mention Craigory's dumb variation of Plato's cave.

Kulkarni, tipping his drink back and forth, said, "So Craigory's book doesn't exist. Okay—but if it did, how would it go?"

That, I didn't expect. "What do you mean?"

"I remember thinking, when I first heard of it, that Plato's cave is such a weird Rube Goldberg idea." Kulkarni's debate-club rhetorical perversity tended to emerge after his third gin and tonic. "What's the motivation? Who benefits from chaining up people underground and making them watch shadows on the wall?"

"So your objection is economic?"

"Or it's a wrong turn in philosophy from the start, that all the engineering details of Plato's cave are worked out to the last detail, chains and shadows and puppets and fire and stuff, but the question of why it's there at all isn't touched. Why put on a puppet show for prisoners? Where do the puppeteers come from? Who's paying them?"

"They're enthusiastic volunteers?"

"No, no, just forget about the puppets and the puppeteers. The prisoners too. Our man Craigory is right, the shadows are the heroes here." Kulkarni ordered another round. "So how would his book work, if it existed?"

I enjoyed this kind of nonsense with Kulkarni. "Lots of questions. What happens when a shadow learns it's not real?"

"But the shadows are already kind of real, right? That's Craigory's point," said Kulkarni. "The shadows want things. They have thoughts and intentions."

"But they're stuck in the cave. Half real."

"Say the cave is destroyed."

"But maybe if the shadows escape the cave, they can become fully real."

"Perfect, great, send that to Craigory," said Kulkarni. "A shadow of a lion comes out into the sunlight of actuality, and that sunlight causes it to become a real lion."

"It's like something from one of Renard's books."

"What?"

"Friend from when I was a kid. He liked this kind of thing."

"I was going to say it was right up my great-uncle's alley."

"Maybe Nate could do a concept album about it on his scribbleboard."

And so on.

It was the last time Kulkarni and I had a real conversation.

– – – – – –

Not long after that, something changed in Kulkarni.

I didn't make the connection at first. But in the weeks after we met in Connecticut, Kulkarni spent less time meeting clients for assessments and more time holed up alone in his office. This was back when everyone at Dare to Know worked together in the same building. Not the grand space we used to own in our glory days, but still, a nice rented space downtown.

Kulkarni had started working on something. His office, normally clean to the point of barren impersonality, became infested with scribbled-on papers. He got a hollow look.

He avoided talking to me.

It was as though Kulkarni had caught some mental virus. He began to dress sloppily. At first it was just a wrinkled shirt, an errant stain, the same trousers worn twice in the same week. He didn't shave. Kulkarni had always been impressively buff, going to the gym four times a week, a regular tennis player. That all stopped.

I asked him what was up.

He mumbled something and kept his distance.

So one day after work, I illicitly let myself into Kulkarni's office. There was a sour smell. I looked through the mess of half-full coffee cups, crumpled-up papers, smeared whiteboards. Kulkarni was working his way through some thicket of mathematics. I could see that he had reverted to his original metaphor, his interlocking glass boxes with ever-shifting panes. Reengaging with the primal image that first gave him access to subjective mathematics.

I couldn't imagine why anyone would do that.

Page after page was filled with scribbled geometrical diagrams, more and more complicated, and by their very nature incomprehensible to anyone who wasn't Kulkarni. But I could feel a pattern in it. I could sense how the logic hung together. I could almost sense it drawing closer to me, until it was quivering in my hand . . .

Then it was gone.

Quick as a flash. But I had it. I did have it, for a second.

Then I saw this scrawled on one of Kulkarni's papers:

7/4/1054.

— — — — — —

I meant to ask Kulkarni about that date. The same date on the envelope Xuuzi had handed me in my dream just a few days before that. The date of the supernova. The date I had somehow written myself. But why?

That was when Kulkarni quit Dare to Know.

I didn't understand why. Nobody did.

It was abrupt.

It happened the day after I rummaged through Kulkarni's papers. Kulkarni had acted strangely with me all that week. Avoiding me at work, as though he sensed something about me had changed. Something *had* changed, of course, but I hadn't told anyone about my encounter with Xuuzi the week before. About the weird shit she and I had taken together. About Xuuzi coming out of the hotel bathroom with Julia's impossible hair and dress, about the bronze monsters in a flaming desert of metal, about a ritual in the hotel's banquet hall with everyone from Dare to Know looking like Cahokians, and then Renard appearing, and then all of us becoming

Flickering Men . . .

I will show you the eschaton.

Xuuzi had shown me something, for sure: a nightmare. And the hotel room had been wrecked the next morning. I quietly paid for the room damage, though not on the corporate card, obviously. Dare to Know didn't need to know. Something in me didn't want me to know either. Didn't want to think about it. It had just been a bad trip on her weird shit. The more that night receded into the past, the more it felt like a dream best left forgotten.

But this bad dream slotted in too snugly with other bad dreams. 7/4/1054.

I would ask Kulkarni about it.

The next morning, though, I couldn't find him. When I did spot Kulkarni, I happened to be in the break room with some new interns—for some reason I was telling the interns about the early years of Sapere Aude, the crazy years, stories of how it felt like we used to be something more than just another corporation trying to keep its shareholders happy, mentioning only in passing the freaks, charlatans, and witches that hung around us at the beginning—I was more aiming to give the interns a flavor of what the company was like when it still felt like we stood for something, some ideals, when we were making big technical breakthroughs, when we were explorers and revolutionaries who were going to change the world. I did notice the interns share an exasperated glance—when is this old blowhard going to shut up?—and maybe I was going too far when I claimed that our start-up had almost felt like the Manhattan Project, especially when I told the interns about the night of the infamous Hopkins incident, and I compared it to when they exploded the first atomic bomb in 1945, saying we felt the way Robert Oppenheimer must've felt after the first atomic bomb test in the New Mexican desert, when he famously quoted the Bhagavad Gita: "Now I am become Death, the destroyer of worlds."

Kulkarni was standing in the hallway when I said that.

Staring at me in an odd way.

Like when you unexpectedly see someone you don't want to see.

Kulkarni quit that day. I didn't know at first. I came around to his office later to talk to him and learned it was already cleared out. I asked people where Kulkarni had gone. Nobody knew.

A temp said he had already left, maybe?

I went outside and spotted him.

Kulkarni was across the parking lot with a man who looked like an older relative, a kind of professor emeritus, leather-elbows-on-a-tweed-coat grandfather type—wait, was that actually Kulkarni's mathematician great-uncle? The half-respectable, half-crackpot guy he'd told me about who was trying to derive a mystical glyph to ward off evil?

Kulkarni said something to the old man.

The old man stared at me, agitated.

He waved his hands in the air at me, like he was playing a scribbleboard.

I started walking across the parking lot to them.

Kulkarni helped his great-uncle into the car. He didn't even look at me. Before I reached them, he drove off.

I wanted to ask Kulkarni what the hell was going on.

I called him. Nobody answered.

I went to his house. Nobody home.

I never saw Kulkarni again.

– – – – – –

For what it's worth, I later learned that the "I am Death" quote was almost certainly fabricated by Oppenheimer later. The actual night of the testing, Oppenheimer is only reported to have said, "It worked." And another scientist added, "We're all sons of bitches now."

Actually, it's just me.

I'm the son of a bitch. The destroyer of worlds.

Stop putting it off.

Go to her.

– – – – – –

haven't been paying attention to the road. I have been driving on autopilot through Julia's neighborhood, not even listening to the phone's directions. But now I'm back in the real world, with the cigarettes and lottery ticket from the gas station on the passenger seat . . .

Wait.

I'm somehow pulling up at Julia's house.

How had I found my way here, how had that happened on its own?

But it happened.

Here I am.

Look at her house.

The cigarettes and lottery ticket I just bought are suddenly ridiculous.

Jesus. Her place is *huge*.

I knew Julia and Keith had done well for themselves. Still startling to see it with my own eyes. I don't want to be here. Be honest: Julia knows quite well things didn't work out for me. I don't want to see her pitying smile. Painful for her too. And Keith, who'd gone from shitty midwestern improviser to jackpot-level screenwriter, and then, even more improbably, on to film producer, I can already see Keith backslapping me with a, How's the Grim Reaper business, man? Those trains still running on time?

Well, no, Keith, for me personally that train is now officially twenty-five hours late.

Make an excuse.

Turn around. Go home.

But the blue envelopes—

It doesn't matter. Put the car in reverse. Back out.

My phone buzzes.

A text from Ron Wolper. *I understand you're in town. Please come by the office at 2 tomorrow.*

Wait—how does Ron Wolper know I'm in town? Well, Dare to Know headquarters *are* in San Francisco. Julia is probably still in touch with the old gang, she probably mentioned to someone that I was coming to town and Ron Wolper heard it through the grapevine. Plus Lisa Beagleman probably has lodged her complaint by now. I'm surprised it took Wolper this long, then.

Two o'clock meeting, though. That means Wolper isn't taking me to lunch. Ominous. Well, whatever Wolper wants to say to me, minus the courtesy of lunch, I've got an ace up my sleeve.

Because I'm dead.

Because the books are wrong. Because there's an error in the thanatons. How many other times have the thanatons spoken inaccurately? Never, as far as I know. Maybe I'm the first? Maybe the whole system of thanatons has become unstable, maybe it's about to break down, maybe I'm the first chink in the armor?

"You gonna stay out there all night, big guy?"

I look up.

Keith is silhouetted in the door, holding two beers, a big smile on his face. A daughter behind him in pajamas shrieks and then disappears.

Too late to back out now.

For years it bothered me that the fairy-tale by-product of my calculation of Julia's death date never had a proper ending.

Of course, that was because I had never properly completed her thanaton calculation.

But examining the vectors of symbols up to that point, I could make a probabilistic case that the story would go in a certain direction.

In the fable, the king and the princess get trapped inside an enchanted hill, hypnotized by their own fears and fantasies, which become semireal in the darkness—so many dreams that the king and princess are hypnotized, and eventually don't even recognize each other, and are trapped under the hill forever.

But the story wasn't over. Because the calculation wasn't over. Out of the various possibilities hinted at in the symbols, out of the remaining elements that still had to be slotted into place like leftover Scrabble letters, I calculated this as a likely ending:

Once during the night, or during those thousand years, the princess discovered another man who lived in the darkness, a man who was not the king—a little wizard with black eyes and a great staff of carved iron.

The wizard's iron staff was attached to many iron chains, and each chain was in turn attached to a dream that was now living under the hill with them. As the wizard moved his staff, the chains rattled, forcing the dreams to move under his command.

And so the princess learned that her dreams, and the dreams of the king, and the dreams of their dreams, were enslaved to the secret wizard's will.

But one day, deep in the cave, the princess found the king's lost sword. At first she did not remember this sword. She did not even remember who she was, or why this sword was familiar. But with this weapon in her hand, the princess did begin to remember herself, and the king.

She searched for the king in the darkness.

And just as light was fading outside the cave, she found him.

When the king saw his sword, both he and the princess suddenly remembered themselves fully, and realized that they had been trapped within this enchanted hill for an entire night, or perhaps a thousand years.

Both king and princess ran toward the light, together again. Their dreams and the dreams of their dreams pursued them, shrieking and growling and spurting fire, trying to stop them.

But the king and the princess escaped the hill.

Their dreams and the dreams of their dreams could not pursue them out of the hill, for they were chained to the wizard and his staff. The king and princess now understood how the wizard had imprisoned them with their fantasies and fears, and had fattened himself on their dreams.

But they were only dreams.

And so the king and the princess turned away from the enchanted hill and their dreams, and leaving behind both their fantasies and terrors, they returned to the castle where the feast of a thousand years was prepared for them.

When I finished computing this story, I had a small feeling of satisfaction. Just a few stray threads stuck out from the math, but not many. I didn't have to account for them; they were within the standard deviation. What counted was that the unsatisfying story with a sad ending now had a happy ending.

But not every story can be recalculated.

— — — — — —

Entering Julia's house with Keith:

The happy domestic rush, kids running around and tumbling over each other, not even shy or regarding me warily, just exulting in their natural aristocracy, because of course the world exists expressly for them, they're just romping in their palace. Keith leads me through it all, telling me Julia's upstairs but she spotted you in your car, she saw you idling outside, she realized you probably didn't know exactly which house ours was, our address should be clearer, gotta fix that, hey cheers, drink up, how many years has it been, it's great to see you! Pure Keith, the same innocent goofball energy from before he made it big, trying to make me feel at ease, being humble about his house, as if anything was humble about this place: beautiful fifties modernist lines, old-growth redwood, Japanese elements but not overdoing it, carefully deployed curios but kids' paintings on the walls too, clay wood-burning stove but plastic bowls of half-eaten cereal on the kitchen island, action figures underfoot . . . unfussy, charmingly untidy and alive, effortless. It feels like they're saying: seriously, it's not our money you're looking at, it's just the authentic expression of who we are! And hey: check out these windows! Twenty feet high. The city glittering below, the Golden Gate bridge, the entire ocean. Top of the world.

Do not think of your garbage home. Your condo, obliterated. Don't even remember it. Dead men don't have homes. We walk the land until someone finishes us off.

I'm dead.

Makes me reckless.

— — — — — —

When Julia comes downstairs I'm stunned. She looks better than ever. Like the mask of youth fell away and this is the real Julia. There's a surprising gray streak in her hair that looks like it always belonged there. Fit. Skin glowing. Eyes alive. She's become herself.

She says my name. We hug. My muscle memory is startled, recognizing the shape of her body. I'd forgotten what it's like to hug Julia.

I shouldn't have come.

I have only a certain amount of goodwill to spend here. Julia's it's-been-a-long-time goodwill. And her you-used-to-be-important-to-me goodwill. Keith's you're-the-ex-boyfriend-but-I'm-a-decent-fella-so-I-will-work-hard-to-make-you-comfortable-in-my-home goodwill. Make no mistake: that goodwill is finite as fuck. Stay an hour too long, tell the wrong anecdote, see how chummy Keith will be *then*. Be careful.

Don't be careful.

Have another drink! This ain't no ten-dollar wine, that's for sure. Now we're sitting around the table with the kids. Two adorable daughters, one earnest son, and they're voluntarily eating real food, salmon and quinoa, not screaming for mac and cheese. Who am I, they ask? Oh, Mommy's friend from college. Keith says: If only you lived here in San Francisco!

Framing us as equals. Nice try. I couldn't even afford to rent a one-bedroom here.

Julia answers my question: "No, I haven't seen anyone from the old gang. You know, with kids . . ."

Wait. If Julia hadn't told anyone I was in town then how did Ron Wolper know?

Put a pin in it.

Work stuff—don't even think about it.

It's a strange thing, though. I feel so at ease here—why? Why has my tension melted away, why am I so relaxed?

Then I realize: no computers. And yet they must obviously own computers. Oh—Julia must've turned off all the laptops, shut down every tablet, powered down every phone. Because she knew how they'd make me feel.

She's considerate.

She wants me to be okay.

More than I deserve.

Should I bring up the blue envelopes? Over dinner? No. It could freak her out. Wait till it's just the two of you. But I can't leave tonight without asking.

Presumptuous.

She probably threw away those envelopes long ago.

Maybe this was a mistake.

The dinner conversation goes on and the kids take center stage, as they should. The older daughter is a Girl Scout and she's just built her own computer from a kit. (Julia's eyes flash to mine—will it be okay? Of course it will, her computer's very simple, it barely makes my stomach flutter.) The daughter shows off the computer—it works! Pixels flashing across the screen! She's only ten! Even I am charmed!

But Girl Scout must've learned a few truths about The Way The World Works because her clear young eyes slice right through me. She is not charmed. She correctly intuits I'm a nobody. Well, of course—think about other friends of the family who must've had dinner here, other movie producers, technology honchos, maybe even famous actors. After all, Keith's studio does those computer-animated movies where an anthropomorphized saucepan or cockroach will make you cry more than any human could, the emotional payoff laser-guided, perfect. As for me, I'm just some dude Mommy sidestepped on the way up. So Girl Scout is nice to me, but in a limited way, making it clear her niceness is strictly a function of her graciousness, not reflecting anything about my worth or . . .

Jesus. Get a hold of yourself. The girl is *ten*.

Mambo music! Peppy, sixties-style mambo music! The younger girl just put it on; it's music from Keith's studio's new movie, which he cowrote and which will be released this spring. She tells me the whole plot in the breathlessly self-absorbed way kids have in that they assume of course you must be interested in every little thing they say, although it's disconcerting to hear her gravely yet accurately use phrases like "inciting incident" and "the second act reversal." But she comes by it honestly, like Keith does; it's the air she breathes. This movie, she tells me, is about a fussy anthropomorphized library book that gets stolen from a rare book room by a spunky bookworm girl because the girl is the only one who recognizes the handmade book is in fact an unfinished manuscript by her favorite sci-fi author, a legendary recluse. The unfinished book manages to escape from the girl, because all it wants is to return to its cozy rare book room. But the book gets sidetracked and lost and falls in with some other print old-timers—a motormouth discarded newspaper, a know-it-all volume from a 1960s *Golden Home and High School Encyclopedia* set (from *Nut* to *Pik*), and a comically vain fashion magazine—and together they take a cross-country trip to find that reclusive sci-fi author so the fussy handmade book can have the ending of his story written. Second act reversal: the author's dead! But the journey to find that author ends up taking decades, the whole latter half of the twentieth century rolls past, different styles and historical events, as print dies and is replaced by zeroes and ones, and our four heroes become more and more irrelevant, but guess what—when all seems lost, in the end we meet the spunky bookworm girl again. She's an old lady now, we feel the ache of years, she's a successful author herself but you can tell there's something missing from her life. But by serendipity she comes across our hero, the unfinished manuscript of her almost-forgotten childhood favorite author, now tattered and damaged—but the girl recognizes it and she realizes that *she's the one who must write the ending for her beloved long-lost book!*

Keith's daughter tells the whole story to me in an excited rush. Keith shrugs at me as if to say, trust me, it's more than that . . . or yup, that's it, can you believe I get paid like a king to dream up garbage like this? But I think to myself, I wish I had made something like that, something that my sons could be that excited about. But what could I possibly do that would impress them? The last time I got anything like an emotion from them was when I was pitching at their charity softball game and some smart-ass batter socked a line drive straight at my head. I was knocked flat, went down like a sack of rocks. But even though I remember my sons looking down at me with concern, I couldn't help but suspect what those stares really meant: *there goes our college tuition.*

Those "white trash skanks," as Erin called them, were expensive in the end. Erin righteously sucked away every cent—present, past, and future. Well, what judge wouldn't take her side? I gave her fucking chlamydia.

"Hey?" The grave little boy looking up at me. "You okay?"

Everyone at the table is staring at me. Lurch in my gut. Did I say something weird? Wait, did I actually just blurt "fucking chlamydia" out loud for no apparent reason? How much wine have I had? This wouldn't be the first time . . . not knowing minute to minute what I'm doing. Christ, get it together.

"Uh," I say, weakly.

Here's what's weird: I'm not focused on Julia tonight. I'm more fascinated by her gregarious husband, her charming kids. How wrong is it that I find Julia's kids more compelling than my own sons? It's wrong. I held my own boys close to me when they were babies, I sang them to sleep, I played with them for hours on the carpet, I helped them with their math homework . . . well, who cares. My sons scorn me now, so let me hang out with this ten-year-old Girl Scout who builds computers, let me spitball loglines with this eight-year-old script doctor, let me talk about the meaning of life with this serious little first-grade boy who is looking at me with more emotional intelligence than I've ever—

Christ! Shake yourself out of it.

"Sorry, I didn't get much sleep last night!" I say, with what I hope is a jovial shrug, as though the reason I hadn't slept was—why, I had plumb forgot or something! A careless mistake, and not because I was *mathematically dead*—so should I bring up the blue envelope now? Make it official? Julia, Keith, the whole family gathered around the table, wholesome scene, open it up, read it—surprise! they're dining with a dead man—but no, I just say, "Uh, it's so great to meet you, you should meet my sons, too, they're about your age, actually a little bit older, more into sports but, you know, I should get that computer kit actually, if you could tell me the brand of that, and that library book movie, I can't wait till it comes out, I know my boys loved your other movies, the one with the—the, uh, plants—"

Julia looks at me like I'm insane. She had been to plenty of movies with me, she knows I would loathe the kind of movies Keith makes. But guess what, that first movie he wrote, the one that catapulted him to Hollywood, where he'd been steadily climbing ever since—the movie with the talking plants? The neglected houseplant and the discarded Christmas tree who go on a road trip together? That movie actually made me cry, I admit it, even though the boys hated it, and they made fun of me for crying. They called the movie stupid.

Stupid, huh? Well, guess what: even though my sons are both older than Girl Scout here, they wouldn't be able to assemble a fucking computer if their lives depended on it.

Eventually I put enough words between myself and the blurted "fucking chlamydia" that maybe it's forgotten. The kids are looking at me like I'm normal again. Am I? Fuck it, I pour myself another glass of wine. Julia flicks her gaze to Keith for a second but I notice it. Am I a drunk ex-boyfriend crashing a family dinner now? Is that who I am? No, I'm not! I'll prove how I can hold it together. I'll show them.

Should I ask Julia about the blue envelopes now?

How conceited is it for me to assume she held on to them?

The son asks, You and Mom met in school? Like in kindergarten?

Not quite kindergarten, kiddo! I deflect it classily, though, and I tell a sanitized story of how Julia and I met in college. By the end of it I sense I have Julia and Keith back on my side. The daughters aren't idiots, though; they've figured it out, that this strange man was Mommy's boyfriend once, that this piece of shit could've been their daddy. Keith gets activated for some reason, becomes even friendlier to me. He tells his kids the story of how I hadn't laughed at Julia when her heel broke and she fell in the snow. Well, that's a pretty tame story, and it makes me look good. The kids warm back up to me. This is a roller coaster . . . Wait, why had Julia told the broken-heel story to Keith?

There's not enough time to wonder because now Keith is explaining to the kids what I do for a living, and how Julia used to work at the same company, selling the time and date you die. This interests the kids—so I'm one of *those* people. And that reminds me, I remember reading an interview with Keith online somewhere—fine, let me fully admit it, for a while I was absolutely cyberstalking Julia and by extension Keith, even though each internet session would end with computer nausea, and even vomiting from being online that long. But I couldn't stop hate-reading everything about Keith, baffled by his semifame. Mercifully in the interviews Keith never said writer clichés like "my characters have lives of their own, I just listen to them" or "I get my ideas from my dreams" (he said he didn't recall his dreams), but in one interview he was asked about Julia's time at Sapere Aude, and he said, "My job is similar to what my wife used to do at Dare to Know, I guess. Because every truly deep story puts death at the center, right? A story is a machine for reminding you that you're going to die. We feel like we have infinite time, infinite resources. But we don't. I'll let you in on a trick. Here's how to write any story and make the audience feel something. Take two characters. Make them care about each other. Then have time pass. It can't help but end up sad."

Garbage! Pretentious *and* childish. I hated Keith even more after reading that. "I'll let you in on a trick"—fuck you. A story is a "machine," a story is an algorithm—Christ, stay in your lane. It made me want to go back in time, to visit college-age me and Julia as we were watching one of the dumbass movies she would drag me to and whisper to my younger self that, guess what, you will lose Julia to a guy who creates crap like *that*.

But how different are you from him? Keith makes stories act like algorithms; you make your algorithms act like stories—I mean, your thanaton algorithm metaphor *does* take the form of fairy tales, right? And anyway, who's laughing now, or crying actually, because Keith's movies actually work for me, I cried at the Christmas tree movie, so give Keith credit, that interview was obviously just Keith's stream-of-consciousness way of talking, he wasn't afraid of being a clown, Keith deserves this beautiful family, this beautiful house, he deserves Julia. He's a better man than me.

What on earth am I thinking about?

I excuse myself and go to the bathroom.

Standing there, pissing, the world floating and spinning around me, a little bit of vomit rising up, I realize only now that I am truly trashed. Humiliating. Drunk dead man in the bathroom. I'll bet you anything by the time I come back to the table, all three children will be safely packed off to bed, out of my toxic presence. I've disgraced myself. How bad was it? I'm looking at my face in the mirror. It might've been really bad. Dead eyes, dead mouth, dead face. You've been dead for more than a day, now. You're giving off death rays. You make living people uneasy and they don't know why. You think there's still a chance of Julia showing you that blue envelope now? Good fucking luck. In my pocket I still have the cigarettes and the lottery ticket—what did I think I'd prove with those? Like Julia wanted to be reminded? Julia never looked back. She was never nostalgic. Well, you know what? Julia *should* look back, she *should* be nostalgic. Previous versions of Julia and me still inhabit their locations in space-time; they still love each other. Our past selves don't know what they'll become, but we should acknowledge those past selves, we should honor them, they still exist in a way.

Flush. Shut up.

When I come out of the bathroom it's just Julia in the dining room. But she's not putting away the dishes, or bustling about, or making herself busy, which would be an implied signal for me to leave. She's just sitting at the table. She has her own glass of wine. The wreck of the dinner strewn around the table.

"Let's go out on the deck," she says.

So we go.

On the deck I say, "Where's Keith?"

"Putting the kids to bed."

Now the conversation will die. Over dinner we'd already talked through all the catching-up-with-you stuff, carefully avoided anything that would make either of us uncomfortable. Now we're standing outside on the deck, just the two of us gazing out at the city, the bay, not looking at each other. I realize we had relied on Keith to keep the conversation going—Keith's good-natured laughing at my jokes, his urging Julia to tell such and such an anecdote, his saying to the kids *you'll love this*, his pulling all the different strings of the conversation together. The dinner conversation had been script-doctored by Keith on the fly, and he had stage-managed Julia and me and the kids so ably that I hadn't even realized it. It was merciful of him to do it, he must've sensed what would happen if he didn't intervene, but now I knew what would happen, and it was this: the exhausted silence between Julia and me.

Standing outside on her deck, the bracing air sobering me a little, freshly amazed and humiliated by the magnificent view. I should be leaving. But I can't leave without asking her about the blue envelopes. I look at Julia and feel the cigarettes and lottery ticket in my pocket again, and in a panic of awkwardness I just take them out.

She looks startled.

I'm an idiot.

She doesn't take them. She doesn't even move.

I put the lottery ticket and the cigarettes on the table between us.

Like old times?

"Jesus Christ." Julia exhales. "I quit smoking fifteen years ago."

What did I expect? The cigarettes are radioactive with embarrassment now. And come on, a lottery ticket—look at this house. She needs money?

I'm creepy. I'm a creep.

"I shouldn't have come," I say.

"No . . . no," says Julia.

We stand there for a while.

Julia says, "I hate to see you bro-ing down with him."

This I didn't expect.

After a second I say, "You'd rather Keith and I be tense?"

Julia takes a few moments to choose how to phrase it and finally lands on, "Keith is friendly to everyone."

I feel the hammer of that. We stand there for a while again. Cold now. Well, I did come all the way out here. Might as well ask her now. Get it over with.

"Hold on," says Julia, and goes back inside.

She's gone longer than I expect.

She comes back out with a lighter. Not a regular lighter but one of those long-range gas barbecue lighters the size of a curling iron.

"I couldn't even find any matches." She laughs—laughs?—and opens the pack of cigarettes I gave her. She takes one out and lights it with the absurdly big lighter.

She smokes for a while.

I say, "I'm sorry I was ridiculous in there."

"What are you talking about?"

"In front of your kids," I say. "Kind of drunk. Saying nonsense."

"The kids loved you. Keith too."

I look at her. Wait. She's not just being polite. She's smiling. Genuine.

I misread every cue tonight, maybe. Understood nothing.

"Ugh," says Julia. "I can't even finish this."

She stubs the cigarette out. Not even half smoked. Looks around for someplace to put it. Why doesn't she flick it twenty feet away from her, like she used to? Um, because she's not a nineteen-year-old idiot? Even still, it's absurd what she does now: she actually puts the extinguished cigarette in her pocket.

She shivers.

"We should be going in," she says.

I turn to her and say, "So I looked myself up."

– – – – – –

Of course she immediately knows what I mean.

She doesn't go in. She just stands there.

"And?" she says tonelessly.

I say, "Do you still have our envelopes?"

Of course she knows what this means too.

"Yes," she says.

"Have you opened them?"

She is invisibly pulling away. I see why, in her eyes—why'd I even mention it? What am I doing? Why am I really here? Look in her eyes *now*. Nice going, asshole! I had thought I'd made a fool of myself before, alienated everyone; it turned out, miraculously, that I hadn't but now I truly *have* fucked up because now Julia is looking at me with something worse than disdain.

The way she's looking at me, what does it mean?

"Can I see them?" I say.

"Our envelopes?" she says.

"Yes."

"You want me to get them?"

"Please."

She leaves the deck again. Goes back inside.

I'm shaking. Why shaking? Because if the date Julia calculated twenty or so years ago matches what I calculated yesterday, then I really *am* dead somehow. It can't be a fluke. Or this is the first time thanaton theory is wrong. But that's even more unthinkable. I know thanaton theory backward and forward. For a thanaton prediction to be incorrect would be a whole different level of wrong, it wouldn't even be one plus one equals three, it'd be one plus one equals every single thanaton in the universe exploding like a bomb.

One plus one equals . . . I feel the idea coming back, the eschaton idea I'd had while driving here. Connecting to the broader ideas from my old papers in my condo last night in Chicago. Standing here on Julia's deck, already Chicago feels like a lifetime ago. But those old calculations clicked with something else inside me. Something new is bubbling up.

July 4, 1054.

Cahokia, supernova . . .

I'm a little dizzy.

Let it come.

I take out a cigarette.

I try to light it with Julia's lighter. Guess what: it's literally the first cigarette I've ever tried to smoke in my life. Emphasis on *tried*. Because I can't figure out how to light it. The breeze keeps blowing out the lighter. I end up sticking the singed cigarette in my own pocket.

Movement out in the darkness. Looking down into the forest below the deck, someone's moving. Somebody's down there. Maybe somebody taking a walk? No, the trees are too dense, why would you walk down there? Someone chasing after their loose dog? No, they're moving too slowly. In a hoodie . . . Some kid slipping out of the house and getting high on his own?

Not a hoodie.

Not a kid.

Someone in a cloak. A ragged man.

Looking straight up at me.

Then gone.

"Were you just trying to smoke a cigarette?"

Julia, out on the deck again.

I'm still off-balance from what I've just seen. "Yes."

"Since when do you smoke?"

"I don't."

"Oh."

A moment goes by.

"I couldn't even manage it now," I say.

"What? Why?"

"I couldn't light it. The lighter kept going out."

Julia laughs.

I say, "How do you make it light?"

"You suck in while you're lighting it."

"Oh." I think about it. "Why does that work?"

"You're the physics major."

This is the old Julia; this is the old me.

Good old times.

She has both blue envelopes. So she did keep them. Not at the bottom of some box in the attic, either. She must've known exactly where they were.

Did Keith know about them, too?

Was Julia *expecting* me to ask for them tonight?

In the forest below there are two ragged men now. Someone else in my peripheral vision. Does Julia see them too? They're in the trees, hidden. They're waiting. Waiting for me to leave?

Julia tries to give me my envelope.

I don't take it.

I know those men.

Julia looks impatient. "So take it if you want it."

I recognize those men around the house from Minneapolis.

"Why do you want it anyway?"

My heart is in my throat. "What?"

"You said you'd already looked yourself up. Then you already know when you'll . . . you know."

She's still holding my envelope out to me. Why are Minneapolis people skulking around outside Julia's house? I look again.

Now they're gone.

I don't take it. "Um. You open it."

Irritated now. "*Um.* I don't want to know when you'll die."

"Please."

Julia frowns.

But she does it. She opens my envelope. She unfolds the paper inside. One last multiplication to go. Just like me, she'd left that final step undone. Didn't go all the way. She takes out her phone, turns it on. Does the arithmetic on the calculator app.

She stops.

She calculates it again.

Stops again.

She stares at me.

− − − − − −

What had I expected? I think, as I drive away from Julia's house. Julia had looked at me like a dead man. Knowing I was dead. Or quasidead. Dead as far as the thanatons were concerned. Well, whatever death stuff was on me, she wanted it away from her house. Away from her kids. Away from Keith. Out of her world.

"So it's true," she said.

"So what is true?"

She didn't say. She just said:

"You should go."

Not frightened. But looking at me like I was a ghost. Maybe she'd glimpsed the ragged men around the house, too. Were they there for me? Had the ragged men been there, waiting for me to come? Would they depart with me, too?

I said, "Okay, so. I'll see you later."

Julia said, "I don't think so."

The finality of it.

I said, "Is this it?"

Julia just stood there. Cigarettes and the lottery ticket on the deck table. They won't be touched again. Everything I touch is death. My gifts are death. I am death. The real end of us.

She said, "Please go."

No sympathy for a dead man.

"Okay," I said. "Well, have a nice life, Julia. You have a beautiful family. Perfect son. Two perfect daughters."

Julia said, "Three daughters."

For a second I didn't know what she meant.

She stood there, arms wrapped around herself, the hollow look she had at her wedding, when she—

Then I knew.

Julia said, "You remember when we broke up?"

It flooded my brain.

"I think, deep down, you knew."

I didn't want her to say any more.

"I still think about it. I was actually convincing myself to be excited about it. I wasn't sure so I didn't tell you. Then you broke up with me. So I went ahead and got the test. It was positive. But I thought, there was no way I was going yoke myself to your miserable shit for the rest of my life."

I couldn't meet her eyes.

"I was twenty-five years old. I didn't know anything. I was too scared to take care of it properly. So that day I ran five miles, as hard as I could. And I ran five more the next day. And I ran even harder the day after that. It probably didn't change anything, maybe it would've happened anyway, but do you want to know how it feels to have a miscarriage into a toilet?"

I didn't know, I didn't know, I don't know.

"There's a little bloody dead creature floating there. I could've held her in my hand. I should've. I don't know if it was a girl or a boy. I thought of her as a girl. Then I couldn't stand to look at her anymore and I flushed her down."

I saw Julia's own blue envelope on the table. It was open.

I saw the letter I had written to her.

Destroyer of worlds.

I said, "I wish I could have met her."

"Just go," said Julia.

— — — — — —

Keep it together. Drive straight. You're drunk. Just get back to your hotel. Where's the hotel? No idea. This isn't your city, you don't know the way. Your phone knows where the hotel is. Just put the address in, listen to it. As sick as it makes you.

I had always wanted a daughter.

My phone isn't even speaking directions at me. I must've fat-fingered the settings. It's babbling in some language I've never heard—a guttural tongue, like the phone is reciting a thousand ancient foreign names, or relentlessly counting down in some exotic number system.

What would you have named her?

Would she have looked like you?

Or Julia?

Or someone who almost looked like Julia, but except her eyes?

Like maybe she'd have your eyes?

The phone stops talking. I glance: it's almost out of batteries. Wait, and my headlights aren't on! I'm driving without headlights? Turn them on!

A ragged man stands by the side of the road.

Swerve. Almost hit him. Heart in throat. Keep driving. Who the hell was that? Look at dashboard. Car almost out of gas. How? That can't be, I had a full tank when I drove it off the rental lot this afternoon. And yet this car is almost out of gas.

You and Julia and your daughter. Living in Bloomington together. We would have figured it out.

Rearview mirror: another ragged man.

Keep going.

Stop at the gas station. Put my credit card in the pump.

Declined.

What? Try again.

Declined. Different card.

Declined.

Holy shit.

Debit card then.

None of my cards work.

What is happening?

We are going to die, she had said. What is your name? I had said. I was never even named, she had said. And where did she come from, who was Xuuzi really? A bloody ghost climbing out of a toilet, growing larger, slithering out into the world. Then hunting me down. You're a piece of shit. Nice car, Daddy. I'm the other woman.

Beep beep beep. How will you pay?

Fuck. How much cash do I have?

Less than twenty dollars.

A ragged man is standing just outside the range of the gas station lights.

Watching me.

Get back in the car. Breathe. How do I get back to my hotel? Can't trust phone's guidance. Phone wants to kill you. Figure it out on your own. Never had a sense of direction but must try now. The look in Julia's eyes. Not contempt. Something else. Wine buzz gone. Panicked sober now. Oh shit oh shit oh shit. None of my credit cards work, I have less than twenty dollars, so how will I even pay for my hotel room?

How drunk am I?

Had Julia been waiting to tell me about our baby?

How often had Julia read my letter to her? Had she only opened my envelope tonight? Or had she read my letter before?

Julia at her wedding, watching those children dance.

Dream come true.

I have to go to the bathroom again.

From the pump, I spot a ragged man standing at the gas station's restroom door. Watching me.

Oh no.

Get out of here. Key in the ignition. Turn it.

How far? Just go.

Go go go.

Julia had said, Just go. Looking at me like she didn't even know me. But Julia did know me. I had never really known Julia. I had never seriously tried. And when Julia didn't act like the Julia in my head anymore—I threw her away.

You will never see her again.

My bladder's really bursting. Pull off onto the shoulder, anywhere. Here is fine. Park the car on the side of a hill. Blunder out into the darkness, staggering. How long have I been driving? Where am I?

Pissing off the side of the hill.

Eschaton calculations crowd through my brain again. Push them out of your mind. Focus: figure out the timing with Julia. Is it possible, what she said? Right before I broke up with her we had been apart for about two weeks. When would she begin to show, if she was pregnant? When would she start to feel sick? She was sick at Cahokia, don't you remember? Shit. Shit shit shit. You idiot. Idiot. It's possible she had been as much as ten weeks along. How old would our daughter be now? Like, twenty-five years old. Don't even think about it. If she hadn't miscarried, would she have gotten an abortion? Probably. Get everything associated with that dickhead out of me right now.

Antiperson.

Create an antiperson.

Stop thinking about her. Getting high with Xuuzi on the hotel bed. Particle, antiparticle, eschaton, anti-eschaton, king, princess, me, Xuuzi—

I finish pissing.

Someone is behind me.

I turn around.

Nobody there.

Zip. Wipe hands. Get in the car.

Drive.

There's a ragged man coming out onto the road, in the rearview mirror. Keep driving. Don't look back. Minneapolis, years ago, the ragged men hanging around the hotel. I know when they show up. When the gates of the chthonic crack open. It's happening now. Everything is coming together. Somebody somewhere is finishing a set of steps. Somebody somewhere is snapping off a rat's head. Eschaton equations multiply in my brain, waiting for me to touch them, to work with them. To do the math makes the math come true. The paradigm shift is coming, the next leap forward.

The equations line up, one leading to the next, spelling it out.

What is the eschaton?

The eschaton reveals itself when thanaton theory fails.

When does thanaton theory fail?

7:06 p.m. Last night. Outside Chicago. When I spun off the road. When I became dead and alive. For me alone the calculations blow up. For me alone there is division by zero, irreconcilable infinities, a rip in the fabric of thanatons.

What is the eschaton?

The eschaton is the king who dreams.

Where is the eschaton?

The eschaton is here right now.

I'm driving but my mind is pulsing with math. Road whipping past, speeding into darkness. Wind whipping through the car. I feel the exhilaration, the wild fresh hope welling up.

Kill it?

Ride it.

Write it down. Go, go, right now.

I pull up to my hotel. How did I find my way back? Don't care. Barge into my dingy little room, get to work. Fill the hotel notepad with equations, diagrams. Chasing down the eschaton. Figure it out. Plug the time I died into the equations; reverse everything; work backward to the original derivations. Go down to the night manager at the front desk. Get another notepad. Get twenty! Back in the room, drinking coffee, on the trail of it now, back to work, I'm not even working, the work is just happening through me, something huge is trying to enter the world, a vast invisible thing so I just try to get out of its way, I make myself the door the vast invisible thing can pass through. Something is trying to get itself born through me, to make itself real, even as something else tries to stop it. It's the world itself struggling against me. I'm caught between two energies, pivoting off both sides, zigzagging back and forth, the opposition between the energies pushing me further and higher, eschaton, anti-eschaton, take a break, take a walk down the hall, standing in front of the hotel ice machine, *chunk-chunk-chunk*, *chunk-chunk-chunk*, finding the rhythm, disassembling the eschaton equations in my head. Getting farther from shore. The hallway of locked doors. This hotel is full of death. Walking back to my room, all at once I know when every guest here will die. They will all die at the same time. I pass the night manager and I know his death clearly, too, no calculation required, because now I feel thanatons surging all around me like a fizzing sea, thanatons streaming after thanatons, the geometry of them wobbling and gushing.

But never touching me.

Everyone in this hotel will die tomorrow.

Except me.

Because the eschaton isn't a particle.

It's a person.

An eschaton and anti-eschaton are born at the same time; they diverge. A universe flourishes between them. The king and the princess enter the enchanted hill; they lose each other in the dark. Dreams flourish. The king and princess find each other again and they leave the hill. The particles plunge back into each other and annihilate each other. The universe is annihilated, too.

I am the eschaton.

The eschaton is not a particle. It is me.

I go into bathroom. Shaking. Every particle has its antiparticle. So who is the anti-eschaton?

But I already know who.

Her.

In the mirror I see myself but it's not myself. Behind me the shower curtain moves. There's a ragged man behind it. I leave the bathroom, go back to my desk. Shut up and calculate. But someone has moved my stuff around. There is nonsense on my paper that I hadn't written. Wait, it's not nonsense, no actually it is nonsense, but it puts my mind in a new place. My ability all comes rushing back. I'm scrawling across the papers, I barely understand my own math but to do the math makes the math come true. There's a ragged man sitting on the bed behind me. How did he get in my room? Don't look at him. You invited him in. Eyes on your work. The ragged man creeps closer, he's standing right behind me now. Something that had been forming inside me for years, now brimming over. The ragged man is leaning over me, I smell his musty breath, so close.

The thing that had been forming within me is showing itself. Is this how it felt for Stettinger? Did Stettinger go through this?

Burning up. Fever.

Get up.

Hang "Do Not Disturb" on the outside door handle.

Everyone in this hotel is going to die tomorrow.

Lock the door.

I feel all the thanatons around me, buzzing and prickling.

They are *unstable*.

I look at the equations. In clear math, I've laid out how it works. Over hundreds of years, thanatons naturally break down. Stumbling and collapsing into more and more degraded versions of themselves. All things being equal, in fact, there should be no thanatons at all anymore—by this time, every thanaton in existence should have already collapsed, disintegrated, vanished. Gods, heroes, men, chaos.

Except the universe can't exist without thanatons.

So something must be refreshing the thanatons.

I feel it in myself.

I can calculate it.

I already feel the shape of it. Like a story, like a metaphor. For the thanatons to reboot their cycle would require a massive amount of energy.

The kind of energy that's generated when the eschaton and anti-eschaton meet each other at the world's end.

When I meet the anti-eschaton.

A possible solution: bring the eschaton and anti-eschaton close together, thus stirring up that necessary energy, *but then* separate the eschaton and anti-eschaton *before* they end the world—yes, that's it. I push forward, keep searching, keep writing, go faster. And all at once the answer drops out.

I've hit the target.

I've got it.

I read it again.

How can the thanatons be refreshed?

By bringing the eschaton and the anti-eschaton close together and using the energy between them to perform a Great Calculation.

What is the Great Calculation?

Subjective mathematics that involves mass actuation of thanatons.

What is a "mass actuation of thanatons"?

A giant amount of human death.

Step away from my desk.

Back to the bathroom. A giant amount of human death. Legs weak. The sacrifices in Cahokia. Splash water on face. This time my shower curtain is open. There is a living baby lamb suspended over the bathtub. Each of its legs is held by a steel clamp that is part of a larger apparatus screwed into the tiles. The lamb is attended by another ragged man. The lamb is struggling, its eyes are wild, it stares at me like it knows me, it's emaciated, missing an ear, its body is completely laid open, skin sliced aside and pinned back, but it's still alive, blood streaming down the drain of the bathtub, its heart still pumping, organs writhing against each other, its little tongue moving. I look into the lamb's eyes, watch the struggling animal held over the bathtub by a network of steel wires and clamps.

Lamby-Lamb opens its mouth, and the vast invisible thing begins to speak.

- - - - - -

When did the current generation of thanatons begin?

In Cahokia. The day of the supernova. July 4, 1054.

At what stage in their life cycle are the thanatons now?

Thanatons are now in their final stage.

When will the thanatons collapse?
All of the thanatons will collapse tomorrow.
What will happen if the thanatons collapse?
The universe collapses with them.
How do we keep the thanatons from collapsing?
A Great Calculation.
What is the Great Calculation?
You already know this.
What is a "mass actuation of thanatons"?
You already know.
Who is going to do a Great Calculation?
. . .
What is going to happen tomorrow?
. . .
Is the world ending?
. . .

– – – – –

wake up on the floor.
My hotel room is full of light. Birds are singing somewhere outside. It's eleven in the morning. I'm still wearing yesterday's clothes. My body is covered in a sour film from last night's wine and coffee and sweat.

It's a normal day.

I get up, bones aching. I move around the room.

Everything is clean. I don't remember cleaning it.

I go into the bathroom. The bathroom is all in order. No bloody lamb skewered on poles in the bathtub. No ragged men.

I come back out into the bedroom. All the pages of my calculations from last night are neatly stacked on the desk. Equations, lines of symbols, spinning out crazier and wilder as they go on.

No need to look at them again.

I know.

Strange how calm I feel.

I take a shower. The warm water hits me and the steam rises around me. I scrub myself down. I wash my hair.

Then I do it all again.

Savor it. How many times in my life have I showered like this and really appreciated it? How many times have I taken the time to enjoy hot water, privacy, soap?

This is my last shower.

I get out. I dry myself off. It feels good.

Good-bye, showers.

I look at the stack of calculations on the desk.

It's all there. How everything will end. How it all must end, today. I had mathematically derived it in the equations, but now I can feel it around me. The thanatons are almost dissolved and the universe is showing its age all at once. It's too old. Forced to live longer than it should. It's an ancient tapestry that's been rotting on the wall for centuries, ready to fall to pieces, the world is an aged sickly animal that just wants to lie down, wants so badly to sleep. Everything in my hotel room is hollow and insubstantial, straining to persist. This bed. The desk. These curtains. Nothing holds them up from inside anymore. Matter itself is starting to falter. Existence had been living on a precarious line of credit that has finally run out.

Today is the last day.

— — — — —

call Erin in my hotel room.

"Hi, Erin."

"What's wrong with your phone?"

"What do you mean?"

"I've called you like five times," she says. "It doesn't even go to voicemail. I just get disconnected. My texts come back 'failed to deliver' or something."

"Oh—uh—"

"Where are you?"

"San Francisco."

Exasperated: "San *Francisco*?"

Too hard to explain. "Hey . . . are the boys there?"

"It's Saturday, remember? They're at soccer practice. Why are you in San—"

"I'll tell you later. Or actually—uh—"

"What's going on?"

I will never see Erin again. Never see the boys again.

"Do you think we can all talk on the phone later on?" I say. "All four of us? Like, together?"

She senses it. "What's wrong?"

"Nothing. I just wanted to talk to you and the boys."

"I'm at the grocery store. I've got to go."

"Wait. No. Erin. Not yet."

A sigh, hundreds of miles away. But maybe something in my voice makes her not hang up.

"Will you be back in Chicago before Christmas, at least?" she says. "Because you have the boys this year. You do remember that, right?"

I can't answer that.

"Are you still there?"

"Erin?"

"What?"

I say, "Do you remember that Christmas Eve when we went to 7-Eleven?"

"What are you talking about?"

"Your family didn't have a party that year, nobody else was doing anything, but you wanted to do something special, so you made a reservation at um, um—"

Impatient. "Of course I remember."

"But then something went wrong with the reservation and we had no place to eat that night and we were all starving."

"Because someone else with our last name made a reservation there, too. The restaurant got mixed up." Baffled, then defensive. "That wasn't my fault."

"I'm not saying it was. And so we ended up at 7-Eleven—"

"Uh-huh—"

"—we ended up at 7-Eleven and the boys had corn dogs for their Christmas Eve dinner and we had that terrible frozen pizza."

"Ha. That's the only Christmas Eve the boys ever talk about."

Pause.

"They talk about it?" I say.

"And then we went back home and watched the end of *It's a Wonderful Life* and the boys fell asleep between us."

"And I held your hand."

Pause.

She says, "Yeah, I remember."

Pause.

"Hey, Erin?"

Pause.

"Erin?"

My phone died. It was at three percent power when I made the call. I had plugged it into the wall in my hotel room, thinking it would charge. Apparently it hadn't been charging. I jiggle the charger in the phone.

Nothing.

I pick up my room phone.

Except I don't know Erin's number, ridiculously. It's trapped inside my phone. And my phone is dead.

Maybe the problem is my charger. I can get another charger.

With what money?

I had wanted to talk to Erin again. To talk to my boys one last time. Not happening now.

They deserved better.

I leave my room.

I walk past the hotel's front desk, where I will never pay, and I go outside.

San Francisco is chillier than yesterday. But peaceful, everything's normal. I feel a slight buzz, a little hum. The first crack in everything. The beginning of the crumbling. Can't everyone feel this buzz, this hum?

The sound of thanatons running down, dwindling, fading.

I get in my rental car.

The engine doesn't even turn over.

Try again.

I turn the key. A grinding, defeated sound.

But I'm supposed to meet Ron Wolper at Dare to Know in an hour. At two o'clock. Wait, why would I waste time meeting with Ron Wolper on this, the last day of the world?

Well, why not?

It doesn't matter what you do.

Eat your shitty panini.

I twist the key in the ignition one last time. The car sputters. Then nothing.

Actually it's fine. I have time.

Until 2:33 p.m. We all have until then.

I get out of my car and I start walking to Dare to Know.

I never return to that hotel.

Every trip is one-way.

— — — — — —

own the beautiful winding streets of San Francisco, past the elaborately restored houses, up and down flower-lined hills. Dare to Know isn't too far from my hotel; it's downtown, it's walkable. I can almost kind of see it already, between buildings, far away: a mod fortress atop a hill, at a skew angle to the grid.

As I dip into a different neighborhood, the temperature drops. I wish I'd worn a jacket. The air is gray and tired, as though everything around me already knows it's on its way out. The world is exhausted but it's still trying. It's keeping up appearances. Lisa Beagleman. So many puh-puh-puh-puh-proms not happening now. The predicted death dates of so many people changing from whatever we had said to *today*. I didn't handle Lisa very well so let me make up for that. Maybe I can reassure the whole universe now a little.

2:33 p.m. and then it's over. But it's okay. You had a good run, world. We'll go out together calmly, with some dignity, some sense of occasion. We'll help each other through it.

I'm passing people in the street, all going about their ordinary lives. Should I tell them? No. What's the point? You want to spend your last few hours insisting to strangers "the end is near"? You don't need to convince anyone. You know it in yourself. Inside you is the hole in everything. The eschaton. It's splintering, it's widening.

And anyway. Look in everyone's eyes.

We all know it's coming, deep down.

We've all been waiting for it.

Wanting it.

2:33 p.m.

I'm hungry but I have almost no money. I end up walking into a McDonald's. My last meal is really going to be a McDonald's hamburger? Fine, whatever. And yet even this cheap shitty hamburger is somehow pretty good. My last hamburger. I sit there, chewing, looking out the window. Almost nobody else in here. Like some folks got the memo early and raptured themselves out of the world before it ended.

What will happen after the world ends? Will the eschaton continue to exist, will I be conscious in any way? Will I remember this world after I meet the anti-eschaton, the anti-me, after we come back together?

How will I meet her?

Will she just appear, and then it's all over?

The thought is too big.

Do I really believe any of it?

Look at the McDonald's cashier. She's talking to her friend who just walked up to the register. A whole life that has nothing to do with me. I am soon going to end her, end her friend, everything. What will happen to that cashier and her friend? How much of her will stay real? Or is she just a dream I had, or a dream of one of my dreams, a shadow stuck inside an enchanted hill?

What time is it?

I stick my charger in the wall and try to recharge my phone. Nothing. I jiggle and kink the cord. There is a momentary flash. But the phone won't charge. Or it'll charge for a few seconds and then stop. Nothing works. The car, the phone, the credit cards—every machine is working against me. Matter itself is fighting me.

But not fighting that hard.

Deep down, it wants to go.

It's not just Erin and the boys I want to call. I want to call Julia, to apologize for last night. Did I disgrace myself at dinner? Did I actually drive to my hotel blackout drunk? I want to call Kulkarni, if

Kulkarni was still in touch. But he isn't. Who, then? I want to call . . .

The cashier and her friend laugh.

I'm alone.

Buying that hamburger put me under ten dollars. No credit. So I have literally less than ten dollars in the world. Six dollars and change now: two quarters, a dime, a nickel, a penny. I look at the coins until they stop meaning anything.

I walk back outside.

It's still about an hour's walk from this McDonald's to Dare to Know. The world itself won't last through this afternoon. So let your eyes take it in. Smell the unremarkable air. Listen to the everyday traffic, run your hands on the ordinary brick walls, touch this tree's normal bark. All about to be swept away. Whatever comes next won't include this. It won't include me or anything I see. We've had our turn. The next universe is around the corner, waiting in the wings. Impatient.

I walk.

- - - - -

'm at the bottom of the hill of Dare to Know.

This neighborhood is crowded with people for some reason. All kinds. Homeless-looking men, tired clerks, sharply dressed financial types, shiftless teenagers, business-casual project managers, schlubby programmers all milling around, as though waiting for something. I had thought the city felt empty before, but apparently everyone has come here. Wait—was there supposed to be some event today? A protest, a demonstration? Possibly. It wouldn't be the first time.

The people waiting at the bottom of the hill are oddly quiet. Moving aimlessly, sometimes murmuring to each other. Something empty and tense in this crowd, almost mechanical . . . then

I get it, they're all pretending like they're suffering from Sapere Aude syndrome! It's part of one of those anti–Dare to Know demonstrations. I've watched enough protests like this. I focus on one guy in particular, a man in his sixties with a buzz cut and a gut, sweatshirt, pleated khaki shorts, junior-high gym teacher type, not someone you'd expect to participate in street performance art, but even he has the same lifeless vibe: like a neglected video game character who had slipped into an idle-loop subroutine, shuffling back and forth. He won't look into my eyes.

Well, duh. I'm the weird one, trying to look strangers in the eye.

Good luck, protestors. You have less than an hour.

I look up.

Dare to Know is an unusually shaped building atop the hill. I start walking up the stairs and I feel the echo. I'm walking up Monks Mound alone while pregnant Julia waits in the museum and the sky is gray and drizzly. I'm walking up Monks Mound on July 4, 1054, surrounded by throngs of Cahokians as the sky is broken open by a supernova—maybe that's the real reason we smear the sky with fireworks on the Fourth of July, to satisfy a pattern that's older than the country itself, an unconscious urge, a primal sense that on *that* night of the year, the sky must be made to light up as it did on that night, a thousand years ago. If nature doesn't do it, we'll do it ourselves.

Sense of occasion.

The thanatons refreshed. The world continued.

Not today.

I break away from the crowd and climb the enchanted hill.

— — — — — —

E ven though I'm late Ron Wolper makes me wait.

Classic Wolper.

When I first walked into the forcefully tasteful lobby of Dare to Know, I had been certain that my eschaton proof was correct. Punch-drunk with discovery. Almost light-headed.

But now that I've been sitting in the lobby for fifteen minutes, waiting for the irritatingly casual receptionist to get someone to escort me to the meeting room . . . the more I wait, the more my calculations feel ridiculous.

Maybe I'd made a mistake.

Had I really proven anything?

Deep down I must not believe it, not actually. If I truly thought the world was about to end, why was I spending my final minutes in Dare to Know's lobby? 2:33 p.m. . . . I don't even know what time it is. My phone is dead. And there's no clock in here.

I went wrong.

Mistake. I get up from the couch. Walk around, a little wobbly. Were my calculations a mistake?

Receptionist side-eyes my jittery pacing.

Whatever. I can't sit down.

Atmosphere at headquarters saps my confidence. Life in sales is so hand-to-mouth, it's easy to forget I'm part of a global multimillion-dollar company. Well, headquarters reminds you of that like a kick in the teeth. Ruthlessly sleek building atop a hill, arrogantly turned at an odd angle to the rest of the city. I've visited here only four times in my life but this lobby is freshly redesigned every time. Always in a way both fastidious and laid-back, as if to welcome you with a *Hey, kick back, just chill!* but also to warn you, *Yeah, um, so just make sure you chill the correct way.*

I don't belong here.

Spent too long away from the heart of things. Chicago doesn't feel like the sticks but it kind of is, isn't it? Rooms and hallways in this place are modish in ways I can't quite grasp. Passing executives look like hip grad students.

And so many computers. The nauseating blitz of their calculations are rapid needles stabbing into my head. Don't they have staff here who can do subjective math? They must not have any, or they'd all have run for the door long ago. Computers prickle and squeal in every direction, jabbering, chopping, roughly shoving around data, a mathematical racket that's nearly intolerable.

So nobody at Dare to Know HQ can do the simplest thanaton calculation. All of them managers and admin.

Just then an intern casually wanders in. She stops to chat with the languid receptionist, another real go-getter.

"Did you see all those people outside?"

"Yeah, do you know why?"

"No, do you?"

"Some kind of demonstration, maybe?"

"God, again?"

Math static blasts my ears. It's hard to put two ideas together, to maintain a train of thought. Jumping lights. I can't keep the calculations straight.

Have I deluded myself?

The intern is saying my name.

"Uh, right this way, please?"

I pass through the doors and walk down the hall. Waiting for the elevator with the intern, I glance at some meeting happening behind a fishbowl window. Hard not to hate everyone in that conference room immediately. All of them nerdy and yet fuckable in a way that doesn't make sense . . . Seriously, go look at old pictures of most of the people who actually built this company. Blattner and Hansen. Ziegler. Hopkins. Even Hutchinson. All of us dumpy compared to these poised, beautiful meta-nerds.

A sick cloud of computational buzzing scraping all around me.

Will this elevator ever come?

In this glass-walled conference room a dozen people sit around a large table, pretending to care about some dipshit's PowerPoint. One woman is separate from them—she sits far from the screen, outside the table's circle, in the corner of the room, looking bored. She has dyed black hair in the kind of severe haircut that only looks good if aggressively maintained but she's not maintaining it. Wearing a Smiths concert T-shirt that can't possibly have been authentically obtained. Maybe twenty-five years old.

She sees me.

The elevator doors open.

And I mean it felt like she saw *me*.

The intern guides me into the elevator.

The girl catches my eye. Holds it.

Holy shit.

It can't be.

The doors slide shut. But I know who that girl is. Computers buzz screech wail, disarranging my brain. Wait, was I just seeing things?

The intern drawls away as the elevator rises.

There was a look of recognition in that girl's eyes. Impossible. She recognized me.

Xuuzi—

Can't be.

Eschaton, anti-eschaton, elevator, de-elevator, and if the elevator tries to bring you down, punch a higher floor . . .

Was it her?

The elevator doors open. The intern escorts me through a maze of empty white halls. Every office we pass is vacant. Every room unoccupied. This floor is desolate. Where am I being taken? The air thickens with computations, choppy and fizzy.

Wait—should I tell Ron Wolper about 2:33 p.m.?

But I had left my calculations at the hotel.

Send this intern to fetch them, then? To prove to Ron Wolper what I've figured out? No time. And anyway I'm clearly wrong. But no, no, there was something real in those calculations, or I felt it becoming real, as if while I was balancing the equations in my mind, I was also balancing the world outside me, my math pivoting everything, rotating the sea of thanatons around me until I could almost touch the eschaton—like grasping a fish in dark water, I felt its shape, even as it wriggled away—

Focus.

What is Xuuzi doing here at Dare to Know?

A man screams somewhere.

Something is wrong. My head is full of nauseous static. The intern leaves me in an empty conference room to wait for Ron Wolper. After a minute I peek out the door. The floor is deserted. The glass wall looks into the hallway and the atrium beyond. Another window looks outside but the blinds are drawn.

My stomach feels out of sorts too.

What time is it?

I check my phone, reflexively.

It's still out of juice.

But it must be around 2:33 p.m. If my calculations were correct, the world should be ending right around now—but what am I even saying? The fact that I can be so calm about it proves I don't really believe it.

I open the blinds on the window.

The world's going on as normal. The crowd is still gathered at the base of the hill, now shuffling around Dare to Know in a circle. So it must be a protest after all. Though I don't see any signs or banners.

There's something wrong about the way they're walking.

I crouch to plug the phone into the wall. Maybe I can recharge it here, look up the protest online, learn what's going on. Might as well use the phone—I can't feel any sicker than I do now. Of course my back is killing me. Why didn't I sleep in the hotel bed? Why'd I sleep on the floor?

I hear another scream, closer. A woman.

I pause, sweating.

What?

My phone still won't charge. I unplug it, blow air into the plug hole thing, jiggle it around. I find that if I keep pressing upward on the plug after it's inserted, the phone does charge. But I can't keep pressing upward all the time. I wedge the phone between the wall and a plant and the floor so that upward pressure on the plug is always being applied. The phone is charging now, precariously—so long as I don't move anything—

Ron Wolper finds me on the ground, futzing with the phone.

"What the hell are you doing?" he barks.

Ron Wolper. Aggressive mustache, crushing handshake. Not even deigning to offer his hand this time, though. As for myself right now—okay, I get it, I'm wearing the same wrinkled cheap outfit I bought yesterday, I don't look my best. The jolting noise of calculations is making me sweat. Should I ask Wolper about the demonstration or whatever outside, about Xuuzi, about the men and women screaming down the hall? Wait, had I actually heard those screams?

Steady.

I'm supposed to be here.

Ron Wolper had called me in. And I'm ready for whatever news Ron Wolper wants to tell me. Because I have something important to tell him too.

Ron Wolper says, "You're fired."

– – – – – –

This knocks me off my stride.

Ron Wolper adds, "No point in drawing it out."

My mouth is dry. Heart beating hard. Something about Ron Wolper always wrong-foots me. More than just the humiliation of being accountable to a jagoff who was basically a toddler when I was one of the people building this company from nothing.

Because it's past 2:33 and nothing has happened.

But even still, even if I'm wrong about 2:33—

"Did you hear me?" says Ron Wolper. "You're out."

"It doesn't matter," I manage to say.

"Oh brother," says Ron Wolper. "Here we go."

"There's something important I have to tell you."

"Sure. Let's get this part over with."

"It's about the algorithm."

Ron Wolper rolls his eyes infuriatingly. I'm still crouched over the power outlet with my phone. Ron Wolper just stands there. Where do I start? With the eschaton, the anti-eschaton?

I say, "I found an error in the algorithm—"

"Where is everyone?" Ron Wolper steps back, sticks his head out the door, looks up and down the hall, irritated. "On vacation or something? The whole floor?"

"And when I investigated the error, I found out that—"

Ron Wolper turns back to me. "So you looked yourself up."

Puts me out of joint. How did he know?

"Yes, I did look myself up, but here's the thing, it's—"

"At least you're not lying about it."

Oh, Ron Wolper, that smug hostility, I'd forgotten how much you set my teeth on edge.

Ron Wolper goes on. "You do know that looking yourself up is already sufficient cause for termination, right?"

Irrelevant. But push through. For some reason I need Ron Wolper to understand this. Why? Maybe because I haven't really talked to anyone else in person all day. If the world is indeed ending, I can't let it end without human contact with someone who might understand me. Even if it's Ron fucking Wolper.

I say, "The algorithm said I was dead."

Ron Wolper just nods, maddeningly.

"But I'm talking to you, right?" I say. "So there must be something wrong with the algorithm, I mean, I'm standing right here . . ."

Of course I'm not "standing right here," I'm still crouched on the floor with my phone.

I get up.

Okay, *now* I'm "standing right here."

"Sit down," says Ron Wolper.

I sit in the chair.

Ron Wolper does not sit. "There's nothing wrong with the algorithm."

"But listen, it's—"

"Stop," interrupts Ron Wolper. "Yeah, the algorithm predicts when you're going to die. And the algorithm can also predict when you're going to look yourself up."

It takes a second for this to sink in.

Ron Wolper, with maximum condescension: "The time of your death that you derived from those books—*we* seeded that result in there, okay? 7:06 p.m. CST, two nights ago. Yeah. I know it, too. That's not actually the time that you were going to die. It's the time we knew you'd be dumb enough to look yourself up. You didn't get the joke?"

I'm speechless.

"Our message to you? That we knew what you were up to?"

Still speechless.

"It's a courtesy we throw in for every asshole who looks themselves up," says Wolper, sitting down at last. "Ever since that stunt with Hopkins. And you're not the first one. Anyway, you're busted, and now you're fired. On the plus side, though, no, you're not dead. So you've got that going for you."

Ron Wolper is *loving* this. Ron Wolper must've had this meeting marked in his calendar for years. Probably the very first week he came to work for Dare to Know, Blattner and Hansen informed Ron Wolper that this would happen.

But wait—if the Books of the Dead were seeded with inaccurate information—and if they can predict more than just my death, if they can even predict *when I look myself up*—

"I'm the eschaton," I say, weakly.

Ron Wolper chuckles. "What?"

Holy shit, I'm a fool. Everything I thought I'd discovered last night—the galactic scale of its stupidity all comes crashing through to me. There is no eschaton. There is no anti-eschaton walking around either. That girl I glimpsed downstairs wasn't Xuuzi. All my exhilarating inspiration, everything I had oh so carefully deduced last night—it's nonsense. That's why 2:33 has come and gone and nothing happened. Because I'm a fucking fool.

But I know thanaton theory. I know it better than Ron Wolper, I sure as hell know it better than all the poseurs in this building suffused with brain-melting math static that they're too stupid to be bothered by—

Doesn't matter.

I was wrong.

And now I'm fired.

With less than ten dollars to my name.

Ron Wolper opens a drawer in the desk.

It has a paper in it, folded up.

Ron Wolper places the paper on the desk between us.

He says, "This is your *real* death."

The paper sits there.

Ron Wolper gives the shit-eatingest grin I've ever seen.

Don't reach for it.

The paper just sits between us.

Don't reach for that paper.

But I want it.

I want it.

At this moment I want my death so badly that I realize that, up until now, I never truly understood the appeal of what we sell.

But now that my death has become real, now that my own calculation is complete, now that my death has been forced out of an unmeasured cloud of possibilities and pinned to one definite date—

I want that paper more than anything.

The phone on the conference table rings.

"Hold on." Ron Wolper answers the phone. "Wolper."

I look at the paper.

"Uh-huh. Uh-huh. Uh-huh."

Ron Wolper keeps *uh-huh*ing away on the phone. Not paying attention to me anymore. Security will probably come to escort me out of the building. The buzz of electronic calculation intensifies all around me. They've got to know how it affects me. Using it as a weapon.

I know what'll happen next. Once he gets off the phone Ron Wolper will indicate the paper on the table and say, "This is your real death, but it'll cost you." And I will respond with something like, "Cost me what?" And then he'll come back with a number. But there's no number I can afford. What can I offer Wolper—my proof of the eschaton?

But that's garbage now.

Another scream erupts, somewhere else in the building. Ron Wolper notices it. He cocks his head.

Why are people screaming?

Ron Wolper returns to the phone, his voice is different. "Uh-huh."

Some guy runs past the room, down the empty hallway, holding his hand to his mouth.

Vomiting and running at the same time.

What is happening?

Ron Wolper has been on the phone for at least a minute. What is this, some negotiating move? Make me twist in the wind, make me wait for it, psych me out?

At last Ron Wolper puts the phone down.

But he does not say what I expect.

He does not say, "It'll cost you."

He just pushes the folded paper toward me.

"Go ahead," he says. "Take it. It's free."

What's up with his voice?

Wait.

Look at him. He's bluffing. No—something more. Ron Wolper knows something I don't. Something he just learned. Something making his voice catch the tiniest bit.

Afraid?

Never seen Ron Wolper afraid.

Afraid of what?

Look into his eyes.

Ron Wolper's face is pale.

What did they just tell him on the phone?

I have no idea what Ron Wolper was *uh-huh*ing on the phone. I have no idea what's written on that paper.

But I am now absolutely certain it has nothing to do with my death.

Then I realize it.

It is happening.

It is happening right now.

Someone else screams in the hallway, closer.

It *was* Xuuzi in that meeting room.

Particle. Antiparticle. The last step of the proof clicks.

"Is there anyone in this office named Xuuzi?" I say.

Ron Wolper swallows. "What?"

"Or not that—maybe Susan? Suzy?"

Ron Wolper looks away.

The derivation is finished. The proof is shining in my brain. Eschaton and anti-eschaton are both fully in the world now. Me and Xuuzi. To do the math makes the math come true. Because the Great Calculation has already begun. Happening right now in rooms all throughout Dare to Know. The mass actuation of thanatons. The screaming. The dreadful rightness.

Somewhere in this building, I feel her begin to move toward me.

My phone dings. I've received a text.

Ignore it.

"Go ahead," says Ron Wolper. "Read it. Your death. It's free."

Terror in his eyes.

I say, "That paper doesn't have my death."

More people are screaming downstairs. Men, women. They're not even trying to hide it from me anymore.

I say, "I don't know what's written on that paper but it's not my death."

"Pick up the paper," says Ron Wolper.

I say, "7:06 two nights ago wasn't fake. I really am dead."

"Read the goddamned paper," pleads Ron Wolper, voice quivering, and I glance at the folded paper and unexpectedly I see right through it.

I see through the walls around me.

I see every room in the building simultaneously.

I see people being murdered, right now, in various rooms throughout this building. Clubbed, stabbed, poisoned, in the meeting rooms and offices, dozens of human sacrifices are being carried out precisely on time, at this very moment it is happening below me, above me, down the hall from me, people screaming, each computed act of violence cracking open the gates a little more. Consecrating us into a metaphysically destabilizing state. Clearing the way for the ritual.

A Great Calculation.

Ron Wolper is still holding out the paper to me, a paper Kulkarni must've given him, a paper from Kulkarni's great-uncle, I realize now. Ron Wolper is begging me to take the paper but I see through it clearly. It's not my death date written on that paper. It's a sacred glyph whose sheer geometry was supposed to obliterate any evil that gazed upon it.

They thought that would work on me.

Ron Wolper starts chanting the same words my phone was chanting when I was driving back from Julia's. The solemn recitation of the list of ancient names, the counting down of strange numbers.

They thought that would work on me, too.

My phone gets another text. Then another. Ding. Ding. It's the vast invisible thing trying to talk to me, it wants the universe to keep going, it wants to speak reason to me, it wants to talk man-to-man.

Pleading with me.

I stand.

Centuries fall off me.

I feel her coming.

Xuuzi is advancing toward me and the room floods with metallic light. Outside the window new stars have erupted, the people gathered around the hill stare upward, and this room is tipping, tipping over, and as it is tipping it is changing. The floor becomes the ceiling and the ceiling becomes the floor, the walls are turning bronze, then gold multiplying on bronze, gold and bronze walls everywhere, and then we are inside the enchanted hill surrounded by dreams and dreams of dreams, we are atop Monks Mound surrounded by people lining up to be sacrificed, Xuuzi is coming up in the elevator and my phone which is not my phone is ringing, ringing, ringing.

Julia. More texts. Ding. From Erin. Ding. From my mom. Ding. From Martin McNiff. Ding. Ding. Ron Wolper's phone is ringing too. My phone won't stop ringing.

She comes down the hall.

She stops.

She knocks on the door.

Every thanaton in the universe streams toward me, the walls blaze bronze and gold, boiling silver ocean, flaming mountains of brass—

"Read the paper, read it," pleads the melting thing that is no longer Ron Wolper—

Xuuzi says, "Now we are in Cahokia."

And then everything begins to flicker.

- - - - - -

am in darkness, deep underground.

I rise. The dreaming bird cloak is on my shoulders. I can't see a thing. The ground is packed dirt. The world around me black as night. I reach out and feel earth on either side, rough rock, roots, soil. The air dense with bitter smoke. I cough, nose and throat stinging.

I am inside the enchanted hill.

I am in Cahokia.

I hear their footsteps, coming down the narrow tunnels.

They are coming for me.

I rip the bird cloak off my back.

Throw it down.

Everything flickers.

– – – – – –

am pixels. I am a glowing man. I am a collection of squares gliding through darkness. The blocky computer graphics of alligators, spiders, lizards, snakes lurk somewhere, twitching among endless levels.

They adjust their vectors.

They are coming for me.

I sprint through bitmapped floors, I hop over low-resolution piles of skulls and garbage heaps and glitchy trapdoors, looking for her. Where is she?

Everything flickers.

– – – – – –

wade through steam tunnels underneath the university. Dirty water soaks through my shoes. I swing my flashlight and my surroundings jump out of the darkness in fragments, flashes of crumbling brick, pipes diverging in all directions, multicolored graffiti, bundled wires and electrical boxes, looking for Renard—

Renard isn't down here.

I'm alone in the tunnels. I'm lost.

I hear creatures shrieking down the dark flooded tunnels, looking for me.

Where is Xuuzi?

Everything flickers.

– – – – – –

am back at Dare to Know.

I stumble down the bright empty hallways, everything corporate, clean, and sterile. I try door after door. All locked.

Screams up and down the halls.

I can't find her.

Cahokian smoke burns my throat, smelling like the scaly black meat Xuuzi had burnt in our hotel room, the weird shit. I don't remember how I got from Ron Wolper's office to this hallway. My feet are soaked with steam tunnel water, squishing in my shoes. What happened to Ron Wolper? An invisible subroutine draws and erases my bitmap repeatedly as I move through the halls. The smoke makes my head swim. Concentrate. I had been in Ron Wolper's office—there had been a knock on the door, then Xuuzi's voice—

And then the world changed.

A mass actuation of thanatons.

Giant amount of human death.

We are in the consecrated world now.

I hear my name.

I turn. Hutchinson approaches me from one end of the hall, holding up that beaded bird cloak. He is solemn, he is in no hurry. I glance at the other end of the hallway. Ziegler walks toward me, with Gaffney and Hwang right behind him, their heads bowing in rhythm, their hands slightly raised, a holy procession.

I swerve down an adjoining hallway, dashing through the fluorescent-lit maze of white, passing one glassed-in conference room after another. All full. Every department apparently having an all-hands meeting.

Where did Xuuzi go?

In every conference room, a PowerPoint presentation is projected onto the whiteboard:

NOW YOU DRINK THE BLACK DRINK

The employees in the conference rooms drink from their Starbucks cups.

I keep running, looking for her.

Outside the sky is in revolt. Heavens collapsing. Stars catching fire.

In every conference room, the PowerPoint advances to the next slide.

NOW YOU DIE

I keep running.

Every conference room door electronically locks itself. A stunned moment, and then the employees within the rooms are scrambling to their feet, cardboard cups tumbling to the floor. They're staggering for the suddenly locked exits, clawing at the glass walls, but then the black drink kicks in.

Screams.

The project managers in each room take out their knives and stab each Dare to Know employee one by one, precisely on the schedule announced aloud by their phones.

NOW YOU ARE IN CAHOKIA

I am in Cahokia and San Francisco and all the holy places at once.

I scramble through a hallucinogenic fog.

Hutchinson and Ziegler and Gaffney and Hwang are still walking toward me.

Flicker. The four men are now choppily animated sprites jerking through the digital void. A crocodile, a snake, a lizard, a spider.

Flicker. They are four Cahokian priests, forbiddingly cloaked and jeweled.

I'm lost in spinning colors in the black. The taste and smell of Xuuzi's weird shit catches in my throat, the scorched guts of an insect. Fog burns my eyes. I'm clumsy and muddled, my feet heavy.

I stagger, grabbing the wall to stay upright.

In the cave the puppeteers are throwing the puppets into the fire. In Cahokia the pits are filling with bodies, clubbed and stabbed. In the enchanted hill the wizard gloats as dreams butcher dreams. In the video game errors run riot, the code is warping, data crumbling. At Dare to Know death is being dealt in every locked conference room, knife in the heart, club to the head, blood on the computers, blood on the ergonomic chairs.

With each holy killing, the tissue separating the worlds gets a little thinner. Each divinely timed murder cracks open the gates of the supernatural a bit more, brings us more fully into the consecrated reality. So pile it on, overdo it, until nature is overwhelmed and we are free, we are weightless, for a moment no longer bound by physics but by something else.

The dreadful rightness.

I enter a Dare to Know break room. The espresso maker is spattered with fresh blood. Cut-open corpses are heaped on the dining table, staring blankly up at the fluorescent lights. Dead beef, bad food. The refrigerator has a word spelled out on it in magnets, I am startled to see it is my name, but the letters of my name are backward, they spell something else. It's not my name; it's a nightmare word, but that nightmare word is also the secret of the universe.

All of this happened in Cahokia a thousand years ago.

San Francisco will be obliterated soon. Just like Cahokia. Nobody will know or remember what happened here.

Everything flickers.

– – – – – –

'm in the steam tunnels. The water is up to my knees now. Rickety pipes loom out of the darkness, jungles of valves and tubes and knobs.

My flashlight is about to die.

I hear Hutchinson and Ziegler and Gaffney and Hwang coming up behind me, clanging and splashing through the maze of tunnels, catching up. I know what they intend to do.

Bring eschaton and anti-eschaton together, unleash their world-ending energy, divert that energy to revive the dying thanatons. Bring me and Xuuzi together, sacrifice us. Hurl king and princess back down into the darkness of the cave, to wander and search for each other for even more hundreds of years.

But Xuuzi and I have already found each other.

She's here.

Xuuzi is ahead of me in the tunnel.

I slog hard through the water. I'm trying to catch up with her. Xuuzi looks like she's walking toward me but she's somehow moving backward, sliding away from me. The thanaton power surges between us, a wobbling repulsion forcing us apart as if we're the like poles of two magnets, but I'm fighting toward her and she's straining toward me, squeezing the invisible resistance between us, generating more of it.

Colors flower out of the darkness.

I look into Xuuzi's eyes.

Cold. Inhuman.

Something vast and alien but intimately connected to me, as impersonal as electricity and yet buzzing with opaque emotions. I move. The anti-eschaton responds to me. I feel her shape and behaviors shifting in reaction to me, as naturally as wax takes the form of its seal.

The thing I called Xuuzi gazes back at me with fathomless absorption.

King and princess.

I am just as incomprehensible to her.

Then Xuuzi and I break through the last of the energy pushing us apart, eschaton and anti-eschaton, every timeline overlaps in this looping moment, the compressed energy between us spikes, the world rips open, and beyond the rip a glaring metal landscape rolls out to forever. Kingdom of raw gold, flashing purple sky, ocean of molten silver. I thrash my glittering tail, I flex my ridged thorax of iron and gold, I raise my metallic body. What used to be Xuuzi is a creature of brass and silver, jeweled and many armed, spiky golden claws, whirling eyes of flame.

Our hideous kingdom.

Eschaton and anti-eschaton merge.

The king and the princess take each other's hands, the last loose threads come together, and I see how the fairy tale should really end.

In the darkness of the enchanted hill the princess found the king. When they saw each other, the king and the princess awakened, and they remembered their true selves at last.

They rushed to the mouth of the cave. Provoked, their dreams and the dreams of their dreams rose up to stop them, dragons and goblins and warriors and strange beasts, with such a clamor that the very walls of the cave began to shake.

But just as the king was about to depart the cave, he halted. For he recognized the dreams as his. His dreams and the princess's dreams, and the dreams of those dreams, were still trapped here, weak and miserable, chained to the wizard's staff, forced to do the wizard's bidding.

The king hesitated.

The princess tried to draw the king away, to leave the enchanted hill and their dreams behind.

But these dreams were his own.

The enchanted hill began to collapse—

– – – – – –

A deep wrenching—

Hands grab, catch, and then they're all over me.

I'm yanked back into Dare to Know.

Hutchinson and Ziegler and Gaffney and Hwang seize me. They're kicking me as I'm curled up on the gray corporate carpeting in the white hallway. I see smashed-open glass walls, with Dare to Know employees running everywhere.

– – – – – –

The king was overpowered by his dreams, and the dreams of his dreams, who dragged him back into the cave.

– – – – – –

I stare up at the fluorescent lights. There is blood in my mouth, a broken tooth, my eye is crushed. I'm being lifted, taken somewhere. The breaking-down universe can't maintain a single form. Hutchinson and Ziegler and Gaffney and Hwang carry me up stairs of corporate architecture, up dirt tunnels of burning smoky blackness, up through glowing levels of colorful pixels, up the enchanted hill. All four of them are singing in a way I recognize, wheedling and whining, mechanical and insinuating.

They carry me onto the rooftop of Dare to Know.

Chilly wind blows in the dusk.

The green-black sky is crowded with a jagged new constellation. A flaming face leers down from heaven.

Thousands of San Franciscans shuffle around the bottom of the hill. Weird-shit smoke scorches my nostrils, my eyes. Hutchinson and Ziegler and Gaffney and Hwang cross and interlink their arms, chanting their familiar song.

Across the roof, I see other Dare to Know employees carrying Xuuzi.

They got her, too.

And there is someone else.

- - - - - -

he princess was also overpowered by their dreams, and the dreams of their dreams. They brought both king and princess before the wizard, who was busy preparing his spell to make the king and princess forget themselves again, for perhaps a night, or perhaps a thousand years.

But the ceiling of the cave was already breaking apart, rocks and dirt coming loose, falling all around—

- - - - - -

e are atop Monks Mound in Cahokia, a thousand years ago.

We are atop another holy hill, a thousand years before that, and another and another, countless echoes of Xuuzi and me being sacrificed, all timelines overlapping here in this looping moment.

A familiar voice says, "So, anyway . . ."

Renard approaches in the regalia of the Cahokian high priest. As the wizard of the enchanted hill. As Keith the screenwriter. The world glitches, unable to settle on one form. Renard the hairy shaman with a stone knife thousands of years ago. Renard the naked elder skewered with piercings and covered in blue paint even more thousands of years ago. Renard the boy at physics camp.

But he is dead.

But so am I.

"Every deep story puts death at the center, right?" says Renard. "I'll let you in on a trick. One hundred years from now, you and I will be dead. Nobody will remember any of us. A hundred years from now this place will be totally different. There will be a different cast of characters. Take two characters. Make them care about each other. Then have time pass. It can't help but end up sad."

He spreads his arms and waves his hands in the air. Like Gregory playing an imaginary scribbleboard, like Kulkarni's mad great-uncle drawing glyphs in the air—and as if in a mirror, everyone in the mob at the base of Dare to Know spreads their arms and waves their hands in the exact same way.

How much of our lives was ever our own? Did any of us ever make a real decision?

Maybe never.

— — — — — —

The wizard chanted his spells, lulling the senses of the king and the princess to trap them dreaming within the enchanted hill.

For the dreamless wizard collected their dreams, to feast on them.

— — — — — —

Renard drapes the bird cloak over my shoulders. I try to look for Xuuzi but I can't move. Now I am in Cahokia. Mound 72. The sacrificed man wearing a beaded bird cloak lying faceup on a sacrificed woman lying facedown. All around them, other sacrifices of men, women, and children.

This has happened thousands of times.

But we're cutting it close this time.

Renard is assisted by ragged men moving in and out of the unstable darkness. Thanatons near collapse, the world shaky, jolting, glitchy.

The universe aches so badly to end.

He won't let it.

Hutchinson and Ziegler and Gaffney and Hwang have stopped singing. Muddled by the smoke, I turn my head to look at them through the haze.

Their heads and hands are missing. Ragged men place the newly headless and handless bodies of Hutchinson and Ziegler and Gaffney and Hwang upon on a wooden pallet, their arms still interlinked. Put a sticker over them; they have done their work.

Yesterday and today.

Renard's mouth and body are soaked in gore. He holds his arms high.

The crowd below roars, or is made to roar.

Dead beef. Bad food.

The dreadful rightness.

The thanatons are already evaporating. Space-time itself is wobbling, an entire ancient contraption reeling and staggering, about to crash. But he does not rush. Renard turns me around carefully by the shoulders. His fingers trace circles of blood around my eyes. A tunnel of red circles forms at the edges of my vision. Don't look back. I feel Xuuzi behind me, other men are walking her backward toward me, compressing the energy between us. The house of computer graphics is in an uproar, lo-res creatures scurrying everywhere, like someone kicked a pixelated anthill. Renard walks me backward, looking me in the eye. Smaller red circles appear inside the larger red circles, blocking out the world more and more. I can feel Xuuzi even closer to me and power surges between us. Renard pushes me still closer to Xuuzi, squeezing the boiling energy. The thanatons shimmer to new life. More red circles. The crowd has fully entered the ritual. Cahokians circle around the giant mound under an ancient Illinois sky. San Franciscans are circling around Dare to Know.

They lay Xuuzi facedown on the altar.

They lay me faceup on top of her.

The trapped energy pulses between our bodies.

Thanatons guzzle the energy, refreshing the universe.

I'm looking up at Renard. He raises a knife to sacrifice Xuuzi and me in one stroke.

Why both of us at once?

I feel Xuuzi's unseen hand touch mine, from below.

And I know.

From under me, Xuuzi slips something into my hand.

That is, I slip something into my hand.

The red circles on the edges of my vision multiply. Xuuzi and I are the same mind. The red circles telescope my view of the world into a tunnel, crowding around a tiny Renard at the very end. The eschaton and anti-eschaton came from the same origin.

I grip whatever Xuuzi or I put in my hand.

Xuuzi and I are one.

Renard's eyes go wide.

I stare up at him.

Afraid. The naked fear. What I used to see.

I grasp the levers of the universe for a moment and shift them.

In a panic Renard brings down the knife—

That's all, folks!

- - - - - -

The princess had hidden the king's sword in her robes.

Before the wizard could act, before the dragons and goblins could attack, she threw the sword to the king.

The king caught the sword and swung it, knocking down the wizard, then brought his sword crashing upon the wizard's staff, cracking it in half, destroying the chains that shackled his dreams, and the princess's dreams, and the dreams of their dreams. The dreams ran riot around the cave, reeling in astonishment and confusion as the wizard shrieked. The freed dreams cavorted even as the cave's ceiling shuddered—an avalanche, and the enchanted hill trembled—boulders and masses of dirt tumbling from above—

- - - - - -

Inside the black vacuum, jagged pixels mutate and scatter in all directions. Bitmaps collapse, code reverses, truncated sprites flash and jitter, graphics turn to mush, the program is crashing.

Everything flickers.

- - - - - -

In San Francisco, stars come unmoored in the impossibly colored sky. At the base of the hill the people scramble helter-skelter, suddenly freed.

Not for long.

Everything flickers.

- - - - - -

The steam tunnels are nearly full of water. I'm half swimming through it, trying to touch the floor or grab the pipes, but the current sweeps me along. The tunnels are cracking and collapsing and I hear a waterfall ahead. Xuuzi is paddling with me. We plunge through the filthy water and the steam tunnel suddenly opens into blue sky, wild sunlight, a gasp of fresh air—

Everything flickers.

— — — — — —

As the cave disintegrated around them, the king and the princess ran through the throng of their freed dreams, creatures fluttering and galloping and squawking all around them in panic.

The mouth of the cave wobbled, about to collapse. The dreams and shadows stumbled and surged and scurried for the exit. None of them would make it in time.

Nothing in this cave would survive.

The king and the princess took each other's hands, slipped through the collapsing exit, and, leaving their fears and fantasies behind, and the dreams of those dreams, escaped the enchanted hill.

— — — — — —

Under the barren platinum sky.

River of molten silver.

Lonely desert of fire.

It is only Xuuzi and me. Her face is overlapping geometries of spiked brass, multiplying jewels in her eyes. I rear up, my thorax of iron and gold multiplying on bronze, spikes and crests of blinding silver.

The enchanted hill collapses behind us.

The flowering structures of matter, energy, life, intelligence collapse.

Light blasts through the world of shadows.

The dream is over. People are born, and they have their thoughts and emotions and dreams. Life feels so real to them, and then they grow up and die. They never meant anything. All the people I ever knew in that world, and the billions I never knew, all shadows. All vanish with the old universe, a dream forgotten.

Their old world is dimming.

Losing focus.

I'm farther and farther away.

I don't recognize the shadows. I never understood any of them anyway. I am already forgetting them. My mind doesn't know how to feel them, how to find my way in, can't tell them apart. I reach out to the fading world but there's nothing to catch on to. I just slip off. Already I can't even remember a single name or face of anyone I ever knew. None of them were ever even real.

Am I always going to be the good guy in life?

No. Learned that ages ago.

I am Death, destroyer of worlds.

The only real job I've ever had.

Don't look back.

— — — — —

Walking to the party, on an icy hill, one of Julia's heels broke. By the end of the ninth hole Julia and I had forgotten about the goose, we were both trashed, we were just laughing.

Our clothes were off and Julia was standing on the bed wearing only sweatpants, doing fake karate for some reason, I forget why, with a lit cigarette in her mouth.

Julia and I rode our bikes through downtown, which always seemed kind of empty, past the ominous-looking water plant, through the gardens next to the river.

Julia flicked her cigarette butt away. It must've gone, like, twenty feet. How'd she manage that trick? Are you born knowing how?

Julia looking up at the ceiling, looking self-sufficient in her happiness, but I knew the truth. I thought, *that satisfaction is mine. I caused that happiness.*

Discovery in her eyes. Something novel, weird.

Take a little home video in your mind right now. Hold on to what's happening.

Julia smoking. Her eyes on me. As though she had been standing behind me a long time. Looking at me almost as if puzzled, a different way than she had before.

Julia went skidding down hard. Into the muddy, half-melted snow.

− − − − − −

The king let go the hand of the princess and turned back to the enchanted *hill, where dreams and dreams of dreams were about to be crushed forever.*

− − − − − −

Not just *when* you died, and *how* you died, but also *why* you died. The philosophical why. All the emotion I should've felt. The love underneath the love. The appreciation.

One particle gets sucked into the black hole.

The other particle in the pair escapes.

− − − − − −

The king dashed back to the enchanted hill.

He flung aside his sword, ducked under the collapsing mouth of the cave, and lifted it up.

As the king braced his shoulders against the sagging mass of rock and dirt, the dreams were able to swarm out of the falling-down cave, countless shadows escaping into the light, streaming past him.

And as each dream emerged from the cave and into the sunlight, it became real.

What had once, in the darkness of the cave, been the mere shadow of a bird transformed into a true hawk. What was once the shadow of a cup became a real jeweled chalice. The shadows of goblins became real warty goblins, the shadow of a dragon a true fiery dragon . . .

The king strained, holding up the crushing weight.

The wizard came out of the darkness, caught up in the rush of fleeing dreams. He tried to push past the king.

The king blocked the wizard.

The wizard grabbed the king's dropped sword, and with a snarl, the wizard stabbed him.

The king staggered but managed to keep holding up the entrance. More shadows streamed past the king and into the sunlight, all of them converting from vague shadows into vivid beings, each transforming into its own blazing reality, transfigured in the sunlight of the new world.

The wizard plunged the sword into the king, sending the blade deep.

The king fell to one knee.

The last dream escaped from the enchanted hill and flowered into its true self.

The hill was empty.

The Cahokian high priest stabs the bodies on the roof again and again. It doesn't work. He looks up, startled.

Cahokia is empty.

On the roof of Dare to Know, Renard stares around the suddenly empty city.

Nobody is on the roof with him. No crowd circles the hill.

San Francisco is empty.

Keith dashes through his house, flinging open doors, running from room to room. The house is empty. Nobody is home.

Then the furniture begins to disappear.

Then the walls.

The stars in the sky go out.

The Flickering Man flashes through the empty levels of pixels, faster and faster, more and more frantic. Nothing is here. No alligators or centipedes or spiders, no piles of garbage or boxes or skeletons. Empty floors forever and ever.

The floors fade.

The gigantic glowing face in the sky fades.

The empty city fades.

The Flickering Man quivers, wavers, reverses.

He fades.

– – – – – –

Just before the enchanted hill collapses overhead, I glimpse the new world. Pulsing purple sky, silver rivers gushing across a wild desert of flame, ranges of glaring gold mountains.

But no longer empty. The last of the shadowy dreams stream past me into the new world, and as they do they become bright, massive, and solid, blossoming deeply and completely into reality at last.

Kulkarni at last becomes the real Kulkarni, Ron Wolper is now the real Ron Wolper, my parents and sisters and Erin and the boys enlarged and blazing with life. Hutchinson is now the real Hutchinson, overflowing with actuality. Ziegler and Gaffney and Hwang are now the real Ziegler and Gaffney and Hwang. Stettinger is now the real Stettinger. The FARGS and Martin McNiff and Blattner and Hansen and Hannah Rhee and the Dare to Know receptionist are radiating, growing, filling with being. Carl the metalhead and the cashier at McDonald's and whoever her friend was and Lisa Beagleman and super-dad David and weirdos Gregory and Craigory and Nate the scribbleboard player and everyone I ever knew, and the billions I never knew, exit the enchanted hill and go to this new place, leaving me behind as they flower into their real selves, as they proceed to the castle, where the feast of a thousand years is prepared for them.

The real Julia looks back at me, eyes wide, baffled but happy.

Then realizing.

No takebacks.

— — — — — —

n my memory, I dashed down the snowy hill to help her up. The heel of her shoe broke when she slipped down the icy slope, but it wasn't a shoe she cared about. She had bought this cheesy high heel at the same Goodwill as the cheesy dress. It was a joke shoe. But nothing felt like a joke right now. Snow fluttered down from the sky. Julia went quiet and I helped her up and she didn't say anything as we headed into the house where the party was, where we could hear the music from even in the street.

When we got into the party all of our friends were already there, in sex criminal tuxedos and cursed bridesmaid dresses, and we all looked brilliant and terrible. Someone had brewed a plastic punchbowl of something blue and evil. I avoided it but Julia found her way straight to it. Someone was shouting into my ear about a band that I didn't care about. Someone else whispered to me about a girl I wasn't interested in. Julia had disappeared.

I felt like I had offended her even though I didn't know what I might've done wrong. We had only gone out a few times. We hadn't even kissed yet. Was she into me or just tolerating me? Where was she, even? Was she embarrassed, angry? Everyone was dancing in the basement. I went down even though I didn't want to dance.

There she was, not dancing. Something had changed. It was sweaty in the basement. The music was from high school—

Madonna—and without a word we began to dance. We melted into each other in a way that we hadn't yet. The back of her cheap pink dress was still wet from the snow. I felt dirt on my hand, too. We moved together.

At one point the song began to skip, but everyone at the party kept dancing as though it wasn't skipping. We adjusted our dancing to take account of it. We kept dancing for a long time as if we weren't admitting to each other the skipping was happening, but the skipping had its own rhythm and made its own pulsing song. We were conspiring with it by dancing inside it, we were both sweaty and I looked into Julia's waiting eyes.

Only when I'm dancing can I feel this
feel this
feel this
feel this
feel this

Dying doesn't feel the way you think it'll feel. Not enough time for panic, for freaking out, not enough time for your mind to catch up to what's happening. When my time comes, I am calm, I do everything correctly, I keep control as much as possible, even as I think, *This is it. Now I'm dead.*

I kissed Julia. She kissed back.

Then the rush comes.

When the universe has its Moment, there should be a sense of occasion.

ACKNOWLEDGMENTS

Second chances are real! A few years ago, I was on the ropes. A book deal went south, I lost my old agent, and my confidence collapsed—though I was loath to admit it. Everlasting gratitude to my current agent John Cusick for picking me up, dusting me off, and putting me on the right track. John, your enthusiasm and wise guidance have turned everything around for me. Special thanks to Dana Spector at CAA for extending my good fortune.

Tremendous thanks to my editor Jhanteigh Kupihea and everyone at Quirk Books for taking a risk on this book. Jhanteigh, you have energized my words beyond anything I could have done on my own. I have learned so much from your editing. Jane Morley, your copyediting and proofreading have improved my prose and saved me from many embarrassing errors. Ryan Hayes, the cover you designed is perfect: something I never could've imagined, but exactly what I was hoping for. Nicole De Jackmo, Jennifer Murphy, Christina Tatulli, Gabrielle Bujak, and Jamie-Lee Nardone, your powers of marketing and publicity have been awesome to behold. I am lucky to work with such a dedicated team of pros.

I am also fortunate to have many smart friends and family who read early versions of this manuscript and helped with their advice, encouragement, and support. These include Christy Allen, Kate Babka, Matt Bird, Joe Cannon, Noah Cruikshank, John Fecile, Joe Fusion, Rob Goodwin, Keir Graff, St. John Karp, Rob Knowles, Sam Malissa, Chris Norborg, Chris Norborg Sr., Heather Norborg, Jennifer Norborg, Ellen Palmer, Alice Setrini, Abi St. John, Laura St. John, Freya Trefonides, Theo Trefonides, and Brandon Will. If I'm forgetting anyone, I apologize! Thanks particularly to April Osborn of MIRA Books for helpful guidance.

Over the years, I have been fortunate to meet many wonderful librarians who have been generous in their assistance and friendship. There are too many to name here, but I must particularly thank my friends Eti Berland and Betsy Bird.

I am indebted to the archeologists and scholars who have brought to light the story of the Native American city of Cahokia. I was especially inspired by Timothy Pauketat's 2009 book *Cahokia: Ancient America's Great City on the Mississippi* and the more recent work concerning Mound 72 done under the direction of the Illinois State Archaeological Survey by Thomas Emerson, Kristin Hedman, Eve Hargrave, Dawn Cobb, and Andrew Thompson. Of course, the fantastical extrapolations in this book are my own.

I have had many great teachers and professors in my life, but the ones who most directly influenced this book are James Group, J.T. Cushing, and J.B. Kennedy.

At last, I will always be grateful to my mother who never stopped encouraging me, and to my father who showed me how never to lose faith or quit. I love you both.

Finally, my inexpressible love and gratitude to my wife, Heather. Without your love, support, and constancy, there would be no book. I am so happy to share my life with you and our daughters Lucy and Ingrid, who have made my life a thousand times richer than I could have imagined.

READ ON FOR AN EXCERPT FROM *BRIDE OF THE TORNADO*, THE NEXT MIND-BENDING NOVEL BY JAMES KENNEDY

Available wherever books are sold in Fall 2022

They called it Tornado Day but none of us knew what it was about. My parents wouldn't explain. Neither would our teachers. I never remembered having a Tornado Day before and neither did Cecilia or anyone from school.

All that week leading up to Tornado Day Mom and Dad didn't let us eat much. I wasn't even supposed to feed Nikki. Breakfast and lunch were next to nothing, dinner was nothing. Late one night Cecilia and I got so hungry we ate some cereal in her room but it tasted weird. I felt guilty. I ended up throwing most of mine away.

I fed Nikki anyway.

All that week we weren't supposed to watch TV or even listen to the radio. Dad unplugged everything and took the batteries out. The light bulbs too. The VCR was out. The refrigerator was empty.

Mom and Dad stopped talking.

It was the same with everyone else's parents. Someone said it's what you had to do to prepare. Prepare for what? Nobody would tell us.

A killer was coming to town.

That's what we heard. We were all scared. We asked, is the killer coming for us?

They wouldn't say.

The day before Tornado Day all the stores shut down. We didn't have to go to school. The house was silent except for the stutter of rain on the roof and Nikki meowing in the kitchen.

It wasn't much of a holiday.

Growing up, when there were tornadoes, Mom and Dad and Cecilia and I would all run down to the basement with candles and food grabbed from the kitchen, and when the electricity blacked out we'd light the candles and set them up all around the cold gray basement until it flared up like a cathedral. The candles pushed back the darkness and made it dance. Colors multiplied, became richer and warmer. We'd hear the tornado raging outside, pounding at the door, shrieking like it was laughing at us, but I felt safe, locked down in the concrete basement, cozy and cared for, in just enough danger to feel a secret thrill.

I had liked the tornadoes because they forced Cecilia and Mom and Dad and me to be together. We played board games, listened to the radio, Dad told stories—I wanted more tornadoes, more thunderstorms, because I wanted my family to be like this all the time.

But when the lights flickered back on, when the all-clear siren sounded, Mom and Dad would get up from our game too quickly. "Finally!" they'd say; Cecilia too would bolt up the stairs, and then I would be left alone on the basement's concrete floor, surrounded by old exercise equipment and Halloween costumes and yellowing paperbacks, and even though it was my turn, nobody wanted to play anymore.

------

t was still dark when Mom woke us up. Outside it was a raw April morning, black and wet and miserable. Drizzle and fog. Low, heavy clouds. Four a.m.

I stayed under my blankets. After a week of no electricity the light from the hallway looked wrong on the carpet. Too bright, too hard. My Walkman was secretly under my pillow (I'd accidentally fallen asleep with it on), and Nikki was awake but she was just staring at me with her yellow slit eyes. Too early. It was going to be a bad morning, I felt it already. Rushing my shower while Cecilia banged on the door. The upstairs stinking of her toxic hairspray.

Usually Dad was already off to work before any of us even woke up. I never saw him in the mornings, I'd just come into the kitchen and see his bowl of milky cereal dregs in the sink, which always depressed me for some reason.

But this morning everything was different. We actually ran into Dad in the kitchen, and Mom too—usually she slept in, but this morning she was up and about, looking frazzled in her ratty blue robe and curlers. She'd laid out two dresses for Cecilia and me to wear to school for Tornado Day.

I'd never seen these dresses before. Old-fashioned flower-print things. Puffy sleeves. Lace trimming.

Cecilia slammed her door. There was no way she'd wear that crappy dress to school, she shouted at Mom. Everyone would make fun of her, she said.

I didn't want to wear mine either. It smelled sour, like it'd been boxed up for a long time. But I put it on anyway. I cleaned out Nikki's litter box as Mom and Cecilia yelled at each other. I kind of hated myself for it, but whenever Cecilia fought with Mom, something in me just wanted to be really good, to balance the family out.

Cecilia won. Mom said go ahead—fine, don't wear the dress! But you'll be sorry! Now I was the only one wearing an ugly dress but the bus was already pulling past our house, way too early. Cecilia and I had to run to the corner to catch it. We got on the bus and its doors hissed shut.

The morning was still as dark as night.

— — — — — —

It turned out everyone had dressed up for school that day. All the boys wore suits and all the girls wore old-fashioned dresses.

Cecilia stuck out in her normal jeans and black sweater. She hid in the girls' bathroom. Mr. McAllister asked Mrs. Bindley to go in and get her. Some of the popular girls were laughing at Cecilia, and I happened to be standing near them when Mrs. Bindley came out of the bathroom, pushing Cecilia along by her elbow.

As they walked past us Cecilia said to me, "You just keep on laughing."

— — — — — —

We were going to meet the tornado killer.

What tornado killer? None of us knew about any tornado killer. That's how you know he's a good tornado killer, the teachers said—when's the last time you even saw a tornado? We had to admit, not since we were really little. But, we said, you always heard about tornadoes in other towns! Exactly, the teachers said. But not here. Would we recognize the tornado killer? They said, no, it's against the law for the tornado killer to actually come into town. He does his work outside city limits. But today was a special occasion, they said. Today was Tornado Day.

Some of the younger kids were scared. They begged their teachers, please, please, no, we don't want to meet the tornado killer.

Everyone meets the tornado killer, was the firm reply.

— — — — — —

Mrs. Bindley turned off the lights and told us to put our heads down to wait for the tornado killer.

Dumb. We were sophomores. We hadn't been told to put our heads down since fifth grade. But there's only one school in town, and it goes from kindergarten to twelfth grade, so even though our high school was in its own part of the building, the teachers still sometimes treated us like little kids.

The dim classroom smelled like our wet coats. The radiator clanked. It felt like we were all in big trouble.

"TOMATO killer," said someone.

Some kids snorted.

"Cuthbert Monks," said Mrs. Bindley. "Another word and you've got yourself a detention."

Even Cuthbert looked startled at that. It wasn't like Mrs. Bindley to overreact. But it looked like she hadn't slept much either. She kept touching her necklace, turning it over and over.

Cuthbert Monks smirked across the room at Ned Barlow but put his head back down. Cuthbert and Ned had been separated months ago, and Jimmy Swiz, he'd been moved over to Mr. Pettifeg's homeroom permanently.

I kept my head down. Cecilia was in Mr. McAllister's homeroom downstairs—she was a year ahead of me, a junior, but I wanted to go down to her room, to let Cecilia know that I hadn't actually been laughing with those other girls, to tell her that I sympathized with her in her everyday clothes when everyone else was dressed up as if for church, and I was wondering if Cecilia and I could maybe switch clothes, or have Mom bring in a dress for her, when I saw the lights moving outside.

The lights got closer. Wobbling out of the dim woods, coming toward the school. You might've called it a parade but nobody seemed happy to be in it. I couldn't see very well through the watery windows, but it looked like a dozen men, the white beams of their flashlights sweeping through the darkness, swinging and clashing. They were coming toward the school.

They were carrying a box.

– – – – – –

The teachers rounded us up into lines and walked us down to the gym. The bleachers were pulled out. There was a small stage with a lectern set up.

Nobody told us anything about what was going to happen next. Kids whispered to each other, but then the teachers would shush them or give them hard looks. The fluorescent gym lights buzzed. It felt too early to be in the gym. Everything had the strange tingle of a dream.

I hadn't eaten since yesterday.

They separated the girls from the boys. Monks found Barlow and Swiz in the crowd and they were shoving each other and some other kid until Mr. McAllister broke it up. But it wasn't as rowdy as usual. Everyone was a little nervous.

I felt weak.

I got mixed up in the crowd and I ended up having to sit with a bunch of freshmen girls I didn't even know. I spotted Cecilia farther up the bleachers. She was sitting with the same upperclassmen girls who'd been laughing at her before. Now they were all together, whispering. I tried to catch Cecilia's eye. One of the laughing girls saw me and whispered something. Cecilia said something out of the corner of her mouth and they all laughed so hard Mrs. Lubeck had to shush them.

Come on, Cecilia. I'm on your side.

– – – – – –

Sophomore year was a disaster so far, and yet Cecilia just said to me, "The reason you don't have friends is because you don't put yourself out there," and I was like, put myself out *where?* But maybe Cecilia was right. In grade school I had liked being in plays . . . maybe I could be a drama club kid . . . In January there were auditions for the big spring musical. I went to try out.

I didn't know anyone at the auditions. I sat in the dark back of the auditorium. All the girls got up one by one to sing a song from the play, which was *Oklahoma!*. I realized too late that I should have prepared. Like, actually have read the play. One after another, girls got onstage and sang, "I'm jist a girl who cain't say no! Kissin's my favorite food!" as I sank deeper and deeper into my seat. I got up and left before they even called my name.

Cecilia was right, though. I see the drama kids messing around together all the time. They are always having a ball.

— — — — — —

The men came into the gym.

I didn't recognize any of them, or maybe I did. In a town our size you sort of recognize everyone, and yet I didn't quite know these men.

The men had put away their flashlights but they still had the box. The box was as large as a refrigerator, wooden and old and complicated, with carvings and handles and rails, and you could see it had been painted over a hundred times, because where one color had flaked away there was another color under it, and the paint was bubbled and faded and cracked and nasty.

The men set the box down on the stage. All of them walked away except one. That man put a key in the box and unlocked it.

Then he too walked away, very fast.

None of us said a word.

The lid of the box started to move.

Something was trying to come out.

I held my breath. The kids around me, too. Nobody knew what it would be.

But of all the things we had expected—of all the things any of us imagined might've come out of that box—we were all wrong.

It was a boy.

He climbed out. He blinked and squinted at us. He gave a little wave.

I thought, they had to be joking.

This was a tornado killer?